The Secretary

Also by Renée Knight

Disclaimer

Praise for *The Secretary*

"A scintillating double psychological portrait. . . . Knight conjures an arresting ending reminiscent of Ruth Rendell at her flintiest."

—*The Times* (London)

"Knight builds tension in this page-turning story about misplaced loyalty, secrets, manipulation, and class with an alternating time line, slowly revealing what happens when one woman's desire to be helpful and needed ruins her life. Highly recommended."

—*Library Journal* (starred review)

"British author Knight follows 2015's *Disclaimer*, her well-received debut, with a decidedly creepy psychological thriller. . . . Readers are sure to be left breathless."

—*Publishers Weekly*

"A cinematic page-turner steeped in atmosphere and just awaiting its adaptation to miniseries."

—*Kirkus Reviews*

"You will devour this gripping tale of obsession and duty with an ending as dark as it is astonishing. Deliciously addicting!"
—Liv Constantine, bestselling author of *The Last Mrs. Parrish*

"A cool, contemporary, whip-smart thriller."
—Paula Hawkins, author of *The Girl on the Train*

"Knight, whose debut, *Disclaimer*, was highly praised, again shows her skill in creating an absorbing psychological thriller."
—*Booklist*

"Whoa, you are in for a treat with *The Secretary*! Dark and intriguing with utterly compelling characters. I genuinely couldn't put it down."
—Laura Marshall, author of *Friend Request*

"Deceptively clever and so unsettling. I love the way Knight casually slips in a twist that makes you shake your head at how wrong you were!"
—Lesley Kara, author of *The Rumour*

"I started reading *The Secretary* last night and couldn't put it down. . . . Such a deliciously dark, hugely satisfying read."
—Paul Burston, author of *The Black Path*

"*The Secretary* is an excellent, dark and clever thriller with a compelling central character. The story draws you in from the start and builds and builds to an intense and unsettling conclusion. I loved it."
—Jenny Quintana, author of *The Missing Girl*

The Secretary

A Novel

Renée Knight

HARPER PERENNIAL

NEW YORK • LONDON • TORONTO • SYDNEY • NEW DELHI • AUCKLAND

HARPER ● PERENNIAL

A hardcover edition of this book was published in 2019 by HarperCollins Publishers.

First published in Great Britain in 2019 by Doubleday, an imprint of Transworld Publishers.

HarperCollins books may be purchased for educational, business, or sales promotional use. For information, please email the Special Markets Department in the US at SPsales@harpercollins.com or in Canada at HCOrder@harpercollins.com.

FIRST HARPER PERENNIAL EDITION PUBLISHED 2019.

Library of Congress Cataloging-in-Publication Data has been applied for.

Library and Archives Canada Cataloguing in Publication information is available upon request.

ISBN 978-0-06-236236-0 (pbk.)

20 21 22 23 24   LSC   10 9 8 7 6 5 4 3 2 1

To my dearest sister Cathy, with love and thanks.

'For I have sworn thee fair, and thought thee bright,
Who art as black as hell, as dark as night.'
William Shakespeare

1

The secretary is the most dangerous person in the room. I couldn't help smiling when I first read that sentence. It was in one of those old-fashioned detective novels; a cosy, drawing-room whodunnit, its pages littered with dead bodies. I curled up amongst them, pored over the details of their savage ends without feeling the least discomfort, safe in the knowledge that all would be well, each thread tied up, the criminal brought to justice. Three cheers for the clever sleuth. Real life is not like that. There are always loose ends, untidy fraying edges, however hard one might try to keep things neat. And justice? Justice is something I lost faith in long ago. I've read *An Unquiet Woman* countless times now – it's one of the few books I brought with me to The Laurels, and on nights when I can't sleep, it's the book I reach for, it's the book that sends me off.

What made me smile was when I imagined the shocked looks on the faces of the well-dressed ladies and gents gathered in the drawing room as they heard the detective denounce the villain. *'The secretary,'* he said, turning and pointing to the bitter spinster, perched, no doubt, on the least comfortable chair in the room. *'There she sat, as quiet as a mouse, at the heart of events. A silent witness, watching and listening, waiting for her moment to strike. One by one, she took down those who thwarted, used and – most foolish of all for her victims – underestimated her.'*

I have been a secretary for nearly twenty years, so of course I was amused when I discovered the villain of *An Unquiet Woman* was one of my kind. I identified with her, saw defiance on her face as she looked back at her accuser, and I could almost hear, as she must have, the sound of the stopper being removed from a crystal decanter as she was led away, and then her betters drinking a toast to justice as the door was closed behind her. It is a sound I am familiar with – that tinkle of cut glass – a welcome drink at the end of a busy working day. *Christine, won't you join me?* And I always did – I never said no.

An Unquiet Woman was published half a century ago, but being a secretary back then was, it seems, not so different to now. That ability to make oneself invisible. It is astounding the number of conversations carried on in front of us, as if we don't exist. The silent witness is a role I am quite used to. Watching, listening – as quiet as a mouse, at the heart of events – my loyalty and discretion never in question. And yet, loyalty and discretion are qualities for which I have paid a heavy price. I have been humiliated in a most public way.

I hate to think what would have become of me if I hadn't been rescued by The Laurels. I have found sanctuary here. No one forced me to come – it was my own choice, though the circumstances were not of my making. Still, I hesitate to call myself a victim. Let's just say I am taking some time out to consider the next stage of my life. Forty-three is too young to retire.

I have tried to apply a work ethic here at The Laurels, and have set myself the task of putting the past into order. I arrived with carrier bags stuffed full of newspaper cuttings that had littered the floors of my home. I gathered them all up and brought them with me, and now I have unfolded each scrap, smoothed away the creases, and sorted them into chronological order, ready to be pasted into a scrapbook. It's a beautiful, leather-bound volume – the kind you might use for wedding photos. I suppose it's a kind of occupational therapy – every page I complete rewinding the clock and taking me back.

Who knew that Christine Butcher would ever have her name in the newspapers? Or that anyone would be interested in taking my photograph? Yet, there I am. My moment in the spotlight a brief period last year, 2012. Most people probably skimmed through the references to me, their eyes scudding over the words until they came to what they considered the meat of the story. They will have forgotten my name. I am ordinary, only there because I made some questionable choices – choices I suspect many would have made in my position.

2

When I heard I would be working at the head office of Appleton's supermarket chain, I can't pretend I wasn't excited. After all, it's not often you recognize the name of a chief executive or see their photo in the newspaper, but Mina Appleton, daughter of Lord Appleton, chair of the company, was a regular at celebrity parties and a favourite of newspaper diarists. She had her own column too, which I'd read and enjoyed. It offered tips for quick and simple family suppers, sprinkled with casual mentions of famous friends she'd entertained at home.

Not that I expected to have any contact with Mina Appleton herself. I was there as a temp, parachuted in to replace a secretary who was on holiday. It was a matter of pride to me to ensure the absentee wasn't missed, and I made myself indispensable. They didn't want to let me go, so it was only a matter of time before I came to Mina's notice.

I remember the first time she spoke to me. It was lunchtime and, as usual, I was alone in the office, holding the fort while the other secretaries went out. I always brought a sandwich in from home and ate it at my desk, so I could leave on the dot of five. My daughter – Angelica – was four years old, and,

4

back then, I always made sure I was home for bath and bedtime.

'Is he at lunch?' Mina was looking for the finance director – Mr Beresford, it was then. Ronald Beresford.

'Yes,' I nodded, a little star-struck, perhaps.

She went straight into his office and closed the door behind her, and I stood up and brushed the crumbs from my skirt. I could see her then, through the window of Mr Beresford's office. She was going through the drawers of his desk – pulling out bits of paper until she found what she was looking for. I was sitting back down when she came out, pretending to be busy, and I think she forgot I was there.

I could hear her at the photocopier, muttering to herself, and when I looked up she was stabbing at its buttons in frustration. It was only when I unwrapped a ream of paper and filled the tray, then replaced the empty ink cartridge and brought the machine to life, that she turned to look at me.

'How many copies would you like?' I asked.

'Two,' she said, and she watched as I copied, collated, then stapled the documents together. Instinct told me she'd like to take them away in a plain, brown envelope, so I found one, and slipped them in for her.

'I haven't seen you before, have I?'

'I'm just a temp,' I said, though it was not how I saw myself. I was the most reliable and conscientious secretary in the department. 'Would you like me to return the originals for you?' She looked at me and smiled, and it was the most extraordinary thing. There aren't many people who have that gift, but Mina has it in spades. When she shines the full beam of her attention on you, it lights you up inside. Certainly, it made me feel, not special exactly, but as if I mattered. In that moment, to Mina, I mattered.

'Mina.' She held out her hand. 'Mina Appleton.'

'Christine Butcher,' I said. Her hand was tiny in mine.

'Good to meet you, Christine.' She smiled again. 'No need to tell Mr Beresford I was here,' and she held on to my hand a moment longer, then left.

When she'd gone, I returned the documents she'd copied to his office, and Mr Beresford's smiling eyes watched me from the photograph on his desk as I tidied up and covered over Mina's tracks. He'd never know she'd been there, and I smiled back at him, standing with his arm around his wife, his two young daughters holding hands in the foreground. Then I straightened his chair and returned to my lunch.

Two weeks later I received a call from Miss Jenny Haddow – PA to Mina's father, Lord Appleton.

'Mina is looking for a new secretary, and your name came up,' she said. And that was it. Mina must have made inquiries about me. All she would have learned was that I was punctual, efficient and, perhaps, that I was married with a child. She could have had her pick of secretaries, but it was me she set her heart on.

3

'*Welcome to my house! Enter freely and of your own will!*' It was Notting Hill Gate, not Transylvania, and Mina Appleton's home, not Count Dracula's, but had I known then what I know now, I might not have stepped so freely over her threshold.

When I rang her doorbell that Saturday afternoon, it was a bitterly cold day – midwinter – and yet I remember feeling warm as I stood on her doorstep. The heat of excitement at a future I had not anticipated. Quite different to the sweating I suffer now – my body overrun with hormones that make me feel as if I'm being slowly poisoned. Early menopause, I'm told.

I had never been to Notting Hill before, and the discovery of such leafy grandeur in the heart of London was a revelation to me. Mina's house was on a terrace of six-storey, pastel-painted houses facing communal gardens – a privileged space, accessible only to those with a key. Homeowners and their staff.

I was surprised when Mina opened the door – I'd expected a housekeeper at least.

'Here, let me take that for you.' I handed her my coat, and watched as she stood on tiptoe to hang it over a hook. Until then, I hadn't realized how short she was. At work she wore heels, but there, in her own home, she padded around shoeless. Once inside, I realized the house was even bigger than I'd thought, and I paused a moment to take in my surroundings – breathing in the unfamiliar smells, my eyes drawn up to the strange sound of machinery on an upper floor.

'It's a lift,' she explained. 'The house used to be a hotel. The children loved the lift so we decided to keep it. I've just sent them up in it. Shall we?'

I never trusted that lift. It was the kind you find in small French hotels: polished brass, red carpet – fancy but unpredictable – claiming to hold five people but even with two it was a bit of a squeeze.

'Thanks so much for giving up your Saturday, Christine. I know how precious weekends are.'

I followed her, passing the open door of a sitting room – a glimpse of velvet cushions, vast sofas, a fire lit in the grate. We headed down the stairs to her basement kitchen – a place she later described as the heart of her home. I expected it to be gloomy, but she'd done something with the lighting that made it enchanting. As bewitching as anything I'd seen in a theatre, as if the sun had somehow penetrated through the bricks. Over the table hung a milky sphere that made me think of a full moon. The effect was hypnotic. Our kitchen at home had one fluorescent strip. It wouldn't have occurred to us to have anything else.

It was so like Mina to conduct my interview in her home, and not the formal setting of the office. It's the way she likes to do business – softening the edges so commercial transactions appear cosy and intimate.

'Please, Christine, sit down.' I squeezed on to a bench at the table, facing into the room, and watched her take a baking tray from the Aga, her hands draped in a linen cloth. A cascade of golden biscuits slid on to a plate. If I close my eyes now, I can still smell them. It doesn't take much for me to conjure up how it felt, being there that first time. Mina's attempt at humility, her efforts to relax me. She managed to make a young woman of twenty-five – as shy and fearful of being a disappointment as I was, with a CV that exposed my lack of experience – feel at home.

'What can I get you, Christine? Tea, coffee?' I liked the way she kept using my name. *Please, Christine. Thank you, Christine.*

'Coffee, please.'

Through the far window I could see a courtyard where the sun filtered down through a tree so large it kept the small outside space in almost permanent shade. It was a late-flowering magnolia. Its flowers smell of lemon, and if one falls you can sit it in a saucer of water and the scent lasts for a week, long after the petals have turned brown and withered.

Mina joined me at the table and then it was down to business, although I was seduced into believing otherwise.

'How old is your daughter, Christine? It is a little girl you have, isn't it?'

'Yes, Angelica. She's four.'

'Angelica. That's a lovely name. Unusual.'

We sat so close I could see the freckles on her nose, the faint blue beneath her eyes. She wore no make-up. Good skin, perfect white teeth. Her hair loose – strong, natural curls that snaked across her shoulders. She is famous for her hair and even now it amazes me how little maintenance it seems to need. Everything else, over the years, has needed a bit of help, but not her hair. It remains quite extraordinary.

'Milk? Sugar?'

'Milk, please. No sugar. Thank you.'

She poured the coffee and put a cup down in front of me.

'Sorry,' she said, stifling a yawn. 'I was out early this morning in Barnet visiting one of the stores. I'm trying out a new layout – new colours. I want it to *feel* like this,' and she held up her coffee mug – blue and cream Cornish ware. I understood at once what she was after – a cosy nostalgia. 'I say *I* because my father's less interested in how things *feel* – he'd be happy to leave everything as it is, but the business needs to change if we're to build on our customer base.' She nudged the plate of biscuits towards me. 'Please, help yourself, Christine.' She took one and held it in her hand, but she didn't eat anything the whole time I was there. I was famished, having rushed out without breakfast, and took a second biscuit. 'To be honest, I was rather disappointed, so we'll have to rethink the design. One thing you should know about me, Christine, is that it's only when I see something in the flesh that I can be certain it's right. And if it's not right, I'll change it.' It didn't occur to me she was referring to human beings too. 'It doesn't matter to me how many times things have to be redone. I know it must drive everyone mad.' She shrugged. She really didn't care, and still doesn't, if she *drives everyone mad.* It was something I once admired – her ability to simply not care. I am someone who cares very much, and will go to great lengths to avoid irritating others, but then, opposites attract. In that sense, we were the perfect match.

'My father sees it as a failing. *Why can't women ever make up their minds?*' She laughed, fondly, as a daughter might of her ageing father and his old-fashioned ways, and I remember, at the time, assuming she and Lord Appleton had a close relationship. Certainly, it seemed to me as I sat there looking at her – those clear eyes, their whites the palest blue – that all she wanted was the best for the business. 'I like to get things right, that's all. So. Tell me a bit about yourself, Christine. How long have you temped at Appleton's?'

'Six months.'

'Goodness. You must know us well. And where else have you worked?'

I slipped my CV across the table and she glanced at it, but no more than that. Perhaps it was my lack of experience that attracted her. I could be groomed to suit her needs. I wasn't aware back then how voracious her appetite was, and how much she would expect of me.

'What does your husband do? Sorry, you don't mind me asking, do you? Of course it's none of my business.'

'I don't mind.' And I didn't. 'He builds kitchens, bespoke. Pieces of furniture – tables, dressers . . .' Even then, I found myself saying what I thought she wanted to hear. My husband, in fact, fitted off-the-peg kitchens.

'He's a skilled craftsman, then. I admire that. What's his name?' She toyed with the biscuit in her hand.

'Mike.'

'Mike,' she repeated. 'And your parents? I'm more interested in *who* you are, Christine, rather than what you've done. You don't mind, do you?'

'Not at all. My father used to work for a company that produced thermos jugs – you know, for tea, coffee. Jugs, not flasks . . .' She smiled at the distinction, and I was embarrassed I'd repeated Dad's mantra: *Jugs, not flasks, Christine. Thermos jugs for the business environment, not suitable for picnic teas.* 'He's retired now.'

'And your mother?'

'She died when I was eight.'

'I'm so sorry. That's too young to lose a mother.'

I took another biscuit. I grew up quickly after Mum died, learning from a young age not to put myself first.

'Siblings?'

'No.'

'Like me, then, an only child.' She worked so hard to put me at ease. To make it seem as if we shared some common ground. 'I suppose it has its pros and cons, doesn't it?'

I nodded in agreement, but I'd always yearned for a brother or a sister. 'Childcare's not a problem, Angelica's at a day nursery . . .'

Mina held up her hand.

'Christine. Your childcare is none of my business. I wouldn't dream of asking you about it. Now, my turn,' she said. 'My father, as you know, is very much alive. My mother too.' I waited for her to say more, but she didn't. Lady Appleton remained an enigma to me for years, though I tried to fill in the gaps, imagining what she was like. Unfortunately, my powers of imagination are limited.

'I have three children. Twin boys, Henry and Sam, and a daughter, Lottie. My husband works in the City, but . . .' She paused, biting her lip. I came to learn this was something she did when she was about to confide something. 'I want to be honest with you, Christine, and I'm telling you this in confidence. I haven't even told the children yet, but we are going to separate. There will be a divorce. I hope it won't be messy, that he'll behave well, but I can't put my hand on my heart and say he will. My husband is not the easiest of men.' There it was, the first secret between us. There have been so many over the years.

'I think it's only fair to tell you because, if you are interested in this job, you should know that the boundary between my private and working life is fluid. You would be joining me at a difficult time in my personal life, and that's partly why I hope you'll say yes. I need my own assistant. Apart from being chief exec at Appleton's, I have many other commitments and I will need support to ensure the children's lives are disrupted as little as possible. I see it as a holistic role.'

'Mummy?'

Her daughter, Lottie, was in the doorway. A dear, timid thing, waiting to be invited in.

'Come in, sweetheart,' Mina said, holding out her hand, and Lottie scuttled over and settled on her mother's lap.

'This is Christine, darling. I'm hoping I can persuade her to come and work with me.'

'Hello,' Lottie said, her eyes locking on to mine, assessing whether I was friend or foe.

'Hello, Lottie,' I replied, smiling. Friend, I tried to communicate. Mina took an apple from the bowl, and began to peel it with a beautiful fruit knife. She has so many pretty things, but that is one of her favourites. Victorian – mother-of-pearl handle – sharp as anything. I watched the skin curl away from the apple, and then Lottie nibble on the slices her mother passed her.

'As you may know, Christine, I've been sharing my father's secretary, Jenny Haddow, but she's about to retire and it's become clear to me that she's not up to managing my workload too. It's all she can do to keep up with Dad's, even though that has lessened significantly. He's beginning to take more of a back seat – he'll retire in a couple of years. Until then you'd have to work for both of us, but after that . . . well, I'd have you to myself. I need someone by my side as I move forward with the company. Someone young.' She stood up, hoicking Lottie on to her hip and walking over to the Aga to make more coffee. 'Do you know much about Appleton's?'

'A bit.'

'Let me fill you in then. The industry is changing and we need to keep up. It's not just about selling groceries, it's about politics too. Food, diet, health. It's something I feel strongly about. Appleton's has a reputation for treating its suppliers fairly and that's something I want to build on. It's what makes us unique. At the moment, we're not capitalizing on it. Appleton's is a supermarket with a conscience – we care about farmers, we care about the land. I believe we can grow as a business without compromising that identity. Food gets to the heart of how we see ourselves as a nation. What we put into ourselves and what we offer to others.' I should have been suspicious, hearing this from a woman who didn't appear to eat, but I was entranced, and it is an image that has stayed with me. Mina, child on her hip, standing at the Aga delivering her mission statement for Appleton's. Domesticity can be the most marvellous disguise.

She put Lottie down, and returned to the table, leaning towards me.

'Christine, I think you and I would work well together. I hope you'll consider it.'

'Yes, of course.'

'And whatever you decide, it's been an absolute pleasure to meet you properly. Here – you must take the rest of these with you, Angelica might enjoy them.' I watched her prepare a parcel of the remaining biscuits – brown paper tied with a piece of raffia.

'Thank you,' I said.

I remember, as I made my way home, feeling lighter, the future opening up before me. I thought I saw it so clearly.

When the letter with a formal offer arrived a few days later I watched Mike take in the private health insurance and travelling expenses, his eyes darting back and forth over the sentences. When they reached the salary, they narrowed, his sandy lashes quivering like antennae. Then he looked at me and smiled. There was nothing to discuss. He handed me back the letter and I looked at it again. It was from the HR department, but Mina had written a note at the bottom: *I do hope you say yes. Very best wishes*, M. For me, the decision had little to do with the perks, and it strikes me now that, when Mike asked me to marry him, I had to think about it, but when Mina proposed, I accepted at once.

4

'As a PA you need to understand what makes your boss tick. What are they passionate about? What are their interests? They will expect you to know these things without having to tell you. They will also expect absolute loyalty, but I think you are aware of that already.'

A well-behaved and diligent pupil, I'd been described by my teachers at school, and I was no less so under Jenny Haddow's tutelage. I gave her my full attention, resisting the temptation to look around the office that, when she retired, would be mine. It turned out to be sooner than I expected. Mina was keen to get things moving, and I imagine she told Jenny how much her loyalty and hard work were appreciated, and made sure she received a handsome retirement package. Jenny Haddow was old school – she'd never had children, never married, devoting thirty years of her life as secretary to Lord Appleton. It's a record even I can't beat.

She and I were having coffee, sitting either side of her desk, she still in the driver's seat. The door was closed and on the desk between us a tray was laid out with bone china cups and saucers, matching milk jug and sugar bowl, silver tongs and spoons with the letter *A* engraved on the handles. I already knew Mina preferred her coffee in a mug, and couldn't wait to shed these genteel trappings.

I cannot fault Jenny Haddow's instruction. She was kind and polite, but perhaps somewhat cool. It is something I've noticed about the personal assistants to people of influence, and I have met many over the years. There is a reserve about them. About us, I should say. We are friendly enough but, I accept, we can be rather chilly. We are like spies – the longer we serve, the more secrets we hold, and the greater the need for our discretion.

I remember a conversation I had once with the PA to a government minister. He had the most peculiar sexual appetites, although his assistant assured me they never involved her directly – the activities themselves took place outside the office – still, she accepted it as part of her job to make the necessary preparations and to clean up after him. She entrusted me with the secret because she knew, like her, I kept the faith.

'It comes with the territory, doesn't it?' she said. 'A good PA gives unconditional loyalty and those who can't are flushed out. If I ever move on and work for someone else, I'll take his secrets with me. I won't tell my new employer. I can't. If I do, I lose my value and my value is that I am someone who can be trusted with anything.' I've never forgotten that.

Jenny stirred her coffee and I noticed how the tiny diamanté pin on the lapel of her jacket picked up the silver in her hair.

'I can tell you all you need to know about Lord Appleton's likes and dislikes, but with Mina I have less experience. These are things you will have to learn yourself. Still, I can give you one piece of advice in that regard. However close you feel you are to her, however much she lets you into her confidence, you need to remember that you are not her friend. It would be foolish for you to think otherwise and it is vital, if the relationship is to be a successful one, that you remember this. It will allow you to hold on to your dignity. That is important. With your dignity, she will respect you. She needs to respect you, there needs to be mutual respect. But you are not her friend and she is not yours. Never forget that.'

I believe she spoke from the heart, but when I later learned, from Mina, Jenny's true relationship with Lord Appleton, I couldn't take her advice seriously. Now I wish I had. It might have saved me a lot of pain. Yet, Mina and I have never been friends in the way most people understand it. Close, yes, but not friends. Our relationship is more substantial. Personally, I think friendship is overrated. It's not something I've found to be particularly sustaining, and with a life as busy as mine, I simply haven't had the time to invest in it.

'You are there to make sure *both* their lives run smoothly, so they are *both* able to perform to the best of their abilities. Lord Appleton is still chair of the company and so he should be your primary concern. I hope I can trust you to look after him, Christine. You will have a girl to help. A temp for now, but you should make it one of your first priorities to find a permanent, reliable secretary who can assist you. A number two.'

I smiled and thanked her, but Mina and I had already spoken about arrangements once I was in charge. I would work for Mina, and the temp would take care of Lord A.

Mina suggested throwing Jenny a retirement dinner, but she wouldn't hear of it.

'I'd prefer drinks in the office, thank you.'

So that's what we did. A quick drink on her last day. Lord Appleton attempted to say a few words, but he got emotional and Mina had to step in. Jenny said something too, but kept it short and left soon after. And then everyone else drifted off. I overheard chatter in the Ladies the next morning that made me wonder whether they'd all gone on somewhere else, but I never got to the bottom of that.

'By the way, my father and Jenny have been having an affair

for years. That's why his speech was a bit desultory. He's going to be lost without her.' We were in my new office, finishing off a bottle of champagne after Jenny's do. 'Oh, Christine, don't look so shocked. My mother's known about it for years – and she lives abroad anyway so it's really not a thing. You know, I wouldn't be surprised if he moved Jenny into Fincham Hall, now they're no longer "colleagues". Might be a good thing, I suppose. I worry about him living there on his own. It's far too big. And have you noticed how forgetful he is?' She leaned in towards me. 'Oh, come on, you must have,' she pressed, pouring the last of the bottle into my glass. 'I had to cover up for him in the last board meeting. I'm surprised you didn't notice. He spends so much time out of the office on unnecessary visits to suppliers, he forgot about the site we purchased for a new store in the north-west.'

'It must be frustrating for you,' I said, picking up my glass.

'It is. I'm glad you understand.' She touched her glass against mine. 'We've got a very busy time ahead of us, Christine. Here's to the future.'

5

Today is a good day. I am not nauseous and my heart rate is even. I feel calm as I sit and look out on to the gardens. The sun is shining, but I am content to be indoors and feel its warmth through the window. Content for it to come to me. Not in the least tempted to go outside. There are times when I itch to get back out into the world. I am not a prisoner at The Laurels, but I accept I am not yet ready to be outside its walls.

I look down at the clipping in my hand. It is the first photograph of me that ever appeared in a newspaper. At that point, I was still unnamed. The caption reads: *Mina Appleton and her father, Lord John Appleton.* I stand in the background, a grainy shadow, barely there. I can just about make out a glass of champagne in my hand. I trim around the edges of the picture, my hand reassuringly steady. Yes, this is a good day. I turn over the cutting and run my stick of glue along it, then place it at the centre of the page in my scrapbook, and press it down. The *Daily Telegraph*, Tuesday, 3 March 1998. I had been working for Mina for three years by then and thought myself well settled into the job, but in the photograph I look a timid thing. An ingénue, hovering on the fringes.

I remember showing the picture to Angelica: *Look, there's Mummy,* I said, and she kept that photo. It was one of those she cut out and stuck into her own scrapbook. *Mummy at a party,* she wrote in pink felt-tip, though it's hard to tell it's me – my face barely more than a smudge. Mina and her father are arm in arm, she smiling up at him and, if you didn't know better, you might think she still respected him. Poor man. He was innocent of the fact that he would be out of the company within the year.

It was inevitable. Mina had a vision for Appleton's and her father was obstructing it. I felt her increasing frustration, and saw him through her eyes. He was an obstacle. He resisted her ideas for change, and I was in awe of the energy she put into trying to drive her ideas through. She wanted to make Appleton's a market leader. Is that a crime? No. What I didn't understand then was the price we would all have to pay for her ambition.

I remember her returning to the office after a day out visiting suppliers with her father – he'd insisted she went with him, for once – and I knew, by the rhythm of her feet as she passed my office, that it had not gone well. Even with her tiny feet, even on office carpet tiles, I felt her fury as she stomped by. I gave her a minute, then knocked and went into her office. She'd thrown her coat over the sofa and was pacing back and forth in front of the window.

'Can I get you anything?' I asked, knowing she would want a whisky. It was after six. Had it been earlier in the day I would have brought coffee or tea. Coffee before midday, tea post.

'A drink, please, Christine,' she said. While I dropped ice into a glass and poured the whisky, she vented: 'You know, one of them actually called me girly. *Your girly's a chip off the old block,* he said to my father. I think he thought it was a compliment. And I had to stand there and smile, as if I accepted it as one. All day I've been trudging round fields, listening to men bleating on, making excuses about the weather and how difficult it is for them with it being so unpredictable . . . blah, blah, blah.' I handed her the glass and she took a swig. 'Thank you. And I have to pretend to be sympathetic. Make the right noises to show I understand how hard it is for them. Then all the way back in the car my father is lecturing me on our responsibilities, as *tradesmen. We're in trade, Mina, not business. This country depends on those farmers. It's our duty as a seller of food to support the men who toil on the land.* But I *am* in business, Christine. Appleton's *is* a business. I want us to compete with the big players, not fiddle around on the ethical fringes.'

'Top-up?' I asked. 'If there's anything I can do,' I said, refilling her glass.

'Well, if it's within your capabilities to make sure my father's around less, then that would be marvellous, but I suspect that's beyond even you, Christine.' Her edge of sarcasm didn't offend me – she was tired, it had been a long day and I suspected her blood sugar was low. I heard her words as a challenge. It was not beyond me at all. A simple matter of taking back control of Lord Appleton's diary.

I hired the temp who looked after him, and it was within my gift to terminate her.

'I'd like to find you someone permanent, Lord Appleton,' I told him. 'In the meantime, let me look after you.'

'Well, if you're sure you can take on both Mina and me, then, yes, why not? I know Jenny found it a bit of a challenge, but it makes sense, Christine. And perhaps you can help oil the wheels between my daughter and me. I understand Mina's in a hurry to take over, but I don't feel she's ready yet.'

'Of course,' I said, and he trusted me.

It was soon after that that he began turning up late for meetings. Only ten minutes or so at first, but then he missed two crucial votes with the board, and people began to notice. Naturally, he always had an excuse. The wrong time was put in his diary, or he'd been given the wrong location. Once, he sat for half an hour on his own in the fourth-floor meeting room, while the directors carried on without him on the fifth. He was livid and began to point the finger at me. No one respects a man who blames his tools, and I maintained a stoic patience. *He's lost without Jenny*, I said when one of the executives took me to one side. *He's not been the same since she retired.* I was able to prove the mistakes weren't mine, by showing the correct days and times in the diary. Proof of my innocence, evidence of Lord A's sad decline. Playing loosey-goosey with a diary was something I became expert at over the years.

It lies heavily on my conscience to know I was instrumental in Lord Appleton's departure. I may not have had a vote on the board, but I played my part. The end came when, as Chair of Appleton's, he was invited on to the lunchtime news to talk about the company's annual report. I am sure I wasn't alone in thinking it should have been Mina. She was so much more telegenic than her father. The week before she'd made her first appearance on *Question Time* – a last-minute invite. I imagine the other female guest had dropped out. Mina shone like a jewel amongst the grey-haired, suited men and, by my measure, the audience clapped louder for her – bursting into applause every time she spoke. They couldn't get enough of her.

'Make sure Lord A has a look over these in good time, Christine.' I knew the financial director, from my time as a temp, and I took the file from him with a smile. 'I wish I'd been able to hang on to you in our department,' he said. 'You don't know what you've got 'til it's gone, as they say. Tell Lord A to shout if he has any questions, I'm around all morning.'

'Don't worry, Ron, I'll make sure he goes over the figures.'

I took the file into Lord Appleton's office and left it with him to read before he was driven to the studio. Mina only just missed him.

'Damn. I wanted to catch him,' she said, waving another file around. 'He's gone off with the wrong figures.' She slapped the file down on my desk. 'Can you get over there, Christine? Tell him there was a mix-up and we've just got these from Ron. Quick as you can.' I did as I was told, yet I knew if Mr Beresford had made a mistake, he would have rectified it himself at once. Still, I didn't hesitate and jumped in a cab to the television studio, and was shown through to make-up. Lord Appleton sat in a chair, wearing a bib like a toddler about to be fed.

'Christine?'

'You've been given the wrong figures, Lord Appleton. We've just got these from Ron.' I was flustered as I handed the file over, but he remained calm.

'Don't worry, dear. It'll be fine. I've done this countless times.' As I turned to leave, he stopped me. 'Have you seen a live television show before, Christine?'

'No.'

'Well, why don't you stay and watch? No need to rush back, is there?'

So I was there, in the studio, to witness his humiliation as the presenter tripped him up over the figures. They simply did not add up. He stumbled on, trying to correct himself, but came across as defensive. I watched his growing panic. At one point, he looked around in desperation, perhaps hoping I would rush forward and rescue him. I didn't move – mesmerized by the car crash I was watching. The more he floundered, the more he raised his voice, as if that would give him some authority. Instead, it only added to the spectacle.

I left the studio before him, and hurried out to the waiting car. When I watched him come out of the building, I saw he was broken. He knew I'd heard and seen everything, yet he said nothing when he got into the car, turning and looking out of the window, his hands trembling in his lap. It was a cruel and nasty stunt, and although not engineered by me, I performed my role with precision.

Mina repaired the damage to the company when she appeared on the news that evening. She was a natural in front of the camera, and the contrast between her and her father was exquisite. She was calm, measured, and in full command of the numbers. By the end of the week, Lord Appleton had announced his retirement, and no one tried to persuade him to stay. *Such a pity he didn't go sooner*, once-loyal colleagues muttered.

'A small but vital cog in the machinery,' is how I was once described, and I think that's right. I have always taken care of the little things.

6

Sunday Chronicle, 8 August 1999

WHAT I KNOW

MINA APPLETON, CHAIR, APPLETON'S SUPERMARKETS

Born at Fincham Hall in the Cotswolds. Left school at sixteen and attended the DeBeauvoir Cooking School in Lausanne, Switzerland. Appleton's supermarkets were founded by her grandfather in 1925. She lives in London with her three children.

When are you happiest?
In my kitchen. It's the heart of our home.

What is the naughtiest thing you've ever done?
When I was eight I put dye in my father's shampoo, so when he took his seat in the House of Lords, he did it with a blue rinse.

Which living person do you most admire and why?
My father for his capacity for forgiveness.

What is the most important lesson life has taught you?
To trust my instincts.

'*What I Know*'. It's a piece of froth, full of untruths. Mina didn't admire her father, and I doubt he ever forgave her for pushing him out of the company. And Mina's kitchen may have been the 'heart of her home', but it was little more than a stage set – and later did, in fact, become one. And was she at her happiest there? Perhaps – when there was an audience to watch her. I wonder, though, whether she has ever been truly happy. Nothing is ever quite good enough for her. She is a woman doomed to live in a state of mild dissatisfaction. People, places, things – they never manage to live up to her demanding standards.

As I paste the cutting into my scrapbook, the glue bubbles under the words *To trust my instincts*, and I smooth it away with the heel of my hand. Mina's instincts are those of the predator. Like a fox, she is prepared to destroy, even when she's not hungry. Even when she's sated from a three-course meal, she'll still trash the coop for the sport of it. Nothing more than they deserve, she'll tell herself. They're chickens. Stupid and weak.

Yet, I was proud to march by her side, thrilled to be part of the new guard. With Mina at the helm, Appleton's took on a fresh glow, as if it had been sent for a makeover and emerged with a whole new wardrobe that revealed how startlingly attractive it was beneath its dowdy exterior.

She brought in a new team, dismissing the old guard with ruthless precision. It happened quickly. Financial director Ronald Beresford, my old boss, was the first to go. It was easy to blame him for the debacle over the figures, and when he tried to defend himself, his former allies looked away. No one was prepared to stand up to Mina.

On his last day, I went downstairs and saw him through his office window, clearing his desk. I watched as he placed the framed photographs of his family into a cardboard box, knowing security were on their way up to escort him from the building. It's not unusual for sacked employees, those who've had access to sensitive material, to be marched out like criminals. As he closed the flaps on the box, he looked up and saw me, and smiled. He bore me no malice, and, I suspect, understood – as I didn't, back then – that I, too, was one of the chickens. That it was only a matter of time.

Mina replaced him with a whizz-kid from the airline industry – Rupert French. We had a new communications director too – Paul Richardson, a master of his craft, with a whole new department created beneath him. An entire floor of people, beavering away to promote, and protect, the image of the company, and Mina's image too. She has always understood that it's how things appear, and not how they are, that counts. Under Paul's wizardry, Mina became the face of Appleton's.

Paul Richardson and I hit it off from the start. He was one of those people who, however busy he was, always had time to pop his head around my door for a chat. He described me once as an enigma, and convinced himself I was privately educated.

'Oh come on, Chrissie – don't tell me that accent of yours isn't from some posh girls' school. Admit it.'

'Don't be silly, Paul,' I protested, amused.

'Then you were finished off in Switzerland, like Mina?'

'I was "finished off", as you put it, at secretarial college and then straight out to work.'

He wasn't the first to comment on my accent. My own father mentioned it once: *Must be that new job rubbing off on you, Christine.* There's no doubt I blossomed under Mina's influence. Like the business itself, I slimmed down and spruced up.

7

The more Mina came to depend on me, the more my confidence grew. Increasingly, she trusted me with personal matters, never doubting my discretion. Not that she ever needed to. She gave me the passwords to her bank accounts, I was on first-name terms with her account manager, I picked up her prescriptions when she needed them, which wasn't often, but it meant I knew every ailment she suffered from, however intimate. We flourished together, Mina and I. She, undoubtedly, the dominant species. I, like a woodland plant, able to blossom in her shade. I was good groundcover, you might say.

I never found my job boring, though I am well aware there are those who view being a secretary as a stepping stone to something else. Not me. I was happy to serve Mina, and there were many occasions when her simple acts of generosity disarmed me. She gave me a company credit card, so I was never out of pocket, trusting that I would not abuse my position. I collected all the receipts, but no one ever checked them. Someone less honest than me could easily have run up thousands of pounds, and no one would have known. She insisted I hire two girls to work under me, so I didn't get bogged down in admin.

Sarah and Lucy – PAs number two and three, respectively. She even allowed us the use of her Hyde Park flat during a twenty-four-hour rail strike, because she knew it would be difficult for us to get into work in the morning.

'Don't be silly, Christine. There's no need for you to catch a bus at dawn. The flat's only a short walk from the office. Here, take the keys for goodness' sake.' She pressed them into my hand. 'There's room for Lucy and Sarah too.' I had hoped the train strike would deliver the silver lining of a day in the office without Lucy and Sarah.

'It's a shame you had to miss your little girl's play this evening, Christine,' Lucy said, as I stood and looked from the top-floor window of the flat, watching the poor souls below me, struggling to get home before the strike began. I ignored her. 'I'm sure we could have managed in the office without you, tomorrow.'

I tore myself away from the view out of the window, and turned around. They were both sprawled out on the white sofa, giddy from the Appleton's sparkling wine Mina had left us. I was only a year or two older than them, yet I felt like their mother.

'Sure you won't have any, Christine?' Sarah said, waving the bottle around.

'Not for me, thank you.'

I was exhausted. They'd spent most of the evening trying, and failing, to draw me into some indiscretion about Mina. I watched Lucy haul herself up from the sofa, weaving towards the glass shelves where Mina displayed a few tasteful pieces of porcelain and glass. I wondered about warning her of their value. Or explaining to her that some of the objects were irreplaceable. She reached out and picked up a slender tube of coloured glass. Something you might put a single stem in. Lucy was a clumsy girl, and I waited for her to fumble and drop it. I imagined it ricocheting against a shelf, smashing into pieces on the floor. Saw the look on her face, when she realized what she'd done. If she broke anything, I'd have to give her an official warning. Three strikes and you're out, was my unspoken rule with the girls. I held my breath, but she returned it safely to the shelf.

'Well, I'm off to bed,' I said. 'Early start tomorrow. I'll wake you at seven. Night, now.'

Mina had asked me to sleep in her room, the girls in the spare, and I closed the door and leaned against it, relieved, at last, to have some peace. I looked around. I still remember the detail of the room, the shapes and colours of the labels on the tubes and pots of cream on her dressing table – how they were lined up in front of the mirror. I squeezed a bean-sized amount of hand cream into my palm, rubbing it in and breathing in what the label described as Tuscan Summer, and I imagined that's how it might smell, after the rain. A hint of rosemary.

I took a shower, helping myself, as Mina insisted, to the luxury soaps and creams in the en-suite and then wrapping myself in a fresh, white towel, picked up my clothes from the floor, bundling my dirty underwear into a ball and tucking it in the bottom of my overnight bag. I hung my suit for the morning alongside Mina's in the wardrobe, and ran my fingers along the delicate fabrics there – silks, cashmeres, Irish linens. One of her go-to pieces was a pale pink silk blouse and I took it from its hanger. I never wore pink, and wondered whether the colour might suit me, and then I found myself slipping my arms into its sleeves, though I was unable to do up the tiny gold buttons down its front. Mina wore that blouse under a pale grey jacket with white stitching around the lapel and pockets. Armani, I read on the label. The phone beside the bed rang, and I jumped, thinking it might be Mina. That somehow she was watching me.

'Hello?'

'She's only just fallen asleep.'

It was Mike, and I closed my eyes, picturing him leaning against the kitchen counter, the Pyrex dish from the dinner I'd left sitting to soak in the sink, waiting for my return. I always left supper when I had to work late – cooking and freezing meals at weekends, for the week ahead.

'I bet she was excited after the play.'

'She cried herself to sleep. She wanted you.'

'I spoke to her earlier – she sounded fine.'

'I know. I heard her singing her song down the phone to you. But as soon as you said goodbye she was in bits, Chris.'

'But she sounded happy, like—'

'She didn't want to upset you. It's not fair on her.'

'I'm sorry. You know I would have been there if I could.'

'Surely Mina could have done without you for one day? And there was a bloody train strike, as well. She could have given you the day off.'

'Well, she didn't. And there'll be other plays. I promise I'll be there next time.'

'Sorry to go on. It's just Angelica's getting so good at covering her feelings. She shouldn't be doing that at eight, should she?'

'She must have been overtired. It can't be just because I wasn't there. Maybe she's coming down with something. She must have been knackered with all the excitement.'

'I didn't call to make you feel bad.'

'I know.' I was still wearing Mina's blouse, unbuttoned – and I looked down at my stomach, puckered and fleshy from pregnancy. I put my hand on it, as if a bit of Angelica was still in there, somewhere. I'd have plenty of opportunities in the years ahead, I thought, to beam and clap along with the other parents.

'Chris? Are you still there?'

'Yes. I'll see both of you tomorrow evening. I'll get home in good time. Love you.'

'Love you too,' he said.

After returning Mina's blouse to the wardrobe, I put on her dressing gown and listened at the door, to make sure the girls had gone to bed, then went out and poured myself a large brandy. I knocked it back, washed up the glass and put it away. The girls had left the sitting room untidy, so I cleared away their dirty glasses, threw out the empty bottle of fizz, wiped down the coffee table and plumped up cushions. I straightened the vase Lucy had picked up, turning it so it was as I remembered. I was so careful, yet I must have caught the sleeve of Mina's dressing gown on a tiny glass bird. I watched, helpless, as it toppled to the floor.

I looked down at it, lying broken, and felt as if I'd killed a living thing. Its beak and tail had snapped clean off. It was a wren. I stooped down and picked up the pieces, hoping Mike might be able to glue them back together, but when I held them in my hand, I knew it would be impossible. It was too delicate. As I stood up, I stepped back on to a splinter of glass. Tiny, but sharp enough to penetrate the tough skin of my heel. Holding the pieces in my hand, I hopped back into the bedroom, careful not to spot blood on to the pale carpets. I wrapped the broken bird in my dirty washing to take home, then sat on the bed to try to remove the splinter. The more I probed with Mina's tweezers, the deeper it seemed to go, and I gave up and covered it with a plaster. It hurt for weeks – a twinge of pain, every time I took a step. It must still be in there – buried under the skin – though I stopped feeling it a long time ago.

8

The next morning I woke at six thirty, and was out of the door by seven. I left the girls a note, not bothering to wake them – *No rush, take your time* – and looked forward to a peaceful morning in the office. It was a glorious day, and I remember feeling a glow, setting off with a clear sense of purpose to the job I loved. In the light of day I was able to forget my call with Mike the previous evening. Hyde Park was almost empty as I strode across it with the dress Mina had asked me to pick up for her, sheathed in polythene, flying out behind me like a chivalric banner.

I marched on, through some of the most coveted addresses in London. Tree-lined streets, houses with glossy, black-painted doors and polished brass fittings. Some are homes, some offices – the domestic and business worlds nestling up against each other. Unless you know, it's quite hard to tell them apart: businesses disguised as homes with their pretty window boxes – the only giveaway, discreet plaques etched with company names. Up the marble steps of Appleton's, a wave to the security man, the glass doors parting before me.

'You're in early, Christine, even for you.'

'Yes. Busy day.' My days were always busy then.

My first call was to Mina's driver. Dave Santini was my most trusted colleague – my brother-in-arms. Like me, he had been hand-picked, replacing the ridiculous liveried chauffeur Lord Appleton had been driven around by. Mina had hailed Dave's black cab one evening and, by the end of the journey, she'd made up her mind he was just what she needed. I don't know exactly what it was that drew her to him but, I imagine, it was those same qualities of loyalty and discretion she'd detected in me. I believe Dave took more persuading than I had – he'd paid out a lot of money for his cab and spent years doing The Knowledge – but persuade him she did. Years later, I discovered that Dave had run up not inconsiderable debts and that, when Mina hired him, she paid them all off.

The cuttings I have on Dave fill only one page of my scrapbook. Like me, he is there, yet not. A below-stairs figure. Less than a thousand words, and so many of them inaccurate. One ill-informed newspaper reported he'd once worked as a security guard. It wasn't true, he never had, and I resented it because it gave the impression of a man thuggish by nature. I know David Santini as sensitive and thoughtful – a good soul who would never hurt anyone.

I wanted to speak to him before I left for The Laurels, but his son picked up and told me his father was in hospital. A heart attack, he said. When I started to cry, he put the phone down on me. I would have liked to visit Dave, but when I called back, I was told *family only*. Poor Dave. Like me, he could not have foreseen the obligations that came with being a trusted servant to Mina Appleton. He and I were 'the accused', all eyes on us as we stood in the dock. It broke us both.

My collapse had come sooner than Dave's – not long after the trial was over. I remember one morning, walking to the station to catch my train to work. *One foot in front of the other, Christine,*

I told myself. It was the first time I'd left the house in weeks. It was rush hour and the platform was crowded, yet the commuters seemed to part before me. When the train arrived, the seats were snapped up, but as I made my way through the carriage, a man stood up and gave me his. I tried to thank him, but he looked away and I understood why when I saw my reflection in the window. My heart seemed to be in a race with the train and I rested the fingers of my right hand on my pulse. I counted over a hundred and seventy beats a minute.

I felt safer on the Underground. No one offered me a seat – no one really noticed me. I'd become invisible – one of them, a commuter, taking the journey I had taken for years. Yet, as soon as I stepped out at Oxford Circus, I froze. I could feel the irritation of the mob surging around me, and remembered how I too used to get impatient when tourists, or mothers with children, dared be on the street in rush hour, dithering around, holding me up. Now, it was me who had no business being amongst busy, working people.

I could have made that journey blindfolded and forced myself on towards Margaret Street, then Cavendish Square. John Lewis was not yet open, but the staff were arriving and I stopped to watch them go in through the Partners' Entrance, envying them their sense of belonging. I continued on, crossing the road on to Wigmore Street, retracing my old route, and as I walked I felt the lining of my coat flapping against my calves, from where I'd caught my heel in it that morning. I remember the sound of the fabric tearing. On I went to Welbeck Street, passing the dry-cleaner's where I'd collected so many poly-wrapped garments over the years – never mine, always hers. I stopped to look in the window of the stationery shop, like a child drooling at sweets, and had to drag myself away, suddenly frightened I'd be late. I was never late. So I ran, and when I arrived at the building, I was panting, and I realized the unpleasant smell in the street was coming from me. A nasty doggy smell. The clothes I had put on that morning had been lying damp on the floor for a week. I couldn't let anyone see me, so I retreated into a doorway and watched from across the road as my former colleagues walked up the marble steps of Appleton's, the glass doors parting before them, as they once had for me.

Dave's heart was broken. For me, it was my mind. He is unlikely to recover. My prognosis, however, is good. Every day I spend at The Laurels feels like one more step on my road to recovery.

9

Mina's privacy was always something I took great care with, but when it came to the media my hands were often tied. In my view, she had a rather relaxed attitude to the press, frequently going above and beyond what I would have considered reasonable in accommodating their demands. I remember, in the early days, accompanying her to the television studios for the Good Food Awards (she was one of the judges); a straggle of journalists had gathered outside and Mina, noticing some inexperienced photographer fumbling with her camera, actually stopped and waited for the girl to get her act together. Then she made her entrance all over again, while I waited for goodness knows how long in the foyer. *They're friends, not foe, Christine*, she said when she caught me checking my watch.

The media loved Mina, so I shouldn't have been surprised when television producers started sniffing around. By then she had an agent who managed her appearances and, with her natural poise in front of the camera, it was inevitable she'd be offered her own show.

At first I was suspicious. I worried that her privacy would be further compromised – and as it turns out, I was right. If she hadn't become so famous, then I am sure there would not have been such a hullabaloo later. If she'd stayed off our screens then, perhaps, the newspapers wouldn't have been as interested in digging around in her business affairs. My opinion was never sought, though. And when I witnessed the ease with which Mina straddled the worlds of business and entertainment, I was converted to the cause. I saw how those worlds fed off each other. They loved rubbing shoulders; Mina had always known that. She introduced politicians to the mix too, hosting dinners and parties where she moved amongst her guests, binding them together, treating everyone as a friend, yet I doubt any of them really were. For them, Mina was a gateway into a parallel universe – a tear in the stratosphere – allowing their worlds to cross over and mingle under her stewardship.

Mina at Home was the title of her television series. I was there at the recording of the pilot, sitting on a silver camera box, tucked in a corner of her kitchen.

'Why don't you pop by on your way home? Dave can bring you. Say around six?'

She didn't even look up from her desk, and I wonder now why she wanted me there.

'Yes. Thank you. I'd like that.'

I suppose I could have said *No, thank you*. It was not on my way home and I'd already missed Angelica's bedtime twice that week. It might have been good for Mina if, over the years, she learned that the word *no* from me was at least a possibility. I spoiled her, I'm afraid. If I had laid down some boundaries early on, like you do with children, then, perhaps, things might have been different. Instead I pushed thoughts of my own family to one side and hurried down after work, to find Dave waiting for me in the car. I sat in the front, breathing in the seductive smell of the leather seats as we nipped through rush-hour traffic, ducking and diving through the back streets.

'She wants you to pick up a few things for her on the way over,' Dave said, handing me a shopping list.

Back then there was no Appleton's supermarket between the office and Mina's home, so we stopped at a rival store. We had the whole thing off pat, Dave and I. He would pull up on a yellow line and wait while I whipped round with a basket, as if I were like everyone else there, grabbing a few last-minute bits for supper on my way home. When I came out, Dave would pop open the boot and I would decant the shopping into the supply of Appleton's carrier bags we kept there. It was one of the house rules: no rival brand must be seen going in or out of Mina's home. It was second nature to me by then, those innocent little deceits.

I had my own key to the Notting Hill house, and when I opened the front door that evening I could feel heat rising up from the television lights in the basement. After taking a moment to adjust to the new atmosphere, I crept downstairs as quietly as I could and peeked around the door at the confusion of equipment and people, Mina at their heart.

I remember she wore a red shirt I didn't recognize – something from the wardrobe department, I guessed. The top few buttons were undone, so when she leaned over to roll out pastry you could see the tiniest glimpse of her cleavage. Not too much. An audience might believe those buttons had undone themselves. Her hair was loose, breaking all hygiene codes, but I could see what they were up to – it was a form of branding. Those wild curls became Mina's trademark. From time to time she brushed away a stray lock with the back of her hand, and when the make-up girl stepped forward to wipe away a streak of flour from Mina's cheek, the director stopped her. He was quite right, that smudge added authenticity. There she was, Mina in her kitchen, simply being herself.

After about twenty minutes of standing there with the

shopping bags, frozen peas dripping against my leg, I picked my way through the lights to the fridge, tripping over cables and people en route, and succeeded in putting away the shopping without betraying the enemy brands. I stayed for another hour and a half, sitting in my corner, sweating under the lights, possibly a little flushed. I was excited to be part of it, yet I doubt anyone noticed I was there.

10

Here I am. *Christine Butcher, Mina Appleton's right-hand woman.*
My name in print for the first time. I set my ruler on the page
and run a fine pencil around the article, then trim its edges.
Mina is there too. The two of us alone in a photograph – me
standing just behind her right shoulder. It will take up two
pages in my scrapbook – one for the picture, another for the
three hundred words written about me.

The piece appeared in *The Lady* magazine, when Mina's
television show was in full swing. It was one of a series of interviews with personal assistants to people of influence, under the
headline 'The Gatekeepers'. It still cheers me, when I read it.
My moment in the spotlight. When the magazine approached
me, I cleared it with Mina, and she helped me out with a few
choice phrases – things she thought would help show me in the
best light.

*'It's my job to make sure Ms Appleton's life runs smoothly. It's a
very fluid line between her personal and working lives, you see, which
means no two days are ever the same. One minute I might be organizing the agenda for a meeting with the Appleton's board and the next
picking up her dry-cleaning and interviewing a new nanny for the*

children. I see my role as a holistic one.' It was how Mina had described my job, when she'd first interviewed me.

You sound like a bloody lady's maid, was my husband's opinion. Mike thought it didn't do me justice. Perhaps. The truth is, looking after the *personal* side of Mina's life was an important part of my job. It was an intricate puzzle, and I was the only one able to keep the pieces in place. Sarah, my number two, seemed to be constantly off on maternity leave – by then she had two children – and Lucy, though willing, was not the brightest button.

'It must be difficult with such a demanding job, isn't it? You have a daughter, I believe,' the sassy young madam from *The Lady* asked, flicking through her notes. *'How do you manage your own work–life balance, Christine?'*

None of your beeswax.

'Without any difficulty,' I told her with a brisk smile. My private life was not up for discussion.

Work–life balance is not a phrase I have ever understood. As far as I'm concerned, work and life are not two separate things to be weighed up on a set of scales. I admit it was a juggling act, keeping all the balls I had to cope with in the air, and there were occasions when I was a butterfingers. But I am proud of my record. In all my years of service to Mina, I had only one and a half days' absence; even our family holidays were taken the same time as hers.

It wasn't easy for Angelica, having a mum who worked unpredictable hours, and I tried hard to make it up to her. If Mike was out, she and I would curl up on the sofa together and watch TV. When *Mina at Home* was on, she loved the behind-the-scenes stories I told her. How Mina burned her first batch of beetroot brownies. How, when making crème brûlée, she singed her hair with her cook's blowtorch.

At weekends, Angelica wouldn't leave my side. Saturdays she

spent on a stool at the kitchen counter, watching as I prepared meals for the week ahead. Sundays, however, I devoted to her. Then, we would bake treats together – biscuits, cakes, that sort of thing – and the smell of them wafting through the house was a comfort to us both, I think.

'Who are those for?' she asked me once, eyeing with suspicion some biscuits I was wrapping in brown paper. I looked up and saw her consternation.

'Come here, sweetheart,' I said, holding out my hand, and inviting her on to my lap. She was nine by then, but still as cuddly as she'd been at four. I kissed the top of her head.

'They're a present for Lottie, Mina's daughter. She's away at boarding school. You know what boarding school is, don't you?' She nodded.

'I thought we could send some to the boys too. They're not lucky like you – living at home with your mum and dad. The biscuits will cheer them up, don't you think?' She nodded again, and I showed her how to tie raffia bows around the packages, as I had seen Mina do, years back.

With the growing demands on her time, it was difficult for Mina to give her children the attention they needed, and so I did what I could to help. As I wrote notes to attach to the gifts, Angelica locked her arms around my waist, resting her cheek against my chest, and I wonder now if she was worried I might parcel myself up, too, as a gift for those children. It was no trouble, parcelling up a few home-made goodies on my weekends off, then popping them in the post with a note. By then I had Mina's writing down to a T.

11

It has taken me a while to settle in here, but now I feel quite at home. The Laurels lies in a secluded spot and I spend a lot of my time looking from the window in my room, a cup of tea in my hand. Just sitting and watching. I have turned around the chair so it faces outwards, giving me a bird's-eye view.

It was always a dream of mine to, one day, live on the coast. Occasionally at night, when I close my eyes and the wind rushes through the leaves, it does sound like the sea. Sometimes, I can actually make myself believe I am there, although the trees are so close that, when the wind is high, the branches tap on the window and it sounds as if someone is asking to come in, and then I am brought back to reality.

Today a headache gnaws at my temple, so I get back into bed and pull the covers over me. I close my eyes and listen to the leaves outside, hoping they will work their magic. That their sound will soothe the clamour in my head. I try to imagine I am floating, the branches passing me from one to the other, holding me up, not letting me fall. I am feather-light, aloft, and after a while I'm able to open my eyes again. Below me is the past and, from up here, I find it less painful to look at.

I was accused of laying down my family as a sacrifice on the altar of Mina Appleton, and for years I denied it.

'Please, Chris. Tell her you can't go.' It was Sunday afternoon, December, already dark outside. Mike stood over me as I packed for a trip to New York. My flight left at eight that evening. 'You said someone else was going this time. Why the change of plan? And why so last-minute?' It was not an unreasonable question – one that would be asked of me again years later, so long after the event that it took me by surprise. It was phrased differently, but still it was the same question.

It was me who tended to accompany Mina on her overseas trips. We travelled first class, stayed in the best hotels and I don't deny I took pleasure in these perks. As I carried on folding my clothes and laying them in the suitcase, Mike rested his hands on mine, held them gently, then turned me to face him. 'Please, love,' he said. He wasn't angry, he was confused. 'Just ring her now and tell her you can't go. Stand up to her.'

'It's not a question of standing up to her, Mike.' But it was. 'It turns out Lucy can't go, after all. And Sarah's still off. And anyway, it's only four days.' I sounded matter-of-fact, my voice betraying none of the anguish I felt. 'I'll be back at the weekend.' He let my hands go and I turned away, but I could feel him watching me as I zipped up the case. Felt his eyes still on me as I opened the drawer next to the bed and took out my passport.

'I don't know what to say to you, Christine. Surely you see family should come first?' He sounded so lost, and yet it was me, not him, who would live to regret my decision to go on that trip.

'Mike. It's only four days.'

The truth was Lucy would have been perfectly able to go. It would have been her first time accompanying Mina, and I'd spent time prepping her, making sure she understood the responsibility. She was excited. Grateful to me for having suggested she go in my place. Before I'd gone home on the Friday, I went in to wish Mina a successful trip and to make sure she was comfortable with everything. As soon as I walked in, though, I knew she wasn't happy.

She kept her back to me the whole time, refusing to even acknowledge my presence. As I ran her through the schedule again, which, admittedly, was complex – a series of back-to-back meetings, lunches and dinners – she drummed her fingers on the windowsill.

'I'm sorry I'm not able to come with you, but I'm sure Lucy will manage,' I said, not for the first time.

'You've made your priorities clear, Christine, and I won't pretend I'm not disappointed. I'd hoped, given how stressful this trip will be for me, that you might change your mind. However, as you say, Lucy will muddle through.' She looked at her watch. 'Goodness, is that the time? I'm surprised you're still here. Shouldn't you be running home to your family?' I was stung by the scorn in her voice.

I returned to my office, intending to put on my coat and go home, but found myself sitting back down at my desk. I had never let Mina down before – never given her cause to voice disappointment in me. I like to think I hesitated, but I'm not sure I did, when I picked up the phone and made the necessary calls to the airline, booking myself on to the flight. I lied to Mike because I didn't want him to see how spineless I was. I couldn't say no to Mina.

When she saw me waiting at the airport on Sunday evening I read, not admiration exactly in her eyes, but certainly a kind of respect I hadn't seen before.

'You changed your mind. Excellent. I appreciate your professionalism, Christine. It will be good to have your cool head with me on this trip.'

My cool head. Something Mina saw as a quality and my husband a failing.

As I opened the front door to leave, it must have seemed to Mike as if I didn't care. But I did. I really did. 'You can still change your mind, you know,' he said as the taxi hooted outside. It is one of my greatest regrets that I didn't listen to him, that I didn't change my mind.

I slept badly on that trip, and I remember on my last night in New York looking down from the window of my hotel bedroom, the curtains pulled behind me, my forehead resting against the glass. The buildings were lit up with festive colour. I admired that city for putting on a brave face. It was 2003, only two years since the attack that exposed its vulnerability, yet from where I stood it was hard to believe it had ever taken place. Even at four in the morning a sprinkle of cars moved through the streets below, their red tail-lights snaking one into the other. I watched them, sealed behind the double-glazing, the windows screwed shut to stop people jumping out on to Park Avenue below. Something I wouldn't have considered back then.

I returned to bed and closed my eyes – not to sleep, but so I could run through the next day's itinerary. I did this sometimes when I needed to relax. An exercise to put my thoughts in order. I could conjure up a clear picture of Mina's schedule for the next day, the times and names of everyone she was meeting – publishers interested in buying the rights to an American edition of her cookbook. The names of their secretaries too, addresses and telephone numbers – the direct lines and the switchboard. The cell phone of the driver who would be chauffeuring us around. It's never left me, my perfect recall. A photographic memory is still part of my skill-set. Numbers, names, I can rustle them all up with surprising ease.

The itinerary was tight and I knew I'd spend much of the day on the phone – calling ahead if we were delayed, shifting appointments around, making use of the white spaces I could picture in my head. It made Mina believe she had all the time in the world, and certainly she used to glide from meeting to meeting with no sign of stress.

The following day it snowed and I was worried our flight home might be delayed, that I would be away for longer than the four days I'd promised. I couldn't relax until we took off, and then I felt Mina shift in the seat beside me, her eye-mask already in place. Within minutes she was asleep. I tried watching a film, hoping it might help me sleep too, but it didn't, and I couldn't concentrate, so I focused instead on the image of the plane on the screen in front of me, tracing its route as it made its way inch by inch across the Atlantic and home.

I suppose I should have seen it coming. It was spring the following year when Mike told me he was leaving. I was washing up after supper. He said he'd been seeing someone else, that he had fallen in love with her, that he didn't want to lie to me. The truth. I felt it in the cold water that leaked into my rubber gloves.

'Please, Christine. Sit down. Look at me, at least.'

I didn't want to.

'Not once have you ever questioned me about where I've been, why I'm out so often in the evenings. Who I'm with. You're so wrapped up in your job, I wonder whether you've even noticed.'

'Of course I have. I'm tired, that's all. When I get home, I feel so tired.'

'Is it worth it? Your job? We have a bigger house, Angelica goes to private school, but I don't want any of those things, and I'm not sure Angie does either. She'd rather have you. You're never here, and when you are, you're not really present. Our home is a place you drift in and out of on your way to and from work.'

I looked away, and I remember how surprised I was to feel his arms around me. He held me for a moment and then went upstairs and packed a case and left. Ten p.m., Sunday, 18 April 2004. The end of my marriage.

My headache is easing and I open my eyes. I can tell by the way the shadows fall in my room that it is late afternoon, probably around four o'clock. I stopped wearing a watch when I came here, a feeble rebellion, perhaps, but one I relish. I've even taped over the clock on my laptop. It's not that I want to stop time, rather that I refuse to be a slave to it any more. I am quite content to allow it to slip away as quickly or as slowly as it chooses.

12

It still surprises me, looking back, how moments of innocence can take on the appearance of devious intent over the passage of time. How a cynical eye can twist things out of shape, and turn them into something that must be explained and justified and defended.

I remember the weekend of the office move as a pleasant one, not as something to be picked over and dissected.

'It'll be fun,' I said to Angelica on the train up to London. I'd enlisted her help that Saturday. 'You'd like to see where I work, wouldn't you, love? Dave's coming to help and he's bringing his son. You can earn a bit of pocket money. We'll order in pizza for lunch and eat in the boardroom.' She shrugged and turned away. She was twelve, and I'd hoped she'd be as excited as I was to see the new offices Mina had created on the top floor, but not a bit of it. Adolescence had come early for Angelica and, with it, an indifference to me that only hardened over the coming years.

In Lord Appleton's day, the top floor had been panelled in dark wood and hung with heavy oil paintings of country scenes but Mina ripped it all out with the zeal of an invading foreign power. It was as if the shutters of a fusty, old house had been pulled back, the windows and doors flung open and fresh air, at last, let in. It seemed to promise a new era of transparency.

I left Angelica to unpack and arrange the shoes Mina kept in the office – standbys for last-minute engagements – while I went next door to unpack my things. I sat behind my desk and looked out at the clean, bright space and felt a tingle of pleasure. A room of my own. That place was a sanctuary to me. I had more joy in unpacking and setting out my things in my new office than I'd had when we'd moved into our new home.

'Where do you want this, Christine?'

Dave's son was in the doorway, holding a box. I smiled and went over, peeling back the flap. Inside were papers and files Mina had asked me to clear from a drawer in her desk. *Relics*, she'd called them, *from my father's time*.

'They're for the archive, Freddie. Leave them here for now.' I can picture that box, tucked in the corner of my office, and I hear it ticking. At the time, I didn't give it a second thought. 'Why don't you go and see if your dad's back with the pizzas?'

I went to fetch Angelica, and found her wearing a pair of Mina's shoes, sitting behind the desk with her feet up. She swivelled around in the chair and looked at me. In her hand was a pen, and she held it like a cigar, bringing it to her lips and inhaling imaginary smoke.

'Could you fetch me my lunch, Christine? Bring it to my desk. And hurry up about it. I'm starving,' she said.

I laughed, but I didn't find it funny.

'Who are you supposed to be? Mina? She doesn't smoke. Come on. Pizzas are here.'

She kicked off the shoes, then curled her feet up beneath her on the chair, coiling a strand of her hair around her finger. It wasn't a bad impersonation.

'Why aren't you at her wedding?' she said.

I hadn't realized she knew Mina was getting married that day.

'I'm working. This is work, in case you hadn't noticed. Now, come on, let's go and eat.' I kept smiling as I picked up Mina's shoes from the floor and took them to the cupboard. 'You've done a great job here, Angie,' I said, running my eyes over the shelves, hoping to distract her.

'You bought a new outfit, didn't you?'

I crouched down, putting the shoes away, keeping my back to her.

'And a hat. Will you take them back?'

'What were you doing rifling through my wardrobe?'

'I saw the carrier bags – the new stuff didn't make it to your wardrobe, so I guess you'll be taking it all back.'

I stood up and shrugged, not knowing what to say. I was embarrassed, and she saw it.

'I'm sorry, Mum.' She got off the chair, came over and gave me a hug. 'It was only banter.' I wished I'd been able to conceal my hurt better. She was only twelve and I didn't want her to feel bad for me, yet even at her tender age, she'd sniffed out the blurred lines in my relationship with Mina.

'It's fine, love. I'd much rather be here with you than at the wedding.' But Angelica was right: I had bought a new outfit for the occasion. *I need something special. I'm going to Mina Appleton's wedding,* I'd said to the sales assistant, who turned out to be a fan. *I love* Mina at Home, she said. *So much better than that Gordon Ramsay. Are you in television too? Not exactly,* I said, *but Mina and I have worked together for years.* Naturally, she'd wanted to know all about Andy Webster, Mina's fiancé. An actor. He was one of the leads in a television soap opera – quite a celebrity at the time. *You must know them well if they've asked you to the wedding.* I'd shrugged and smiled. I cringe now at the memory.

I sometimes wondered why Mina decided to marry Andy Webster. He was a slip of a man, no match for her. Always struck me as rather fey. Two months into their relationship she'd come into my office, closed the door and perched on the corner of my desk. She sat fiddling with the paper clips from my desk tidy, jiggling them from hand to hand, then threading them into a chain. Itching to talk.

'How was your evening?' I'd booked her and Andy a table at Le Caprice.

'We didn't make it into the restaurant. We turned up, but when Andy saw the photographers outside, he grabbed my hand and pulled me away. We drove to the Essex coast – it's where he grew up. We ended up having fish and chips and a bottle of wine on the beach.' She smiled.

'Quite a change. Was it fun?'

'Yes, it was.' She swung her legs like a schoolgirl, straightening out a paper clip and using it to clean her nails. 'The thing is, he's gentle. Kind. Very, very sweet. But I don't know if I can marry him.'

'He proposed?' I was surprised.

'Yes. What do *you* think of him, Christine?'

I barely knew Andy Webster then, yet she studied my face as if it held the answer.

'You don't like him, I can tell . . .'

'I've hardly met him, Mina.' I smiled. 'Are you in love with him?'

'I don't know. That's the thing.' She was genuinely bewildered. 'I was so young when I married the first time. I thought I was in love then.' She shrugged as if she was still unsure.

'You do seem happy with Andy.'

'Yes, but . . .' She looked down. 'We had sex last night. For the first time. To be honest, it wasn't great . . .' She bit the inside of her cheek. 'Not awful, but . . . you know, disappointing.'

I nodded. I did know.

'I don't want to make a mistake. And the idea of going

through another divorce . . .' She started pulling at her hair. 'Tell me what to do, Christine.'

'Well . . .' I weighed it up. 'You said he's gentle, kind and sweet. So maybe that's your answer.'

I think, in the end, though, it was his particular brand of tabloid celebrity that decided her. Andy was a rough diamond that complemented her more refined image – Swiss education, father in the House of Lords. Anyway, she must have considered him an asset. He was useful to her, let's leave it at that.

I remember him sidling into my office not long before the wedding and flopping down on the sofa. He had come to take Mina for dinner, but she was late back from a meeting.

'Can I get you some tea, Andy?'

'Rather have a gin and tonic, Chrissie.'

'Sorry. That I don't have. What about a whisky? There's a bottle in Mina's office. Shall I get it?'

'Can't stand the stuff. Don't worry. I'm sure she'll be back soon.' He made himself comfortable, kicking off his shoes, putting his feet up, and reading the paper. 'I loved the house in Primrose Hill, by the way.' Mina had set me the task of finding them a new home. 'I think Mina did too, didn't she? Has she said anything to you about it?' The answer was, yes, she had, but she'd dismissed the Primrose Hill house before she'd even seen it.

'No, she hasn't said anything. I'm not sure there was much of a garden, was there?' I said, carrying on with my emails. 'Isn't she after a bit of outside space?' As if I didn't know. Land. She wanted land. And lots of it. A country retreat within forty minutes of London.

'The garden was a decent size. I think that house is just right for Mina and me.' I made the mistake of looking up from my screen and catching his eye. He was gazing at me like a puppy. 'Will you talk to her? Try and persuade her?'

'I'll do my best, Andy.' He wasn't to know the hunt was already over. I'd found the perfect house – one of six I looked at for Mina. Thirty-five minutes from London, set in its own grounds with a fishing lake and fields for horses. Mina loved it, but she swore me to secrecy. Andy couldn't know until the purchase had gone through.

Of course, when he found out he came to accept it, as he came to accept everything Mina demanded of him over the years. And to give him his due, for somebody with such limited acting ability, he pulled off the role of devoted husband convincingly. He was there every day for Mina in court, sitting up in the public gallery, along with her three children. The picture of a devoted family. No, I cannot fault him for playing his part with conviction.

13

Jenny Haddow's name flashed up on my phone.

It was 2005, six years since Lord Appleton retired, and yet his former secretary still rang me whenever he had *concerns* about the business. *He's tried talking to Mina,* was how she always began these conversations. The last one had been only two days before. *Lord Appleton is very upset* – she still referred to him as Lord Appleton, even though they lived together at Fincham Hall. *A gentle word from you, Christine, might nudge Mina in the right direction. All he's asking is that she visit Brocklehurst Farm. See for herself what's happening. We know she's brought in a new head of buying, but maybe she isn't fully aware of how he operates. He's come from one of the big chains, hasn't he? They do things differently there. Perhaps, if you slot something into her diary . . .*

I'd told her I'd see what I could do – not that I had any intention of *slotting something into the diary.* I'd seen Brocklehurst Farm on a list in Mina's office, flagged up as a problem supplier, and knew better than to question the ethics of her new head of buying.

'Christine Butcher,' I snapped that morning, when I took her call.

'Christine, it's Jenny here.' I know, I thought, rolling my eyes.

'What is it, Jenny?'

'I've been trying to reach Mina on her mobile but she's not picking up.'

I sighed.

'John's had a fall.' It was the first time I'd heard her use Lord Appleton's first name. 'He was taken into St Thomas's early this morning. I thought she should know . . .' Her voice broke.

'I'm so sorry, Jenny.' I was.

'I tried Mina on John's mobile too, hoping she might answer that, but . . .'

'She's travelling, Jenny. I imagine there's no signal.' I often lied for Mina – always able to find a nugget of truth in what I said. Mina *was* travelling, but only in the car from her new home to the office – a thirty-five-minute journey.

'The doctors fear he might not recover, Christine.'

'I'll track her down, don't worry, Jenny.' Perhaps I said sorry again; in all honesty, I can't remember. I checked my watch. Mina would be here any minute, so I decided to wait and talk to her, rather than relay the news down the phone.

When Jenny had called I'd been putting the finishing touches to a present Mina was taking to Number Ten, that evening. She'd become a friend of the prime minister, and she and Andy had been invited to join the family for their daughter's birthday. Harriet was about to go off to university, and Mina couldn't think what to get her, so I came up with the idea of a cookbook. Mina's own recipes, handwritten – by me – with charming anecdotes. It had turned out beautifully. Mina would be pleased. *To My Dearest Harriet*, I wrote on the inside flap, and signed Mina's name. I was blowing on the ink when I saw Mina walk past. I gave her a minute, then went through with coffee.

'Mina.' I braced myself to break the news. 'Jenny's been on.'

'Yes. I thought she might have.'

I understood then that she already knew. She must have seen Jenny's messages and decided not to respond.

'I'm so sorry, Mina. I'll clear the diary for you.' I assumed she'd want to go straight to the hospital. 'And I'll call Number Ten about tonight, warn them you might not—'

'You'll do no such thing.' She has a brittle quality when she is upset. 'Get Paul on the phone. Actually, you can speak to him for me. Warn him about my father, and get him to draft a press release in case he dies today.' She looked at her watch. 'I'll go to the hospital shortly. Get Dave to bring the car round. Is the present ready?'

'Yes. Would you like to see it?'

'Do I need to? Just leave it on my desk when you've wrapped it.'

Lord Appleton died soon after Mina's visit. She was almost, but not quite, with him at the end. She was in the car on the way back to the office when the hospital called her, and she phoned me straight away.

'I'll need to have a statement prepared – there are bound to be press at Number Ten this evening. A few moving words. Speak to Paul again, will you?'

'Yes. Mina, I'm so sorry . . .' But she didn't want my sympathy. Not then. I understood how she felt – I'd lost my own dad not so long before, and I found myself writing down a few 'moving words' for her – things I might have said if I'd been called on to deliver a speech about my father. I read it back, then toned it down. When Paul dropped by later, I showed it to him.

'She dictated this to me from the car,' I said, handing him the page I'd written. I watched as he raised an eyebrow, nodded, then handed it back.

'Very good. No need for this then,' and he screwed up his notes and dropped them in the bin.

Lord Appleton's death led the seven o'clock news that

evening, in time to catch Mina arriving at Downing Street, her husband by her side. She looked a tiny figure in her black coat, and seemed almost bewildered by the bank of cameras and journalists waiting for her. As if she hadn't known they'd be there.

If you watch that footage, as I have done online many times, you can see how well the scene is choreographed. Her performance is a master class in restraint and dignity. She walks towards the door of Number Ten, her husband's hand under her left elbow, the gift I'd prepared under her right arm. Then she turns at the last moment and takes a step down, leaving Andy behind her, out of shot. She pauses, as if reluctant to speak – though I'd heard her practise that speech in her office, my words coming out of her mouth and back to me, through the wall – and then she looks down, as if gathering strength, before speaking direct to camera.

'I was fortunate to be with my father when he died. I held his hand and we said goodbye.' She pauses. *'He was a great man, a wonderful father and a loving grandfather. I shall miss him very much.'* A beat, and then she turns and goes inside, followed by the cha-cha-cha of camera shutters.

I have studied that performance, looking for the tell when she lied, and it's hard to see it at first. But now I've found it. Next time she does it, I'll know what to look for.

14

On the train that evening, I felt the usual throb behind my left eyebrow as I approached home – a growing tension that I knew would become a full-blown headache by the time I walked through the door. I could hear Angelica's music coming from her bedroom, and I called up, but she didn't hear. At least, she didn't answer.

There were dirty plates from the supper I'd left, in the kitchen sink. I was late back, and couldn't blame her for eating without me. I washed up, and opened the fridge, but wasn't hungry, so I flicked on the kettle, made myself tea and went upstairs.

'Hi, Angie love. How was your day?' She was sitting on the floor painting her toenails. She didn't look up. I hovered in the doorway – the music drilling into my headache, the acrid smell of varnish in my nostrils. Then I took the plunge and went in, kissing the top of her head. 'Hi, love,' I repeated, raising my voice over the music. She jumped, knocking over the bottle of varnish. 'Sorry, I didn't mean to startle you. Why don't you put something down? To protect the carpet.' I set the bottle of nail varnish upright again. 'Can I get you anything? Cup of tea?' She shook her head. She needed something, it was clear, but I felt ill-equipped to provide it. Not her fault. Mine entirely.

'How was your day?' I asked again.

'Boring.'

I approached my fourteen-year-old daughter like she was a wild animal – careful not to provoke, but at the same time, longing to stroke her. So much of her was still a child, and yet I knew her teeth and claws could be lethal.

'I'm sure it wasn't that bad,' I said. She bristled with irritation.

I was useless. I should have put my arm around her, sat down and listened to her music; instead I retreated to the doorway. I felt de-skilled at home. There were no guidelines to follow, no contract of employment to refer to. I was always a better secretary than a mother.

'I might have a bath and an early night,' I said. 'See you in the morning?'

'Night, Mum.'

'Don't be too late, will you,' I said. 'School tomorrow.'

It was midnight by the time she turned off her music, and I fell asleep, but then woke at two. I could hear her voice through the wall, chatting on her mobile phone. She'd nagged me for it when she discovered Mina's daughter, Lottie, had one. The two girls had spent a day in the office, a few weeks before – Mina's idea. *They do it in the States. Bring your daughter to work day.* Much as I'd been dreading it, the day passed without incident, and Mina seemed to think it had been a success. All the way home on the train, I remember how Angelica had gone on about Lottie's phone. *She's older than you*, I'd said. *She's had one since she was twelve*, Angelica countered, and in the end I gave in.

I got out of bed and knocked on her bedroom door, then went in.

'Angie love, it's two in the morning. We agreed. Phones off by eleven.'

'Can you hang on?' she said to whoever she was talking to, then turned to me. 'In a minute,' and went back to her call. 'Anyway . . .'

'No, now,' I said, standing my ground.

'Oh fuck off,' she muttered, but not quietly enough for me to be able to pretend I hadn't heard her.

'Don't speak to me like that.' I tried to produce the authority I had at work – a no-nonsense tone I used when dealing with Sarah or Lucy. 'Did you hear me, Angelica? Now, switch off your phone.' With my daughter, it had no effect. She started giggling, then pulled the duvet up, snuggling down with her mobile.

'Sorry about that . . .' she whispered to her friend.

I pulled back the duvet and snatched the phone from her, my fingers shaking as I switched it off.

'What the fuck? You can't do that!' she yelled, trying to grab it.

'I just did.'

'Give it back. You can't tell me what to do.'

'I'm your mother. It's my job to tell you what to do.'

'Your job? Being my mother? Don't make me laugh! I've seen your job. You're pathetic. You just run around all day, doing as you're told. Bring your daughter to *work* day? I wish you hadn't – it was embarrassing.' I looked at her, my hands trembling, then I turned and walked out. 'You cow,' I heard her say as I closed the door, her voice thick with tears.

After that, home and work became like two continents, moving inexorably apart. For a while, I managed to keep a foothold on each, but in the end, I jumped off one and on to the other. It was not a conscious choice, yet I allowed my home to drift away and didn't notice until it had gone.

15

The road approaching Minerva is lined with tall hedges, behind which lie substantial homes. Converted barns. Swimming pools where orchards once grew. Horses in fields where cows once grazed. Minerva stands out, with its high, red-brick walls and wrought-iron gates – the letters *M* and *A* twisted through their centre. Minerva is the house I found, although Mina chose its name. When I looked it up, I learned Minerva was a Roman goddess – one I found difficult to pin down. Wisdom? Commerce? The arts in general? Even war. Take your pick.

It was the place Mina chose to work from in the weeks following her father's death, and I preferred it to the office. I appreciated its more intimate setting. At Minerva, Mina and I shared her study – her seated at the desk, me at a small, baize-covered card table by the window. If I had to work late, I'd sleep over in the pink room – a small bedroom, down the landing from Mina's. I kept a toothbrush and pyjamas there, which Margaret, the housekeeper, would wash and return to my pillow, ready for next time – *Christine's room,* she used to call it.

It was us staff – the housekeeper, the secretary, the gardeners, the driver – who were the family that filled that big house.

The children – all teenagers by then – were still at boarding school, and rarely home for weekends. Andy spent Monday to Friday in the Hyde Park apartment, performing his role as Mina's husband only at weekends, escorting her if they went away, or playing host when she entertained at Minerva. To the outside world, they still appeared a happily married couple.

Dave picked me up in the mornings, and I remember the whip of pleasure as the car pulled up outside my house. Like a child looking back at summer holidays, I recall the sun always seemed to shine. If I close my eyes, I can still smell the piney scent of the cut-out Christmas tree that hung from the rear-view mirror, mingling with Dave's aftershave and the leather of the seats. I'd watch my own house disappear from view, and sit back as Dave's capable hands steered me through traffic, the muscles of his forearms flexing, the light catching the hairs on his tanned skin. It was a seductive way to begin the day. Most people talk longingly of that Friday-afternoon feeling. For me it came on Sundays, with the anticipation of the week ahead. Thank God it's Sunday, I used to think. I was often alone at weekends – Angelica choosing to spend more and more of them with her father and his new partner, Ursula.

I opened Mina's front door with my key, a cursory knock on the study door, then in to find her already at her desk.

'I've started on the guest list for my father's memorial. I was thinking the Wallace Collection for the venue. Dad was a patron there, and it's around the corner from the office. Could you give them a call? Speak to the keeper of pictures – Cathcart, I think he's called – he was a good friend of my father's.'

'Of course. Have you had coffee yet?'

'No – I asked Margaret to wait for you.' She smiled. 'Will you carry on with the guest list, and I'll get on with my calls.' She picked up one of the three mobile phones on her desk.

That morning, she was on the phone non-stop. One call after

another, speaking to her head of buying, director of communications and finance director – Stephen, Paul and Rupert.

'. . . the new suppliers are in place, aren't they? So a fax will do. To the Frasers and the others on the list . . .'

I heard, but I didn't really listen.

'Rupert? Can you get me figures on the value of the land. Call me when you have them.' I made a note to myself to give the finance director a nudge, if he didn't call back within the hour.

I was able to take Mina's emotional temperature by the tempo of her voice. That morning, I picked up a hunger in it. An urgency for something she wanted but didn't yet have. How complacent I was – tickled by the honour of helping plan Lord Appleton's memorial. It was the kind of thing a family might do together, but Mina had no siblings, and her mother was absent, so, in a way, *I* was her next of kin. Lady Appleton had flown over from her home in Geneva for the funeral, but was refusing to return for the memorial, and I was disappointed, only because it might have been a chance to meet her at last.

Margaret arrived with coffee.

'Will you both be wanting lunch here today?' she asked.

'I think so. Sandwiches in the sunroom for me, but I'm not sure whether Mina will join me. I'll let you know later. Why don't you make enough for Dave, too.' We worked well together, Margaret and I, both mindful of the hierarchy. I don't think she ever resented serving me.

I had lost track of who Mina was speaking to, though I detected her increasing impatience.

'So? Do something about it.' I took over her coffee, and noticed she'd been writing on a pad – a list of names, and beside each, a doodle. At first, I couldn't work out what they were – idle scribbling, I thought – but then realized they were tiny animals. She turned, saw me looking, and ripped the page from the pad. At the time, I thought it was because she was embarrassed by their clumsy execution. Her other phone rang, and I reached for it, but she got there before me. Mobile phones are the curse of the modern PA. How are we supposed to be across everything, if we are not the ones fielding our employer's private lines?

'Alex. Are you sure? It sounds too good to be true. Yes, I like the sound of it very much. Let's talk later.' I found out later that Alex Monroe was a specialist in tax law.

'Rupert hasn't called you back yet,' I said, when she came off the phone.

'Sorry?'

'With the figures you asked for. Shall I call him and get them for you?' I hoped the figures might give me some insight into the morning's business.

'No, thank you, Christine. Can I see the guest list?' She held her hand out and glanced through it. 'Good. Now, I need to show my face outside. A photographer from the *Mail* is here – they're doing a feature on the gardens. Join me, will you?'

'There's a youth from the Haven charity too,' I reminded her, following with the tray. 'The PR department thought it might add something to the piece.'

'Right.'

'And Margaret's wondering what you want to do for lunch.'

'A sandwich in my room, I think, Margaret,' she said to her, as we walked into the kitchen. At the back door, she turned to me. 'Here, Christine. These should fit you. It's a mudbath out there.' She handed me a pair of boots, stooping down to put on her own. I was taken aback sometimes by these acts of kindness. The boots were brand new. The type worn by the country set. She didn't call them a present, or say she'd bought them for me, but I was sure she had, and when we returned later I wrote my initials on the inside. I couldn't bear the idea of someone else putting their feet into them.

The gardens had been transformed since I'd first viewed the house. Then it had been overrun by leggy, bolting roses and brambles, a rather tragic tennis court and a cracked and empty swimming pool. Now, there was order to it. The lower lawns were surrounded by pyramids of yew, a pond sat at their centre, with a statue of Minerva rising up from its depths. It was something Mina had brought back from one of her trips to Italy, and I can't say I was overly fond of it. To me, it looked like something you could have picked up from a garden centre. But Mina liked it, and that's what mattered.

Over the years, I saw Minerva's gardens spread as Mina purchased more land from the adjacent properties. Two out of three of her neighbours agreed to sell her chunks of their gardens, so she could control the view from the house and secure her privacy. There was only one refuser – a house that backed on to the north-east corner of the grounds. The owners were rarely there, living abroad for most of the year. Even so, Mina planted one hundred silver birch trees to screen the house from her view. In winter, when the trees were bare, it seemed as if that house crept closer, playing its own secret game of grandmother's footsteps. I remember once, looking out of the window in the pink room, and noticing its black windows through skeletal branches. If I could see it, then it could see me, and I remember thinking, evergreens – leylandii perhaps – would have been a more effective way of keeping the neighbours at bay.

We found the photographer on his hands and knees beside a patch of green shoots in the vegetable garden.

'Morning,' Mina called. 'Are you getting everything you need?' I hung back, watching him scrabble up to greet her, brushing down his trousers, disarmed, no doubt, by her warmth. He suggested a picture of her with the boy from the charity and she chatted to the youngster as if they were old friends, despite the fact I'd had to remind her of his name only a few moments earlier.

Later, while Mina rested upstairs, Dave and I ate our lunch in companionable silence in the sunroom. The heat through the glass roof always sent him to sleep, and I sat and watched him for a while, then took our dirty plates through to Margaret. We were as foolish as each other, me the secretary, he the driver; both beguiled by our surroundings like the peacocks that strutted across the lawns. They've gone now, those peacocks. Mina had them removed because she couldn't bear having such highly strung creatures shivering around the place.

'Why don't I take that up?' I said to Margaret, as she put the finishing touches to Mina's lunch.

'Well, if you wouldn't mind. Then I can start thinking about her supper. Try and get her to eat that bit of cake too, will you? If you ask me she's too thin.'

I slipped off my shoes at the bottom of the stairs, my heels pink from where the boots had rubbed. They were only half a size too small. I knocked on her door.

'Yes.'

Mina often sounds scratchy when she wakes from a nap. She relaxed when she saw it was me, and I waited for her to sit up against the pillows, then set the tray across her lap.

'Sit for a moment, will you, Christine?'

I was always happy to keep her company.

'I don't remember ever feeling so tired,' she said.

'It's harder, I think, the death of a parent, when you don't have brothers and sisters to bear it with you,' I ventured.

'Yes, you're right about that.' She picked up her sandwich, then put it down again. I was tempted to go over and feed her. *Come on, just one mouthful.* I watched her poke at the cake with the fork. Margaret had put out a pear too, and I recognized the dainty knife I'd seen in Mina's Notting Hill home. I remembered how she'd peeled an apple so the skin curled off without breaking. I'd taught myself to do the same.

'I'm so sorry your mother wasn't able to stay on after the funeral, Mina. I suspect you would have liked to have her with you now.'

'God no,' she said. 'We're not close. My mother's a cold-hearted woman. She's never been there when I've needed her – even as a child.' She pushed her tray to one side and looked at me. 'And your mother, Christine. It was cancer, wasn't it? That took her from you.' She spoke as if we were both orphans – as if her mother had died too.

My hands started to sweat – the anxiety I always felt when I thought of my mother, soaking into the arms of the chair. I imagine it's still there – my shame absorbed into the deep red plush of Mina's upholstery.

'No.' I felt unable to say more, and perhaps that's what sparked her curiosity. She left her bed to come and sit near me, perching on the stool at her dressing table, and turning to face me. I found it hard to meet her eyes, and looked down, imagining how nice it would be to sink into the thick pile carpet and disappear.

'An accident?' My mother's death was something I never talked about.

'Yes, it was an accident.'

'Oh, Christine.' I heard the rustle of tissues being pulled from a box, then felt them thrust into my hand. 'Take your time,' she said. 'It might be good for you to talk about it.'

I thought, *Perhaps it might.* So, I took myself back to the leaves on the pavement. Autumn. Five thirty on a Wednesday afternoon.

'Mum always picked me up later on a Wednesday because of

music practice. I used to play the piano.' *She has promise*, my teacher had said. Mum had ambitions for me, but I stopped playing when she died. Later, I transferred my skill on the piano to a typewriter keyboard.

'What was she like, Christine?'

I tried to conjure up my mother's face, but I had wiped it from my memory long ago. I'd always resisted looking at photographs of her, I think because I believed I didn't deserve to. That I shouldn't be allowed to hoard her image in my head.

'It's hard to remember – it was such a long time ago.'

'How old were you again?'

'Eight.'

'Aah, yes. Too young to lose a mother.' It was what she'd said when she interviewed me. The exact same words. 'How sad, you don't remember her face. So. You were on your way home from school . . .' she prompted gently, coaxing me on.

'Yes. It was only a short walk home. Fifteen minutes, with one busy road to cross. I wasn't allowed to cross it on my own. That's why Mum always picked me up. When we were halfway across, a lorry came out of nowhere. It hit her.' Mina passed me another tissue.

I remembered the roar of the lorry, and how I had watched my mother disappear beneath it. It seemed to me, as a child, as if she was being eaten alive.

A flash of my mother's face came to me, then – as if she was there in the bedroom, listening to me tell the story of her death. And then I realized it was my own reflection looking back at me from the dressing-table mirror, behind Mina. *You look just like your mother, Christine*, people used to say. As I looked at the image, it changed to me as an eight-year-old – a slimy trail of snot running from my nose. I wiped it with a tissue. It seemed as if Mina had conjured up ghosts from my past.

'I don't understand, Christine. Your mother was hit, but you weren't? Did she push you out of the way?'

'I don't remember.'

'Perhaps it would help, Christine, if you tried to.' I closed my eyes, and heard the clock by the bed, ticking away the seconds.

'I was already on the pavement, on the other side of the road, when she was hit.'

. 'So, you ran away from her? Crossed the road on your own?' I wanted Mina to comfort me – rest a reassuring hand on my shoulder – but she was puzzling over the story, trying to pin it down. 'And your mother went after you?' She waited for me to fill the silence. And I obliged.

'Yes.'

'How awful. Terrible for you, to carry that guilt around with you. I can see it's really stayed with you.' She furrowed her brow, tilted her head – gave all the signs of compassion. 'But you were only a child, Christine. You really shouldn't blame yourself.'

She swung around to face the mirror.

'God, I look terrible,' she said.

'I'm sorry I got upset, Mina. I never talk about it.'

'Really?'

She puffed out her cheeks, and applied blusher.

'What about your father?'

'Not really, no.'

'How sad. It might have helped you to hear that it wasn't your fault – or at least, that he didn't blame you for her death. I'm guessing that's what lies so heavily. You'd like to know you had your father's forgiveness.' She smiled sadly at me through the mirror. 'Don't look so worried, Christine. I don't think any less of you. You were only a child. And it's our secret. I'm touched you trust me with it.

'Now. Will you take the tray down with you, when you go?'

16

I hoped Lord Appleton's memorial would go some way to restoring his reputation – for people to remember what he had been, not what he became. Perhaps I was trying to assuage my guilt over the way he'd retired from the business. I felt a heaviness on the walk to the Wallace Collection that evening, but it was mitigated by a small good turn I did on the way. It was nothing really. A dropped glove – me seeking out, and finding, its owner. Yet the gratitude I received from that stranger – a warm smile, a thank-you – sent a terrific shot of well-being through me, and by the time I arrived, I felt lighter.

I wanted Lord Appleton's face to be the first thing guests saw when they arrived at the memorial, so I'd had a series of slides of him in his prime projected on to the back wall. When Mina walked in, I watched with anticipation – not expecting tears but, perhaps, a flicker of tenderness. What I saw was defiance.

As the room filled, I took a glass of red wine up to the first floor and looked down. I couldn't help admiring my efforts – the string quartet playing Mozart, the glorious arrangements of flowers, the elegant canapés served on silver trays. I was more comfortable up there, out of the throng, and wondered whether Jenny Haddow felt the same – ill at ease amongst the guests. I'd spotted her earlier – elegant in green silk – standing alone, watching from the wings. We are neither fish nor fowl, us PAs. Not quite family, not quite friends.

I searched for Mina in the crowd, and found her directly below me, chatting to the chair of a rival supermarket – one of the giants she would have preferred not to invite, but, on balance, was persuaded she should. She loathed that man, and I could tell he was boring her rigid, yet you'd never have known it. The signs were there, provided you knew how to read them. She was itching to get away. I watched as she narrowed her eyes, like a cat smiling, then touched his sleeve – a brief brush of her hand – and off she went, as fluid as a dancer, working her way through the crowd until she settled in the arms of the prime minister's wife. They kissed and, I imagine, the PM's wife apologized again for her husband's absence. Mina concealed her disappointment beautifully. It doesn't do to make those more powerful than you feel guilty – she understood that. It builds resentment, and then they have a tendency to turn on you. Or, worse still, keep their distance.

As the time for speeches drew near, I watched Mina move forward. When she opened her mouth to speak, so did I – my lips shadowing hers. I knew that speech by heart, and though not every word was mine, I'd injected some of her father's pet phrases into it – ones she'd hated when he was alive, but now he was dead, delivered with grace.

'My father was proud to be in what he described as trade. Trade was trade and not business to him and I am so grateful he taught me to appreciate the difference.

'He was a great believer in the ideas of the revolutionary philosopher Thomas Paine. Dad talked of the universal harmony between the farmer who sells his wheat and the merchant who buys it. He was a tradesman with a conscience, believing that profit should not

come at a cost to others. It is a belief he instilled in me at a young age, and something that remains the central ethos of Appleton's today.'

Afterwards, I made my way back down to the main hall, wanting to catch Jenny Haddow before she left. I found her saying her goodbyes to a man I didn't recognize, and hung back until he'd gone.

'Jenny, hello.'

'Christine.' She seemed pleased to see me.

'I just wanted to thank you for your help on the guest list.' I'd run through it with her, and she'd given me a few suggestions.

'Oh, my pleasure. It was nothing.'

I asked who she'd been talking to.

'Clifford Fraser? His father, John, was one of the names I gave you, but sadly he wasn't well enough to come. Clifford's his son – he's in charge now. The Frasers have supplied Appleton's for years.'

'Ah, yes, I know the name . . .'

'And yet not the face. That saddens me, Christine.' I bristled. 'Forgive me, I'm being nostalgic. Mina's speech was touching, but I wonder whether that harmony she spoke of – between Appleton's and its suppliers – is a thing of the past.' She took my hands in hers, and I felt the tremble of her age as she held them. 'Anyway, I must be off, but thank you for organizing such a wonderful occasion for Lord Appleton. He would have been thrilled. You've done a super job.'

'Can I get you a car, Jenny? Are you going back to Fincham Hall?' She looked at me in surprise.

'Oh, no. I'm back in my flat. I'll pick up a taxi on the street. Thank you, all the same. And goodnight, Christine.' She gave me a peck on the cheek, then left.

What happened next is a matter of record, although not one that tallies with mine. I saw Mina with Clifford Fraser, the man

I'd seen Jenny talking to. From where I stood, they seemed to be engaged in an animated conversation. As I looked at him, there was something that reminded me of my father. He was much younger, of course, but I recognized the painful effort he'd made, dressing for the occasion. A jacket, not a suit; the trousers a darker shade of blue. When I looked closer, I wondered if, like Dad's, it might once have been a suit, but the jacket, worn more often, had faded as a result. The knot of his tie was too small and his hair, though brushed, seemed glued to his head. My father didn't have much hair, so too much hair product was never an issue for him.

Someone must have knocked into Clifford Fraser, because he lurched forward, spilling his drink. It wasn't his fault, and I don't believe any of it went on Mina, but it must have alarmed her, because she let out a yelp. Clifford Fraser looked mortified and tried to apologize, but Mina grabbed Andy's arm and clung to him as if she was in distress. Her husband led her away and, as she passed me, she hissed in my ear, 'Get that man out of here!' The expression on her face was that of a woman who'd discovered something rather foul smeared under her nostrils.

'Mr Fraser,' I said, taking his arm. 'Let me help you find your coat.' His eyes followed Mina.

'I only wanted to talk to her. My father and Lord Appleton were old friends.'

'Yes, I'm sure they were,' I replied. I saw Mina have a word with Angus Cathcart, the keeper of pictures, and then he in turn had a word with one of the security men. I didn't want the evening spoiled by unnecessary fuss, so I steered Clifford Fraser away. We'd almost reached the stairs when he twisted around to face the room.

'Your father was a good man. He would have listened to us!' he shouted, and a few heads turned, but Mina seemed to have vanished. The security man pushed forward, roughly grabbing Mr Fraser's arm.

'There's no need for that,' I told him. 'The gentleman is just leaving. Isn't that right, Mr Fraser? Now come on, let's go and find your coat.' I wanted to protect the dignity of the evening, and thankfully he allowed me to lead him up to the lobby. He was the worse for wear, unsteady on his feet, but no more than that. I'd almost got him to the cloakroom when he pulled away again, trying to make his way back into the main room.

'Mr Fraser, please,' I said firmly. He stopped at once and turned around, and I saw tears in his eyes.

'I just want a meeting with her, that's all.'

'It's been a long night, Mr Fraser. Let me organize a car to take you home.' I collected his coat from the cloakroom, and led him outside, hoping the night air would brighten him up. There were a couple of photographers lurking on the corner, so I walked Clifford Fraser in the opposite direction and waited with him until the taxi came.

'Fraser's is one of Appleton's longest-serving suppliers, isn't it?' He looked delighted to have it acknowledged. 'I'm Christine Butcher – Mina Appleton's personal assistant,' I said, holding out my hand. He grabbed on to it, his eyes lighting up. He'd had no idea who I was. The influence I might have. 'I'll see what I can do about setting up a meeting, Mr Fraser.'

'Thank you, Miss Butcher. I'd really appreciate that.' He clung to my hand like a lifeline, and I felt the same shot of pleasure I'd felt earlier, when I'd returned that stranger's glove.

'I'll be in touch,' I said, and helped him into the cab, then waved him off. The next morning, I slipped a date into the diary for two weeks ahead.

17

'What the fuck is this? Oh for God's sake. Don't just sit there, Christine.' It was rare for Mina to swear. She saw it as a sign of weakness, a loss of control. Her finger stabbed at the screen of her desktop. 'This, here. Him.'

I was sitting on her sofa, and we'd been going through the diary for the day – a moment I usually enjoyed. I went and stood behind her and saw that, while I'd been running through today's agenda, she'd skipped ahead to the following week. My stomach dropped when I saw *Clifford Fraser, eleven o'clock.*

She turned around and gave me a look that confirmed this was more than a petulant outburst.

'I don't want that man anywhere near the building. What the hell were you thinking?'

'I'm so sorry, Mina, if I'd known—'

'If you'd known? For God's sake. Just deal with it. And close the door after you.'

I left her office, grateful it was too early for the girls to be in and witness the scene. As I sat down behind my desk, my hands trembled, and I had to wait for them to steady before picking up the phone.

'Good morning, may I speak to Mr Fraser, please? It's Mina Appleton's office.'

'Yes, this is him.' It wasn't. The voice was too old.

'It's Clifford Fraser I'm after.'

'This is John, his father. Can I help?'

'No. I need to speak to your son. Is he there?'

'Is that Jenny?' There was warmth in his voice.

'No. Miss Haddow left some years ago. I'm Ms Appleton's assistant.' There was some confusion on the other end, then a woman's voice came on.

'Hello? This is Sally Fraser, Clifford's wife.'

'I'm calling from Mina Appleton's office. I'm afraid there's been a mix-up. We're going to have to cancel your husband's appointment.'

'But it's not 'til next week.'

'I'm aware of that.'

'It was all arranged.'

'Ms Appleton is no longer able to see him.'

'You can't do that.'

'I assure you, I can.'

'He spoke to her personal assistant himself.' I heard her shuffling papers. 'Christine Butcher – yes, here it is.'

'There's been a mix-up. So, no longer possible.'

'He could do another day.'

'We're cancelling, not postponing.' I put down the phone and erased the name *Clifford Fraser* from the diary. When I looked up, Lucy was arriving.

'Morning,' she said, with her usual toothy smile, poking her head round my door. 'Everything all right?' She glanced over to Mina's office, and I left my desk and saw the blinds were pulled down.

'Absolutely fine. She's on a conference call. Could you get me a coffee, Lucy? I haven't had a minute this morning.'

'Sure,' she said, and scooted off.

I returned to my office and closed the door and, in a rather dismal display of solidarity, pulled down my blinds too. When Lucy brought in my coffee, I saw Mina pass by the open door. She was wearing her coat, but I knew she had no appointments out of the office that morning. I'd had the day mapped out. Lunch at her desk, and then a three o'clock with the TV production company. 'Where's she off to?' Lucy asked. I had no idea.

'A last-minute meeting. Not sure what time she'll be back.'

I expected Mina to phone in, but she didn't, and as the day went on I felt a growing nausea. I even wondered whether I might be coming down with something. At around six thirty, Angelica texted, asking what time I'd be back. It wasn't like her, and I was cheered by the thought she wanted me at home. *Leaving soon,* I texted. *Everything OK?*

Tell you later, she replied.

See you around eight thirty xx

If I left at once, I'd be home before then.

I put on my coat and went into Mina's office. I always made sure it would be as she'd like to find it on her return. It was a mess – an untidy display of that morning's fit of temper. Ink had leaked on to the blond wood of her desk, and I saw she'd been chewing the end of a pen. There were bits of plastic on the floor around her chair, where she'd bitten pieces off, then spat the splinters out. Screwed-up balls of paper littered the carpet where she'd tossed them at the bin and missed. I got down on my hands and knees, gathering up every tiny shard of plastic, picking up the balls of paper, unfurling and reading each one, in case it was important.

'You're still here.'

I wondered how long she'd been standing there, watching me on all fours, crawling on the floor around her desk. Long enough to take off her coat and drape it over her arm.

'Just having a tidy before I leave.'

She didn't reply, but stayed in the doorway watching me until I stood up and moved away from her desk.

'Sit down, will you?' She nodded to the sofa, closing the door and crossing over to the window, her back turned towards me. She was so slender I could see her shoulder blades moving beneath her sweater, like two wings, folded away. 'I was going to speak to you tomorrow morning, but as you're still here, I might as well do it now. I assume you're not rushing off.' I still had my coat on and hesitated – thinking of Angelica waiting for me at home. 'If you need to leave, just say so.'

'No, it's fine.' I tried to sound breezy, but no doubt failed. She turned around, slinging her coat on to the sofa beside me, walking to her desk, and sitting down.

'It's about this morning. The business with the Fraser man . . .' She talked to her computer rather than me, sending off a couple of emails. 'It's been irritating me . . .' She logged off, then looked at me, and I was about to say something but she raised her hand and stopped me. '. . . more than irritating me, actually. It's been buzzing around in my head all afternoon.' Under her desk, I saw her slip off her shoes and curl her legs up beneath her – a manoeuvre only a woman of Mina's tiny frame, or perhaps a child, could manage with such elegance on a swivelling office chair.

'As I said, it's been buzzing around in my head – an unpleasant distraction – and I resent the intrusion. That's the point, I suppose. There are more important things I should be thinking about.'

More important things than you, a voice in my head sneered. My phone rang in my pocket.

'Do you need to get that?'

'No.' I switched it off without even checking to see if it was Angelica.

'Where was I? Yes. An unpleasant distraction. It's made me ask myself what kind of person it is I want working with me. And the answer? Someone I can be confident has my back. Not someone who is complacent and careless.' She looked so comfortable, curled up like a cat on the chair. 'I don't like complacency, Christine. It makes me question a person's loyalty.' It hung there between us, that question of loyalty. 'When someone's been with you for a long time, someone you've grown to trust, who's been part of your team for years, they become like family. And, like family, you put up with things that perhaps you shouldn't. Overlook mistakes, or pretend not to notice, because you've come to know that person well, and assume they have your best interests at heart. That their intentions are good . . .' She spoke slowly, considering every word, and every word she spoke sucked the air from me. My working life flashed before me. And yet I couldn't think of anything I'd done that Mina would've had to *overlook*. My record was faultless. Apart from today. One appointment in the diary with a man she didn't like. I clasped my hands on my lap to keep them still. 'The problems begin, I think, when that person becomes over-familiar, takes things for granted, small liberties that at first seem like nothing. It's only when you look closely at them that they become impossible to overlook.'

It's a habit of mine to drift off when I'm distressed. I saw the cleaners arrive in the outer office, a husband-and-wife team, one emptying the bins while the other vacuumed. I realized Mina had stopped talking and I turned and saw she was watching me, her fingers cantering back and forth on the desk. She took a breath, or perhaps it was a sigh – even now I find it hard to think clearly about that evening.

'You see, it's not just the incident with the diary today.' She picked up a pen and doodled on a pad. 'There was something that happened some years ago. It bothered me at the time, but

I decided not to say anything. I wanted to give you another chance. I worry now that I was too trusting. Perhaps you don't remember it, Christine, but I can tell you, it has stayed with me. A niggling little doubt at the back of my mind that has now come to the forefront again.' I held my breath. 'I allowed you, Sarah and Lucy to stay over in my Hyde Park flat. I think there was a train strike – some reason you couldn't get home. So I offered my hospitality.' She looked at me, her head cocked to one side. '*Do* you remember, Christine?'

'I think so.' So this was it. My only other mistake. She'd had to go back a long way to find it.

'You think so.' She put down her pen and looked at me. 'I left you in charge. I trusted you. It's disappointing, to think my trust was misplaced.' I felt myself grow hot and, no doubt, my face reddened – my skin betraying me, as it has, since childhood. 'One of you went through my clothes, I suspect even tried a few things on. My perfume was used. These may seem like petty things to you, but it's not a nice feeling to know that someone has been nosing through one's private things.' She'd invited me to make myself at home. *Mi Casa Su Casa*, I think was the phrase she'd used. I prickled with shame. 'An ornament went missing too. A glass bird. It was valuable and, more importantly, a favourite of mine. Perhaps it got broken. Perhaps you'd all drunk too much of the champagne I left. Or maybe someone took a shine to it – took it home with them. I hesitate to accuse anyone of theft. Whatever happened – the point is, it was covered up. And that's dishonest. Wouldn't you agree?' I nodded, unable to speak, sickened by the knowledge that, for all these years, Mina had been saving up this one transgression to use against me. If she'd questioned me at the time, I would have owned up. Now she had turned my foolishness into a switch to cane the backs of my legs. 'I won't tolerate dishonesty, Christine. I left you in charge. I assumed you would take responsibility for Sarah and Lucy. And this business with the Fraser man – well, it's made me question your loyalty again. The fact is I've lost confidence in you.' She stood up and walked to the door, opening it for me to leave. I couldn't move. 'We'll talk again in the morning. I'd like you to go home and think about what I've said.' Her blue eyes fixed on me, and I forced myself to my feet, and walked towards her. 'I need to know I can count on you when it matters. That you are someone who is prepared to go that extra mile. It saddens me to think you might not be.'

'I'm sorry, Mina,' was all I could manage.

'Yes, I'm sorry too, Christine. It would be a pity to lose you.'

I heard the door close behind me and, as I walked towards the lift, I saw the new version of myself she'd painted. *Over-familiar, complacent, disloyal, untrustworthy, dishonest.* I rushed into the loo and was sick.

As usual, the house was in darkness when I got home but, for once, I was grateful Angelica wasn't downstairs to greet me. I'd have time to gather myself. No need to trouble her yet with the impending loss of my job. I tried to find a silver lining – I'd have more time to spend with her. I switched on lights, took off my coat, then checked my face in the hall mirror, practising a bright smile.

'I'm home,' I called out. I went up and knocked on her bed-room door. I could see light coming from beneath it and went in. I smiled. The room was tidy, and I assumed she'd done what I'd been asking her to do for months. It took a moment for me to realize she wasn't there, and that the room was so neat because her things were missing.

I remembered, then, that my phone was still switched off, and when I turned it on I saw six missed calls from Angelica. She hadn't left any messages. I phoned her back at once, but she didn't pick up. It was only when I went back downstairs, I found her note on the hall floor. I must have stepped on it when I came in. *'I've moved in with Dad.'*

I sat on the stairs and cried. Perhaps, if I'd come home when I promised, I might have been able to persuade her to stay, but instead I'd let her down again. And I knew, in my heart, she would be better off with Mike and Ursula. She deserved more than the home I'd given her.

I lay awake all night – the silence of the house closing in on me. I looked at the clothes I'd chosen for the morning, hanging on the wardrobe door. An empty suit. My dismissal would be quick, I knew that. Mina didn't like people hanging around. No need to work out one's notice. Her words rang through my head: *It would be a pity to lose you, it would be a pity to lose you –* over and over. She'd said *would*, not will. *It would be a pity to lose you.* A glimmer of hope. Perhaps, a second chance.

The next morning, I was ready for her when she walked in.

'I see now, Mina, that I should have come to you before about Lucy. I've been covering for her for some time, now – correcting slip-ups that I chose, as you say, to overlook. She's sloppy – always has been. There's no gentle way to put it. I hate doing this – loyalty is something I take as seriously as you do – but I realize my loyalty to Lucy has been misguided. She's not up to the job. She's a liability. The appointment with the Fraser man confirms that, and I can only apologize that I didn't correct her mistake before it came to your attention.' Mina sat back in her chair and, though she tried to cover her surprise, I saw it there. She didn't think I had it in me. 'I've already spoken to HR and between us we've worked out a package. They agreed with me that severance would be best. She'll get a good pay-out, but no call to come back at us with a claim of unfair dismissal.'

'I see. And you're prepared to handle this, Christine?'

'Absolutely. I'll take her out to lunch – to make the process smoother.'

She smiled, nodding her head. She was impressed.

'If you're sure. I'd hate you to do something you felt uncomfortable with.'

'Absolutely,' I repeated, returning her smile.

Lucy was sitting at her desk, unaware that when I invited her out to lunch that day she would not be coming back.

'Might as well bring your coat, Lucy. My treat, but probably best to bring your handbag too.' I'd taken Sarah into my confidence, and she took an early lunch. With Lucy going, it would mean a pay rise for her.

I booked a table in a nice restaurant, serving up Lucy's dismissal with an expensive bottle of wine. She drank most of it.

'Lucy, you mustn't take it personally. It's just that Mina has lost confidence in you. You know how she is. She can be very exacting. For my part, I've found it a pleasure working with you.'

By the time dessert came, she'd shed a few tears, and I gave her hand a squeeze.

'You're not being sacked, Lucy. It's just time for you to move on. I'm sure you agree it's a more than generous payout. And I'll make sure Mina writes you a glowing reference. Now, drink up. Here's to your future. I know it will be a bright one.'

18

'My guess is? It's one of the big chains whipping up some disgruntled little shit.'

Five o'clock on a Monday. I was standing outside Mina's office, balancing a tray of Waterford tumblers, a bucket of ice and a bottle of whisky, wondering how I'd manage to open the door. It was dear Paul Richardson, Mina's communications director, who came to my rescue. He looked up, saw me struggling, and leapt to his feet, opening the door and shooing one of his team out of my way – a young buck he'd lured from a tabloid newspaper to work for him.

They'd been in there for hours, and there was a lot of mess from the food and drinks I'd brought in. I moved around as quietly as I could, collecting up dirty plates and cups, making myself as unobtrusive as possible. The atmosphere was electric, something I'd noticed over the previous weeks when there'd been more meetings than usual with Mina's top team – the tranquillity of our offices on the top floor injected with a harsh, frantic energy. Certainly, levels of stress were heightened over that period, but I can't say it was unpleasant. I rather liked the sense of urgency, and I think it aroused in me an instinct to close ranks and protect Mina.

'Let's calm down,' Paul said, as I poured drinks, placing glasses into outstretched hands, the conversation carrying on as if I wasn't there. 'I've seen this before in the airline industry, and in telecommunications. You get the big boys flexing their muscles when they see a rival succeeding in doing what they've failed to achieve. It's the holy grail, Mina. A healthy profit and goodwill from the public. They want it. They don't have it. Appleton's does. Appleton's has you. So, I'm afraid, it will get personal.'

'Who is this Ed Brooks, anyway? And when did the *Business Times* start doing investigative reporting?' Mina asked. I set down her whisky, noticing spots of blood on the skin around her thumb from where she'd picked at the nail, a tell when she was stressed. The newspaper article sat on her desk. '*Mina Appleton Accused of Bullying and Hypocrisy*', read the headline.

'He's new.' This from the thrusting young buck in PR. 'Trying to make a name for himself. Who reads the *Business Times* anyway? As I say, in my view it's just some disgruntled little shit whining to an ambitious hack.' I could smell his twenty-a-day habit on his cheap suit. Paul raised his hand for calm.

'I can see it's upsetting for you, Mina. You've had, and continue to have – let's not forget last Sunday's profile piece – a good relationship with the media. This will pass, I'm sure of it.'

I wasn't so sure. Two weeks before, Margaret had come across journalists ferreting through the bins at Minerva.

'God knows how they got in.' Mina had seemed genuinely perplexed when she told me about it. 'I can see I've been rather naive.' Not naive; complacent.

'You say that, Paul, but how can you possibly know?'

'Trust me,' he said.

'I agree with Paul.' Rupert French, the financial director – a man whose weight went up and down like a yo-yo. No doubt he'd wolfed down more than his fair share of the biscuits and sandwiches I'd brought in. 'It's no coincidence these stories started appearing soon after the annual figures came out.' He positively ballooned over that period. 'The business has grown and continues to do so and, with the greatest respect to your late father, Appleton's was never considered a threat before. Now it is.'

'Don't underestimate journalists. Particularly ambitious ones.' The young buck reached for the whisky bottle. 'I'll see what I can find out about Ed Brooks. You know they've found a way to get into people's phones?'

I made a mental note to order in more food.

'Now let's not get hysterical.' Douglas Rockwell was a barrister friend of Mina's, whom she'd asked to sit in. He was around a lot during that period – dinners, visits to Minerva, breakfast meetings. 'Phone-tapping is illegal.' He poured himself water. 'It's nearly six. Let's see if it's made the news.' He reached for the remote control and turned on the television. I watched, next door in my office.

The story was the third headline:

Pressure grows on Mina Appleton. The Businesswoman of the Year denies allegations of unfair practice.

'*Some of your suppliers are accusing you of dishonourable working methods, Ms Appleton. Of not practising what you preach.*'

Mina looked startled when the microphone was pushed in her face. The reporter had confronted her on her way into the building. One negative piece in a newspaper, and they'd all begun sniffing for blood. I thought Mina handled it with dignity, gently moving the microphone aside.

'*All I can say is that there is absolutely no truth in any of the allegations made in one newspaper, through an unnamed and uncorroborated source. There is nothing more I can add at this time.*'

She gave a polite smile and appeared serene, but I saw the pain in her eyes, and felt a surge of tenderness. I switched off the TV and watched as, one by one, everyone left her office, until only Douglas Rockwell was left. I popped my head around her door. Mina was in full flow.

'I'll sue. They don't have anything. An anonymous source feeding a green journalist.' She pulled at a strand of hair behind her ear.

'Take care, Mina. In court you'd be under oath,' he warned. She looked up and saw me in the doorway.

'I'll order in a light supper, shall I?'

'Oh for goodness' sake! Go home, Christine. And close the door behind you.'

It was frustrating not to have been able to do more. I so wanted to do my bit, and yet it seemed all I could offer were beverages and light snacks. My time would come soon enough, though.

On the tube that evening, I sat next to an elderly man, smartly dressed for an evening out, his blazer adorned with badges and ribbons – RAF, I saw from his wings. I smelled soap from where he'd spruced himself up: Imperial Leather. When he got off, we exchanged a smile and then I noticed, too late, that one of his badges had fallen on to the seat. I got off at the next stop and hurried to the Lost Property Office at Baker Street, but it was closed. The next morning, I was there, waiting, when they opened. They knew me well at Baker Street. *Morning, Mrs Butcher, what do you have for us this time?* I'd taken to allowing extra time on my commute, so I could perform a good deed on my way to and from work. The sense of well-being it gave me became a craving. In fact, I'd go so far as to say I was rather addicted to the smiles and thank-yous I received from strangers.

19

It took me a while to venture out into the gardens at The Laurels. I remember the first time, I had to force myself to put one foot in front of the other, but now I am quite the adventurer. I have become more comfortable in my surroundings, and it's now part of my routine to take a stroll before breakfast. Not far, just a short walk to stretch my legs, never straying beyond the confines of the perimeter fence. I look forward to these walks. They help clear my head and make me feel less cut off. Reminding me, there is still a world out there. I've gained in confidence; in fact I would go as far as saying, I've gained more confidence than I ever thought possible, and can feel myself transforming from the shivering wreck I was when I first arrived.

This is my second walk today. A stroll after lunch. There is no wind, the air is still, not a leaf stirring. I stand for a moment, close my eyes and listen. I hear the purr of wings as a pigeon flies over, then settles in a tree. A soft coo as it makes itself comfortable. It's the little things you learn to appreciate. I open my eyes and look up at the sky and see the clouds are brooding. I suspect we are in for a storm. I look down at the fence and reach out and touch it. Wooden stakes with wire running between them. It doesn't take much to move one of the posts back and forth. It's not so solid in its foundation. The wire too is feeble, and I rest my foot on the lowest rung, and tread it into the mud.

The air cools, and then a few spots of rain fall. Time to go back inside. I will enjoy listening to it patter against the window as I sit with my scissors and glue and work on my scrapbook. Here it is. The article by Mr Ed Brooks that kicked everything off.

Business Times, 24 March 2009
Ed Brooks, Chief Investigative Reporter

MINA APPLETON ACCUSED OF
BULLYING AND HYPOCRISY

Appleton's supermarkets, a business that has become synonymous with fair trade and good practice in an industry often accused of undercutting farmers, is being accused of subterfuge, bullying and dishonesty by a long-term supplier.

Several farms, according to this newspaper's source, have been forced to sell their land at below the market rate because of Appleton's unfair practices. It is rare for farmers to speak out against supermarkets for fear of reprisals. The charge of hypocrisy is directed at Mina Appleton herself, whom the source describes as 'a ruthless, greedy operator'.

Lord John Appleton, who died four years ago, was an outspoken advocate for fair working practices, an ethos his daughter has exploited in her branding of the company . . .

In it goes, and then over the page, my own snippets. Small breaths of fresh air.

THE KINDNESS OF STRANGERS

Thank you to the kind lady who handed in my father's RAF wings. He's eighty-three and it means the world to him to have them returned.
  His daughter Barbara, Tring, Hertfordshire

My first mention in the 'Kindness of Strangers' column in the free newspaper I picked up on the tube on my way in to work. I checked for my name every morning, but I only received two acknowledgements, despite the number of good deeds I performed over the years. Still, they give me a boost, even now, as I lay them out on the page.

THE KINDNESS OF STRANGERS

I would like to thank the kind lady who stopped me in Oxford Street and gave me plasters for my heels which were sore from stupidly wearing new shoes to work.
  Sandra from Bucks

I remember noticing the bleeding heels of Sandra from Bucks as she walked ahead of me on the stairs, up from the underground. I lost her in the crowd at the top, and had to chase her down.

'These might help,' I'd said, holding out two plasters. I always kept some in my purse, for just such a situation. I was out of breath, panting like a dog, and she looked startled, but then, when she saw what I offered, she beamed at me. When I walked away, I felt the warmth of her smile on my back. I admit, I did it for the rush. I was a junkie to the goodwill that came my way.

I flip back and forth between those two pages in my scrapbook – the *Business Times* and 'The Kindness of Strangers' – me and her. I see now my addiction was the subconscious at work. My benevolent acts were an attempt to inject some goodness into my life. I didn't know it at the time, but greed and deceit had already insinuated themselves into our cheery, bright offices. I was a fool not to see it, yet I must have sensed it – phone calls, snatches of conversation – and then I read it in Mr Ed Brooks's article, but I didn't believe a word of that. All that article did for me was to make me more determined to defend Mina. I saw myself as her protector. I was the one who took measures when those journalists rifled through the bins at Minerva. *Leave it to me*, I'd told Margaret. I had cameras placed around the perimeter walls, a new alarm system installed. I hired two men to patrol the grounds from dusk 'til dawn. It was a shame to see that lovely house turned into what must at times have felt like a prison to Mina.

20

An old man standing in the rain outside the Appleton's building. Too early yet for him to be admitted. The doors locked to outsiders. For me, however, they slide open – the security man inside giving me a smile – and I sweep past that old man without a thought. It is only when I am inside and turn around, shaking off my umbrella, that I notice him. I am curious, perhaps, but no more. He tries to shelter in the overhang of the building, unable to use an umbrella because both his hands are holding a box. That is what he's trying to protect – not himself. He is drenched. He must be cold too. It is a bitter day and, as I remember it now, I see his hands are red from it. He's not wearing gloves. He was used to braving the elements. He spent his working life outdoors. I force myself to relive my unkindness in vivid colour, squeezing out every moment of it.

When I go down to reception, later in the morning, I notice he has made it inside, and sits in one of the Barcelona chairs, nursing the box across his lap. I see the box contains fruit – each piece wrapped in dark blue tissue paper. Appleton's latest commercial is playing on the television. Pastures bathed in golden sunlight, orchards bursting with fruit, weathered hands picking crops still wet with dew, and then those same pears and apples being laid out on supermarket shelves. A mouth-watering fantasy, Mina's voice running under the images. *'Fine food at the right price for you, our customers, and for our farmers too. At Appleton's we make it our business to be fair to all.'* She sounds kind, soothing. Anyone would trust her.

I go back up to my office, and when I come down again, it is lunchtime. I am hungry, and go out into the sunshine for a sandwich. When I come back the receptionist calls me over.

'He won't leave, Christine.' I turn and see the old man is still there, lost in thought. 'He wants to see one of the buyers, but he hasn't got an appointment, and I can't persuade any of them to come down,' she tells me.

'Leave it with me,' I say, and approach him with a smile. 'I'm afraid there's no one here who can help you today.' He looks up at me, and I smell the rain on him.

'I picked them this morning,' he says. 'As sweet as you'll find anywhere.' He unwraps a piece of fruit, and I see it is a pear, buffed and shiny.

'I'm sure they are. You don't have an appointment, though, do you? And, as I said, there's no one free to see you.'

'I was hoping Miss Appleton might try them. If she tasted one, she'd know.'

'I'm sorry, but she's not here. Why don't you leave them with me?' I need to get rid of him before Mina returns. She is coming in at four. There is a press conference at four thirty.

'I don't mind waiting.' He is reluctant to hand over his treasure.

'She won't be back today,' I lie and, still smiling, hold out my hands. He relents, and passes the fruit into my safekeeping. I keep smiling as he pushes himself out of the chair.

'I'd like to leave her a note,' he says, so I bring him a pen and paper and he writes something down. I never find out what it is. He leaves, having waited for six hours.

I take the box to the receptionist and watch her unwrap three pears, adding them to the perfectly red apples and perfectly round oranges already in the glass fruit bowl. No bananas. I take the remaining fruit up to the office kitchen, and stick a note on the box. *Help yourselves.* Some of it is eaten, but they are a fussy lot and reject what they see as inferior produce – pears with small brown blemishes. I eat one with my sandwich. It is delicious. It really is as sweet as you'd find anywhere. His note got lost somewhere along the way – I was a busy woman with more important things to think about. It was just another day in the office.

When Mina arrived to address journalists on the steps of the Appleton's building, I'd forgotten all about the man with the pears.

'Thank you for coming. I won't keep you long. I am here to say that, this morning, I instructed my lawyer to serve a libel action against the *Business Times* for its untrue and damaging statements against myself and Appleton's. I am afraid I can say no more at the moment, only that I vigorously deny these vicious allegations, and I am confident the truth will come out in court. Thank you for your time.'

21

It took a month for the case to come to court, and when it did, I barely saw Mina, but we spoke most days. I followed the trial in the papers, and watched on the news as she went in and out of court, saying nothing but looking calm and dignified. She called me one evening, when I was about to go home.

'Christine. Good, I've caught you. I've booked a table at The Ivy. Andy's out tonight. I'd love to change out of my court clothes – would you mind bringing something over? Jump in a cab. I'll meet you there.' Mina hated eating alone. I picked an outfit from the clothes she kept in the office, and arrived at the restaurant before her.

A waiter showed me to the table.

'Can I get you something to drink?'

'Just water, please. Sparkling. Thank you.' A few heads turned when Mina walked in a short while later. She grabbed the clothes and nipped off to the Ladies to change.

'Was that Mina Appleton?' I looked up from the menu. A woman – an ordinary member of the public – stood over me with an eager expression.

'Yes,' I said, without thinking, and she hurried off in pursuit.

'That's better,' Mina said when she returned, settling down and ordering a whisky and ice. The autograph-hunter was back at her own table, showing off her trophy to her friends. 'No peace for the wicked,' Mina whispered, turning away from them. 'So, how are things, Christine?' I filled her in on the day, passing her a file the finance director had asked me to have her look over. While she flicked through it, I opened the menu, glancing down and deciding on the soup, followed by fishcakes.

'Excellent,' Mina said, and I closed the menu, and took the file back from her. 'Aah, there she is.' She stood up, smiling and waving, and I saw a youngish woman – attractive, slim – heading to our table. 'Stella, good to see you,' Mina said, kissing her on both cheeks. 'This is Christine, my assistant. Christine, Stella Parker.'

I stood up, and shook her hand.

'Nice to meet you, Christine,' Stella said. I took a step away from my chair.

'Stella has been my life-saver. I think you're the reason I've stayed sane, you know,' Mina said, pulling out my chair, so Stella could sit down. 'Thanks for dropping off those things, Christine. Would you mind?' She held out her court clothes for me to take away.

'Nice to meet you, Stella,' I said, managing a smile. 'Have a good evening,' I added. As I walked away, Mina's voice followed me.

'I hate eating alone, Stella. So pleased you were free. What shall we drink? White? Red?' While I waited for the attendant to bring my coat, I looked back and saw them, heads bent together, like old friends.

They weren't old friends, though. I'd never heard Mina mention Stella Parker, and I looked her up when I got home. *Nutritionist and healer,* her website read. *Trained in conven-*

tional medicine, Stella has developed her own unique therapies . . . Testimonials claimed she was a *miracle worker – a guru – her hands worked magic.* She sounded like some kind of witch, and when I sat down to beans on toast that night I was full of resentment.

I logged into Mina's personal account, noting the payments to Stella Parker, and cancelled the next one. I was fairly certain Ms Parker would be too embarrassed to bring it up with Mina, and would have to call on me to help. Which she did, and I was full of apologies – banking error and all that. *I'll sort it out, Stella, don't worry.* I didn't appreciate until later that she was worth every penny Mina paid her.

On 14 July 2009, Mina was awarded damages of £100,000. In his summing up, the judge criticized the *Business Times* for refusing to retract the story when they had the opportunity, and for forcing the matter into the courts. He described Mina as a good and decent citizen who'd fallen victim to a bullying and vicious press.

'She appears to have been targeted for no better reason than that she is a successful businesswoman. This was little more than a witch-hunt.'

Mina did not attack Ed Brooks, the journalist, or the newspaper he worked for. Instead she stood on the steps of the High Court with her silent, supportive husband and thanked the jury and the judge for their sensible and clear-thinking decision.

'In spite of the last few weeks, which have been upsetting not only for me but also for my family and for all those who work at Appleton's, I still believe in freedom of the press. But I am grateful that the truth has won out. I will donate the money I have been awarded to the Haven charity. Thank you.'

Mina asked me to organize a lunch to thank everyone who'd

supported her through the trial, and anyone looking in through the windows at Minerva that day, the sun shining down on the guests, might have thought us a strange assortment. Stella Parker was there, sitting next to Mina's barrister, Douglas Rockwell. And the stylist who'd helped plan her outfits for court was chatting away to Rupert French, the financial director. I suppose you could call it a democratic spread. Even Sarah was invited, though it was difficult for me to find a day when everyone was free and, sadly, in the end, she was unable to attend.

It was a lovely occasion, and, as I rose from the table to go and call in the cars to take people home, Mina touched her knife against her glass.

'Christine, sit down, will you?'

I did so, embarrassed when everyone turned to look at me.

'And lastly, but by no means least – I would like to give special thanks to Christine for organizing this wonderful lunch for us all and, more importantly, I want to thank you, Christine, for your unwavering loyalty and support to me throughout the trial, and beyond. I really don't know what I would do without you.' She raised her glass, her smiling eyes meeting mine. 'To Christine,' she said.

I no longer drink champagne. Just the smell of it turns my stomach.

22

A week after the lunch party, Mina and family flew off to the Caribbean where they'd been loaned a house by a wealthy friend. There were a few journalists at the airport when they left, and the photographs that appeared in the papers show a tight-knit family, smiling at the camera, shoulder to shoulder. Yet it took some doing to corral those children into going on that trip. They were young adults by then, but still very much tied to their mother's purse strings – a detail they had to be reminded of when they started coming up with various excuses why they couldn't go. As always, when push came to shove, Mina's children put on a good public show for her.

Mina insisted I have some time off too, and I thought about going away somewhere but, as is the way, I came down with a nasty bug on the Sunday evening and spent most of that week in bed. By Friday, I had forced myself to get up and dress and felt better for it. And then, as the day wore on, I felt well enough to take the train up to London and go into the office. Sarah had been in all week and we'd spoken several times, nevertheless I wanted the peace of mind of seeing for myself that all was ready for Mina's return.

When I walked into the office around four, Sarah had already left – it was Friday, after all. I wasn't sorry to have the place to myself. I checked my messages – nothing important – and went into Mina's office and settled myself behind her desk, a good position from which to survey the room and make sure everything was in its place. She was always so particular. The books and magazines on the coffee table, neatly stacked, the cushions on the sofa flush, the blinds on the windows hung at half-mast.

I was surprised when Dave walked in a short while later. It took him a moment to notice me there, and when he did he jumped out of his skin.

'I thought you were on holiday.'

'I wish,' I said. 'I came down with a bug, and had to cancel my tickets to Vienna.' There were no tickets to Vienna, never had been, but Vienna seemed like the kind of place Dave might expect someone like me to visit. The opera, a bit of culture. We looked at each other, me behind the desk, him standing stock-still in the middle of the office. 'I didn't expect you to be in either,' I said.

'Mina asked me to run a few errands while she was away.' Still, he didn't move. I'd worked with Dave a long time, and could see he was holding something back. He seemed to be plucking up the courage to move and, when he did, he came over to Mina's desk, opened a drawer and took out a bunch of keys. I recognized the leather tag of Lord Appleton's old Jag hanging from them. He didn't offer any explanation and I stayed quiet – a trick I'd picked up from Mina. If you leave a silence long enough, people feel compelled to fill it.

'She wants me to go to Fincham – check over the place. I better get going. Friday-night traffic and all that.' Fincham was Lord Appleton's old home in the Cotswolds – the house Mina had grown up in. I looked at my watch.

'Well, you're not going to beat the traffic now, so you might as well have a cuppa before you go. I'll put the kettle on. Why don't you go and sit soft in my office?' I could be quite persuasive when I wanted to be, and I knew something was troubling Dave. Over tea and biscuits, I managed to coax it out of him.

'Mina wants me to have Lord Appleton's car. The Jag. I've always admired it, but . . . I don't know . . .' He seemed reticent, but I could see by the way he played with the leather tag on that bunch of keys how much he wanted that car.

'You know how generous she is. Just accept it graciously, Dave. If it makes you feel better, I'll come to Fincham with you.' I'd never been to Mina's childhood home and I longed to see it before it was sold. Besides, the thought of going home to my empty house was bleak. An impromptu trip to the Cotswolds was beyond tempting.

'No, Christine. I couldn't ask you to do that. It's a long drive.'

'Exactly. I can't have you falling asleep at the wheel. I'll come and keep you company. Besides, if *I'm* there, you could take the Jag away, and then I could drive the Audi for you. How's that?'

'Well, I'm not sure.'

'Honestly, Dave, I'm happy to – a bit of fresh country air is just what I need after being stuck in bed all week.' And with that I went off to make a thermos of coffee for the journey before he could change his mind.

By the time we left, it was six o'clock and the traffic was thick, but in his expert way, Dave slipped around the back roads and we made the M4 in good time. Neither of us spoke much, but the radio was on and we listened, as we had so many times before, to the Friday-evening drive-time show. Anyone glancing over from a passing car might have mistaken us for a couple on our way home for the weekend.

I see now why that journey aroused suspicion. The pair of us, the driver and the secretary, driving for two hours to visit the empty country estate of our employer's dead father. We were both foolish. We had no idea of the scrutiny our trip would come under, the interest strangers would take in it, the questions we'd be asked, and so we slipped out of London without a clue we were being watched.

We stopped once for petrol before we hit the motorway. I stayed in the car while Dave filled up. Later, others pawed over the details, but I barely remembered that stop – snippets, that's all. The sound of petrol going through the pump. Dave's hands in silicone gloves – he always wore them when filling the car. His jacket laid out on the back seat. I saw him through the window of the petrol station shop, picking up a few bits and pieces, but I was preoccupied texting Angelica, and then reading her texts back to me – both of us chatty in a way we could never quite manage face-to-face. Then I poured coffee – one for me, one for Dave, which I left in his cupholder – and so I really didn't pay attention to what he was up to. The Jaguar, I understand now, came with strings. It was a reward, not a gift.

When he got back in the car, I smelled mint on his breath, and he reached his arm across the back of my seat and twisted round, expertly reversing the car with one hand.

As we drove into the countryside, the air inside the car changed, bringing with it the smell of damp, mossy ground, and I felt a thrill of anticipation as we headed into unknown territory.

'I wonder what it's like,' I said.

'Big. Creepy. It's too dark now, but when you drive here in daylight you can see the house on top of the hill.'

'You've been here before then?' I tried not to sound put out. I organized Dave's schedule each week, and I'd never put in a trip to Fincham.

'Yes, two, maybe three times? I brought Mina up here after

her father died and helped her clear out a few things.' I wondered if it was Jenny Haddow's things they cleared out. It should have bothered me more. It should have made me think about what else I didn't know.

We turned off and pulled up in front of a set of iron gates, padlocked shut. In the beam of the headlights I watched Dave take the bunch of keys from his pocket and hold them in the palm of his hand, fingering through until he found the right one. He pushed open the gates, first one then the other, and we drove through. I only had a quick glimpse of the house because he pulled up around the side and parked.

'This is where he kept the car,' Dave said. Stables, converted into a garage.

I followed as he pulled open the doors and flicked on the lights. Lord Appleton's car was an old XJ6, and I watched Dave run his hand along its side, stroking it as if he worried it might bolt in fright. Any qualms he'd had in accepting Mina's gift seemed to have disappeared on our journey up. He sat behind the wheel, and I noticed him hold his breath before turning the key in the ignition. How he must have wanted the engine to fire into life so he could drive it away there and then. It was dead. Barely a sound came from it.

'What a shame,' I said. 'Looks like we'll have to stay. You can arrange for it to be towed in the morning.' I was determined not to have had a wasted journey – I so wanted to see Fincham in daylight.

I'm surprised now, how uninhibited we both were, walking into that grand old house. Mina had always made me feel at home at Minerva, and I saw no reason why she would feel differently about her childhood home. We walked into a vast hallway, Dave trailing behind me like a child scared of the dark.

'I can see why you didn't want to come here on your own,' I said.

The furniture in the hall was covered in white sheets. Paintings had been removed from the walls, leaving ghostly trails. There were so many doors, to so many rooms, all dark and closed up and I tried, but found it difficult, to imagine Mina as a child running around the place.

I followed Dave across the hallway, our feet clicking on the tiled floor, then silent as we walked along a carpeted corridor, worn and stained from decades of staff treading back and forth from the kitchen to the main house, fetching and carrying food and drink. I see us now, Dave and I, following in their footsteps.

It was a very different house to Minerva. The kitchen at Fincham was utilitarian – scuffed lino tiles on the floor, strip lights on the ceiling that buzzed and flickered – a place very much for below-stairs staff. You'd know your place if you worked at Fincham. I sat at the scrubbed pine table, more surgical than domestic under the harsh glare of lights, and watched Dave open the fridge. It was empty of course.

'What did you buy in the shop?' I asked, hoping he might have thought of getting a few things for breakfast. I regretted I hadn't thought of it myself.

'Chocolate,' he said. 'And Polos.' Dave was addicted to Polos – he'd suck on them incessantly whenever he was stressed. When he sat in the defendants' dock, I noticed the floor was littered with strips of silver paper.

While he checked the window was secure, I went around opening cupboards and found a bottle of brandy, tucked away at the back of one.

'Nightcap?' I said, finding two glasses and wiping them with the sleeve of my coat. It was clear Dave wouldn't be driving again that night, so I poured us two generous measures. 'Cheers,' I said, the liquor burning the back of my throat. 'I think this is for cooking,' I joked, pulling a face. 'Two Go Mad at Fincham!' I felt like a character from an Enid Blyton adventure. He looked bemused. I suspect Dave wasn't much of a reader as a child.

'I better go and do the rounds,' he said, and I followed him back along the corridor, switching off lights as I went, the darkness creeping along behind us.

'It's hard to think of this as a family home, isn't it?' I said, looking up at the grand staircase.

He shrugged. 'For you and me maybe, but they're not like us, are they?' It surprised me to hear him talk of 'them' and 'us' – it seemed so old-fashioned. But I see now, he was right. Lines had been blurred. I followed him up, my fingers gathering dust on the banister as I went.

'This is the master bedroom,' he said, opening a door. The place where, very likely, Mina had been conceived. I wanted to see what it looked like, under its covering, and pulled off its shroud. A four-poster bed, a dressing table, wardrobe, chest of drawers, all in heavy, carved oak. Hanging from the windows, oppressive brocade curtains. A cold room. I imagined Lord and Lady Appleton sleeping in the four-poster – little Mina in her own room, further along the corridor. I turned away and went in search.

Mina's bedroom was right at the end – as far as it could possibly have been from her parents', and I thought how lonely she must have been lying there at night. If she'd cried, they would not have heard her.

I knew what that felt like, lying in bed, hoping someone would come and comfort you. You learn to comfort yourself after a while, and then you learn not to cry at all.

I stood at the window and looked out, but the dark of the countryside made it impossible to see anything. How different it was from the view I'd had, from my childhood bedroom. The street lights right outside meant it was never fully dark, so when

I stood at my window I could see into the houses opposite – the families, eating together, watching TV, and even when they drew their curtains I could see shadows moving around behind the thin, unlined fabric.

I could hear Dave in the corridor outside, opening and clos-ing doors, checking each room. When he reached Mina's, he stopped. I had already removed the dust-sheet from the queen-size bed, made up and ready. I heard him turn the handle and come in – felt him standing there, looking at me. I closed my eyes, waiting for him to close the door behind him. Walk towards me.

'I'd like to be off early tomorrow,' he said. 'I have to take the boys to football at lunchtime. Will you be all right up here? I'm going to sleep downstairs.'

'Suits me fine. Night, Dave,' I said, keeping my back turned.

When he'd gone, I looked around the room. There was barely a sign that it had been a child's bedroom, the toys, of course, long packed away. All that was left were some miniature china animals lined up on the glass top of the dressing table. Whim-sies, I believe they're called. People collect them now, though why, I can't imagine. They look cheap and nasty to me.

I picked up the brush from the vanity set – a miniature copy of the one I had seen on Lady Appleton's dressing table – and ran it through my hair, listening to the sounds of the house. Water running through the pipes as Dave went to the bath-room, the creak of the floors, the rattle of the windows. Under the glass of the dressing table was a photograph. It was the first I'd seen of Lady Appleton, and it's an image that stayed with me for a long time. She seemed to fit the description Mina had given – *my mother is a cold-hearted woman.*

In that photo, she looks more like a fashion plate than a mother, sitting in a garden chair, her hair piled up on her head – sunglasses, lipstick, a cigarette in one hand, cocktail glass in the other. Mina is around four years old, sitting on a rug at her feet. She is in the exact same pose, holding a teacup with her little finger sticking out, and a pencil in the other as if she is smoking a cigarette.

I slipped the photo back and picked up one of the whimsies – a squirrel – turning it over in my hand. There was a label on the bottom, *Brownlow*, written in a child's hand. How sweet, I thought. Mina had named them all, sticking a tiny label on each. The squirrel, a rabbit, a badger, a fawn, a hedgehog and a weasel. *Brownlow, Percival, Simpson, Lancing, Hogarth* and *McTally.* When I went to bed that night I felt their beady eyes watching me through the dark.

Now, whenever I have trouble sleeping, instead of counting sheep, I recite the names of those whimsies in my head and imagine the squirrel, the rabbit, the badger, the fawn, the hedgehog and the weasel marching through the countryside, gobbling it up, their sharp little teeth chewing through the turf.

23

I was looking forward to Mina's return and getting back to some kind of routine. But I could tell, as soon as I walked in on the Monday morning, something was off. She was already there, for one thing, and I'd made a point of being in extra early. The blinds to her office were drawn and, as I took off my coat, I could hear her on the phone, speaking French. She was fluent, from her Swiss education. My French, on the other hand, is limited, and so I heard but did not comprehend the conversation. I guessed she was speaking to her mother – French being their preferred language of communication. It was not a pretty sound in Mina's mouth – more Germanic than Gallic. A reflection, I felt, of their brittle relationship.

I went off to prepare coffee and a fruit plate – a dose of vitamin C to ease the jet-lag I knew she'd be suffering from, having flown home only the night before – then knocked and went into her office.

'Good morning,' I said, setting down the tray and moving across to pull up the blinds. 'How was your holiday?'

I'd expected her to come back rested – the court case was behind her, she'd had a luxurious week in the Caribbean – but she was a bundle of nerves. I smelled it in the air. When she looked at me, my heart went out to her. I saw a distressed child, wide-eyed with fear. She looked from me to her computer screen, then back to me again, and I was reminded of the incident with Clifford Fraser and the diary, but I knew whatever was upsetting her was nothing to do with me. There was no anger or petulance there, only utter helplessness.

'I don't seem to be able to . . .' and she looked back at the computer again.

The more panicked she was, the calmer I became. I poured her coffee, took it over to her with the plate of fruit, and then stood behind her to see what the problem was.

'It's this,' she said, pointing to an entry in the diary from the previous month. A trip to Geneva.

It had been Mina's idea a while back, that Sarah handle all her travel arrangements – *you shouldn't be fiddling around with hotels and flights, Christine. You've got more important things to do –* and I'd relinquished that duty. I'd quizzed Sarah about Mina's monthly trips to Geneva when they'd first started appearing in the diary, and she'd shrugged and told me Mina was visiting her mother. I was sceptical, given my greater insight into that relationship, but if that's what Mina chose to tell Sarah, then who was I to contradict her.

'I want to take it out, all of them, but I don't seem to be able to . . . I'm not sure how to do it . . .' Mina was always hopeless with technology.

'Let me see,' I said and she stood up, offering me her chair. I wheeled myself forward and, as I set to work, I could feel her breath on my neck as she watched my fingers tip-tap across the keyboard. It took me only five minutes to delete all those trips to Geneva.

'There,' I said when it was done, turning around to face her. She looked down at me with such gratitude, and seemed to relax, picking up her coffee and fruit plate and going over to sit on the sofa. I stayed in her chair and, for a moment, it seemed our roles were reversed.

'Thank you, Christine. Perhaps you could put in other entries? So it doesn't look as if anything is missing. You know better than anyone how my days fit together.'

'Of course.' It was like being back at school, doing a piece of creative writing with the teacher watching, the clock ticking. It took another fifteen minutes to invent new, plausible entries.

'There,' I said again, basking in her grateful smile. It was a foolish thing to do. You can delete things from the page, but not the hard drive. Mina didn't think of that, and I hadn't realized I needed to. If only she'd been more open with me. At the time, my own vanity carried me away – the belief that only I could help her. It was me she called on and it seemed such a small thing. The least I could do.

'Do you mind if I ask why? I can't see why visiting your mother is something you need to hide.' I waited for her to share her secret. I imagined a lover perhaps, or some sort of clinic. By then, she was having 'a bit of work done' on her face, although as far as I knew it was always carried out by the two girls I booked to visit her at Minerva. I had noticed how, when she returned from her trips to Geneva, she had a particular glow about her. She looked at me for a moment and then shrugged.

'You're quite right, I shouldn't have to, but my mother called this morning – she's worried that my visits could be . . .' I watched her struggle to find the word. *Misinterpreted* was the one she came up with. 'It's complicated.' That was all she thought I needed to hear. And even later, months down the line, when she discovered that those entries had not vanished into thin air, and that she had to come up with a reason why on earth the diary had been altered, she offered me no further explanation, yet it was me she called on once more to help. And again, I couldn't find it in myself to refuse her.

As fate would have it, Sarah phoned in ill that morning and was off for the rest of the week. I sometimes wonder whether things might have been different if she'd been buzzing around the office.

Mina spent much of the week out at meetings, which wasn't unusual. It was the way she did business, wining and dining politicians and media folk, while her top team handled the day-to-day Appleton's business. Delegation, that was her skill. Yet, even in her absence, I sensed that something still weighed on her mind, that my help with the diary hadn't cured her troubles. I found bits of bloodied tissue in her wastepaper bin, and knew she'd been biting the skin around her thumbnail. On the carpet around her chair, I found strands of hair. She's lucky she has so much of it; I imagine that beneath her abundant curls are tiny bald patches where she tugs and worries at it, pulling out clumps. I found them easily. Dark hair on a blond carpet. Obvious, when you know where to look. It took until the end of the day on Thursday before she finally opened up to me.

'Christine, could you pop in for a moment?'

She smiled, but it didn't fool me. I was shocked by how fragile she looked.

'Will you sit down?' She patted the space beside her on the sofa.

I noticed how she sat on her hands, and knew she was trying to hide them from me. The raw, red skin around her thumbs. She looked down at her knees and I had, once more, a fleeting sensation that our roles were reversed, that I was the stronger one.

'This might sound strange to you,' she said, 'but you are one of the few people I feel I can trust.'

It didn't sound strange to me at all.

'I've just come from Douglas's office.' That was news to me.

She must have squeezed in her lawyer between meetings in the afternoon. We were sitting so close that when she turned to face me I could smell her breath – the fear on it – sharp and acid, rising from her stomach. 'Douglas called me while I was away. He's been tipped off that the police are following up on some information they've been given relating to the libel trial.' She slipped her hand out from beneath her and began chewing on her thumb, and I wanted to reach over and stop her, like I used to with Angelica when she bit her nails. 'He told me the police will be obliged to follow it up, but that it won't necessarily lead to anything. Frankly, it's ridiculous. I had a terrible row with him. Douglas had advised against suing the *Business Times* in the first place, you see. He thought the story would go away in time, but it's *my* reputation, Christine. Not his. The Appleton name is what our business stands on. I couldn't sit back and let it be trashed by some journalist. You understand that, don't you? I had no choice but to sue.'

'Yes, of course.'

'And I won. The judge said it was a witch-hunt. I was vindicated. Now, they're after me again.' She ran the back of her hand across her eyes and a tiny speck of blood from her thumb stained her cheekbone. 'I don't feel safe,' she said. 'I feel as if I'm being watched, as if my phone calls are being listened to – I think they'd do anything to try and catch me out.'

'Who are *they*?' I asked.

She shrugged.

'The police, a couple of the broadsheets. And our rivals, I suspect. Who knows? The mob. This is a witch-hunt. Douglas has advised me to go to the police – he says he's confident he could work out some sort of deal, but why should I? It's absurd. If the police pursue this, it will be a complete waste of public money. They should be out catching real criminals, not people like me.'

'Surely, it won't come to that.'

'I hope it won't. Anyway, I'm not going to go to the police, but I do feel compelled to take steps to protect myself.' She put her hand on mine and stood up. 'I could do with a drink. Will you join me?' I nodded and was about to offer to make them, but she was already there, putting ice into the glasses, pouring the whisky. Then she sat down again, handing me my drink, and twisting her body to face me. She looked at me then, studying my face, weighing me up, and I knew she was deciding how far she could trust me.

'What can I do to help?' I offered.

'You're sweet.' She touched my hand. 'There is one thing. There were some papers from Dad's time that I kept in my desk. If they got into the wrong hands, I worry they could be made to look like something they're not. They're private, you see. Not meant for strangers' eyes. There were some old notebooks of mine in there too, I think. You boxed them up for me when we moved offices.'

'Yes, they're in the archive.'

'Are they? Could you remove them? Preferably, out of the building. I'd take them home with me, but I don't feel they'd be safe there – you know how Margaret caught journalists going through the bins.'

'I could take them.'

'Would you?'

'Yes.'

'Home with you?'

'Yes. I'll go to the archive first thing in the morning.'

'Perhaps you could say the boxes contain your things, Christine. I imagine there's some kind of log to fill in?' I felt the old Mina come back into the room. Poised, confident, bold. 'You know I wouldn't ask you to do this if there was anything illegal in those boxes. Top-up?' She took my glass and refilled it.

'I've been meaning to say, by the way. The house in Italy is going to be empty for part of August. I wondered whether you wanted to have a week there? Take Angelica. She'd love it.' I'd seen photographs of Mina's house in Italy, and knew how special it was to her. Close friends and family only. It was thoughtful, and yet I hesitated, doubtful Angelica would want to spend time on her own with me. 'You look worried, Christine. I understand. Teenagers can be tricky. Maybe Angelica would like to go with friends?' She rested her hand on my arm. 'Why don't you tell her I offered the place to you, but that you can't go – and then *you* suggest she take some friends instead? I bet she'd jump at that. Make sure to tell her it was your idea.'

She touched her glass against mine and took a mouthful of whisky; I heard the sound of her teeth biting down on a piece of ice.

'Thank you, Mina. If you're sure . . .'

'Absolutely. You're like family to me – you know that, Christine.' She stood up and reached for her coat, and I finished my drink and got up to leave. 'You know, Christine, thinking about it, it might be best if you get rid of that material altogether.' She said it as if it was an afterthought, her voice as gentle as if we were still talking about the invitation to Italy. 'There's nothing I need to keep, and it'll save me worrying about it. Maybe you could dump it on your way home? Or however you think best. I'll leave it up to you. Think of it as a bit of housekeeping.'

A bit of housekeeping, that's all Mina Appleton asked of me. My crime was to tidy things away.

24

Christine told such dreadful lies,
It made one gasp and stretch one's eyes;
Her father, who, from his earliest youth,
Had kept a strict regard for truth,
Attempted to believe Christine;
The effort very nearly killed him.

Cautionary Tales for Children. A book on the shelf in my bedroom as a child. I remember, soon after my mother was buried, my father picking it up, flicking through and finding that verse, and reading it out – replacing *Matilda*'s name with mine – *aunt* with *father*. I didn't say a word, couldn't look at him, keeping my eyes fixed on the scabs in the crook of my elbow, scratching at my eczema. So, he read it again and again. *Christine told such dreadful lies . . .* At the hospital, after Mum died, I'd promised him I hadn't run out into the road – that I'd held on to Mummy's hand. He knew I was lying, I'm sure, yet I stuck to my story. The truth was unbearable.

As a rule, I'd never deface a book, but this one, I am happy to. I cross out *Matilda* and insert *Mina*. My handwriting is neat, and it sits well on the page. *Mina told such dreadful lies . . .* It scans pretty well. I tear out the page, then trim its edges, and paste it into the scrapbook. *Her secretary, who, from her earliest youth, Had kept a strict regard for truth, Attempted to believe Mina; The effort very nearly killed her. Secretary,* instead of *aunt,* is a bit of a mouthful, but if you say anything often enough you can twist it into shape, and when I discovered how Mina had lied to me, it very nearly did kill me.

I lied too, albeit never to her. We all lied. Dave too. It was contagious. Offices are full of deceit, aren't they? People covering up mistakes – their own or their boss's. Ours was no different, in that respect.

Perhaps Rachel Farrer is an exception. I can't imagine an untruth passing her lips. I lied to her, though, without conscience.

Rachel Farrer's domain was the well-ordered, efficiently run series of rooms in the basement of the Appleton's building. As accomplished as I was in managing time, so Rachel Farrer was with space. When it looked like it was running out, she always managed to conjure up more to store the boxes and files brought down to her archive.

'This'll free up some room for you, Rachel,' I said. She stood over me as I filled in the ledger.

'Only until you return them, Christine.'

'No need. They're full of my old bits and pieces. Old shorthand notebooks, that sort of thing. I haven't had a chance to go through them since the office move. I doubt there's anything worth holding on to.'

'Isn't that for me to judge? There may well be items that relate to the history of the company. If you're not returning them, then I would like to go through the contents and, at the very least, take copies of any material that may be of interest.' She took off her glasses and studied me. She wore them on a gold chain around her neck, and I noticed crumbs caught on the lenses from her lunchtime sandwich.

'Of course you're right,' I said. 'Don't worry, I'll sign them back in when I'm done.'

'Just a moment,' she said. 'These boxes have been mis-labelled.' She put her glasses back on and ran her finger along the entry I'd made in her book, then cross-referenced it with the labels on the boxes. 'Either that or you've picked up the wrong ones.' I should have known I couldn't slip anything past Rachel.

'No, you're right. My fault entirely – they were mislabelled in the office move, and my old shorthand notebooks and per-sonal bits and pieces got dumped into two of Mina's boxes. At least, boxes labelled as Mina's, but in fact they weren't Mina's. I'm so sorry – it's all a bit of a muddle.'

'That's not like you, Christine. Not to notice at the time.'

'Oh, I did, but it was when Lucy Beacham was with us and I haven't had time to sort out all her mistakes. I'm still coming across things.'

'Oh dear.' Rachel Farrer was not happy, but she accepted my explanation and made a note to accommodate the error. 'Here, Christine, you better take one of my trolleys.'

'Super. Thanks.'

I had a driver take me home that evening. Had Dave been available, I might well have dumped the boxes on the way as Mina had suggested. Instead, I took them home with me, stack-ing them in my garage next to a bag of things Mike had left behind. He'd been gone five years and we were now divorced, but still I hadn't got round to getting rid of his unwanted stuff. *Chuck it all, Chrissie,* he'd said. I couldn't though. So I told him I'd take it to the jumble, but I hadn't done that either. Seeing his bag of old clothes upset me that night, and I lay awake, thinking about him and Ursula and Angelica, all snuggled up together in their cosy house. Perhaps it was a vindictive streak that made me decide on a bonfire. *Kill two birds*, was my thinking.

I got out of bed, went down to the garage and carried Mina's boxes, along with Mike's bin bag, into the garden, and set them down on the lawn. I pulled out the incinerator tucked round the side of the shed – the one Mike used to bring out on fireworks' night – he, Angelica and I standing around it waving sparklers. I started with Mina's boxes – wanting to get the blaze going before I added Mike's things. When I took out the first handful of papers, I saw they were contracts. Lord Appleton's signature was on some, Mina's on others, yet I didn't hesitate. I struck the match and set them ablaze. When the fire was going strong, I tipped on Mike's things; I remember my eyes watering from the toxic smoke of the man-made fibres of his clothes. I was about to stamp down the empty archive boxes and burn those too, when I noticed a scrap of paper caught in the bottom of one.

I took it out, and recognized Mina's handwriting. There were doodles too, and I realized they were the same as the sketches she'd made in the study at Minerva, soon after her father died. I shone the light from my phone on it, and saw what I'd missed before. A squirrel, a badger, a rabbit, a fawn, a hedgehog and a weasel. Not very accomplished, but good enough for me to recognize them as the whimsies I'd seen on her dressing table at Fincham. I smiled at the image of her at her desk, those glassy-eyed creatures distracting her as she worked. Beside each animal was the name of a former Appleton's supplier – Clifford Fraser's farm amongst them – but it was the drawings that attracted me, as if the child in Mina had found its way on to the page. I kept it for sentimental reasons. I am a bit of a squirrel myself, and have kept a few mementos from the old days.

25

It was eight a.m. on a Wednesday when they arrived. I still had my coat on. Security called up and tried to warn me, but as I put down the phone the police were already marching through the top floor. I was outraged, not frightened. The cheek of it. I counted five walk past my office to Mina's.

'You are?' one of them said, stopping to lean against my door.

'Christine Butcher. Mina Appleton's personal assistant.'

'This is your office?'

'Yes.'

'I'll need that.' He held out his hand for my phone and I handed it over and watched him go through the call log.

'How long have you worked for Mina Appleton?'

'Nearly fifteen years.'

'She's very demanding,' he said, raising an eyebrow as he scrolled through my calls.

I took off my coat, unwrapped my scarf and, with my other hand, opened the drawer of my desk, taking out the memory stick where I backed up Mina's laptops. He was too busy nosing through my phone to notice me slip it into the waistband of my tights. I didn't consider what I did as an illegal act, merely a precautionary one, and I enjoyed the sensation it gave me, of keeping something back, of feeling the memory stick dig into my skin as I sat down at my desk.

'She calls you a lot. Do you have another mobile?'

'No.'

'We're going to have to take this. And the computers.'

'Why?'

He didn't answer.

'How will I work? Everything's on the computers.'

He ignored my question and walked away. I followed him to Mina's office, watching as gloved hands tipped out drawers, rifled through papers, flicked through notebooks, then dropped them into polythene bags. They pulled cushions from the sofa, unzipped them and shook them out. It was absurd. One went through the cupboard where she kept her shoes, a nasty sneer on his face as he tossed them over his shoulder – ten pairs in the same style but different colours. I was glad Mina wasn't there to witness it. Another kicked over the wastepaper basket in frustration – I suspect, because it was empty. The cleaners had been in, but Sarah told me later that she'd seen the police go through all the bags of rubbish at the back of the building.

'Where's her laptop?' one of them asked me.

'She'll have it with her,' I said. 'If you tell me what you're looking for, I might be able to help.'

They continued to ignore me and refused the teas and coffees I asked Sarah to make for them. She and I stood watching helplessly as trolleys they'd borrowed from the archive were loaded up with computers and files – backwards and forwards they went until they'd cleaned the place out. Meanwhile I fielded calls from members of staff, doing my best to reassure them. I hadn't heard from Mina, despite trying her mobile several times from my landline. It was Dave who finally called me.

'I'm on my way to pick you up. I'll be with you in forty minutes. She wants you at Minerva.'

'The police have been here.'

'Yes. They've been at Minerva too.' He hung up before I could ask any more.

I went down and waited on the street, relieved to be out of the building. People rushed past and the sound and smell of the traffic reassured me that life outside carried on as normal. I expected Dave to come armed with information but he was tight-lipped on the journey up, saying only that the police had arrived at five that morning and that they were still there.

'What do they want?' I asked him.

'Don't worry about it. They won't find anything. We were just doing our jobs, Christine.' And that's true. We were just doing our jobs.

'How's Mina?' I asked him. He shrugged.

'Andy turned up as I was leaving. He's with her now. And that lawyer bloke.' He reached over and turned up the radio for the news. It was the top story: *Police raid the home and offices of Mina Appleton.*

Margaret was waiting for me in the hallway, her eyes red from crying.

'I heard him say she could go to prison.'

'Who said that, Margaret?'

'Mr Rockwell.'

'Where's Mina?'

'In the study with him.'

'Right. Well then, let's you and I go into the drawing room,' and I led the way across the hallway, sensing a change in the house – how it shivered from the assault it had undergone. I hung my coat over the arm of a chair and sat down.

'I thought she'd been murdered. When I let myself in this morning and saw the police.'

'It must have been horrible for you, Margaret. Why don't you sit down for a moment?' I said, and she pulled up a chair closer to me. 'No one's dead and I am sure everything will get sorted out, but you and I need to get on with our jobs. We'll get through this, don't worry.' She was only half-listening.

'They're out in the bloody garden now. Traipsing over everything. The house is a mess. I've managed to clear up a bit down here, but I haven't started upstairs yet. Filthy pigs. I saw one of them stick his hand down the toilet.'

'I'll help you later. We'll do it together. In the meantime, I'd love some coffee and a sandwich. Would you mind? And could you let Mina know I'm here?'

'Yes, Christine.' She snapped to attention.

I heard Douglas Rockwell's voice out in the hall.

'For God's sake, try and talk to her, Andy. I still think we could avoid court if she agrees to meet with them.'

'I'll try, but you know what she's like.' Poor Andy, he had no hope of talking Mina out of anything.

'Yes, you know what I'm like, Douglas.' Mina had caught them talking about her, and I imagined they looked like two naughty schoolboys.

'Just think about it at least, Mina. It could save a lot of pain later.' Douglas was right. It would have saved a lot of pain later.

'I have thought about it and I've made my decision. Bye now, Dougie. Drive carefully.'

I remember smiling – my hands held together, in silent applause. At the time, I admired her for standing up to him, for holding her ground. Now I know it was hubris on her part. There was nothing brave about it. Mina Appleton's image has always been her most precious possession. A sacred object she'll do anything to protect. I heard the front door close behind Douglas Rockwell and sat down and waited.

'Christine,' she said, opening the door. I looked up and saw Andy standing behind her in the doorway, and his eyes met mine for a moment. I'm not sure what I saw in them. An appeal for help? A warning? *Take care, Christine*? He looked as if he wanted to say something, but what, I have no idea. And then she closed the door on him.

She was still in a dressing gown, her feet bare. Her hair a halo of fuzz, a savage look to its usual tamed beauty; faint, blue circles beneath her eyes. She looked fragile, and my instinct to help rose to the surface. We are both Librans, Mina and I, and I see us like a set of scales. The balance was always tipped slightly in her favour, of course, but whenever she weakened, the scales shifted, and I became stronger. I doubt she ever noticed the minor adjustments I made to accommodate her, but any good secretary understands how important it is to keep balance in the relationship. We are dependent on each other – secretary and employer – each meeting the other's needs. A secretary needs to be needed.

Margaret came in with the tray of coffee and sandwiches and fiddled around with plates and napkins. I knew exactly what she was up to – I'd done it myself in the office, hoping no one would notice I was still in the room.

'That's all, thank you, Margaret,' I said. 'Why don't you go upstairs and make a start tidying up? I'm sure you can soon have it looking as if those oafs were never here.'

'Will do,' she said.

Mina sat with a glazed expression, as if she hadn't seen or heard the exchange. I waited until the door closed behind Margaret before speaking.

'I'm so sorry, Mina. It's awful to have your home invaded like this.'

'They're still here, you know. Out in the garden. I don't know what they think they'll find out there. They've even been through the compost. Douglas says it's completely over the top. You'd think they were searching for some drugs haul or something.' She stood and drifted over to the window, her back to me and, again, I felt an overwhelming need to protect her. 'I hear they've been through the office too. Did they take anything?' Her voice sounded small – my own, when I replied, strong.

'Computers, phones. They made a mess but we've cleared it up. I thought you might need this – I managed to smuggle it out.' She turned and looked at the memory stick I held out in my palm, puzzling over it as if it was a strange insect.

'What is it?'

'A memory stick.' I couldn't help smiling.

'Yes. But what's on it?'

'I always back up your laptops and phones. In case you lose them – you know how careless you are.'

She took it from me, looked at it again, then put it into the pocket of her dressing gown.

'I had no idea you did that. Are there any more?'

'No. Only for your desktop, and the police took those, but there's nothing on them they won't find on the hard drive.'

She smiled at me then and seemed to recover, and I felt the scales tip back.

'You really are a treasure, Christine.'

'What are they looking for?'

She turned back to the window.

'I believe it's called a fishing expedition.' Her shoulders rose, then dipped in a sigh. 'I suppose I'd better get dressed. Come with me,' she said, and turned and walked towards the door.

The doors along the landing upstairs were open and she averted her eyes while I looked into each room – my earlier outrage swelling to fury. Paintings lay on the floor. Towels, cotton buds, boxes of tissues, strewn around. All those small, thoughtful touches to make guests feel at home – hand-crafted soaps, creams, bath salts, oils, nightwear – spilled and trodden into the carpets. Books lay face down, dragged from their shelves, and left sprawling on the floor.

By the time we reached Mina's bedroom my fury had turned into a deep sense of injustice. We found Margaret on her hands and knees, picking up hairpins.

'I'll finish up here, Margaret,' I said, and closed the door after her. While Mina showered, I crawled around on the floor, gathering up the remainder of the hair grips and putting them in the silver dish on the dressing table, then I turned and surveyed the room. To the untrained eye, it might have looked as if it was back to rights, but I noticed the details Margaret had missed. I took Mina's nightdress and refolded it, placing it beneath her pillow. I turned around a cushion on the chair by the window so the floral pattern was the right way up, straightened a painting. Only when I was satisfied that order was restored did I sit down.

A cloud of steam crawled over the dressing-table mirror, blurring the reflection into the bathroom. I turned away and gazed into the branches of the magnolia tree that grew below Mina's bedroom window. It was the same species I'd seen in the tiny patio garden of her old Notting Hill home, when she'd first interviewed me for my job, back in 1995. A long time ago, I thought, as spots of rain hit the window and the tree shivered in the wind.

The shower stopped and I listened to Mina clean her teeth, and turned when she came out of the bathroom. She was wrapped in a towel, her face pink, and I was pleased to see she looked more herself as she walked across to her dressing room. While she dressed she talked to me, her voice restored – reassuring and soothing.

'The police are on some sort of archaeological dig. Desperate to unearth something to pin on me.' I studied the leaves on the magnolia, how the rain bounced off their glossy, fleshy texture.

'It suits the common man. A crackdown on the privileged rich. We're all lumped together. Business. It doesn't matter whether you're a banker or a shopkeeper – if you're successful and rich, then you're the enemy.'

She came out and sat at her dressing table, opening a pot of cream and dipping in her fingers.

'I fear it might be a bumpy road ahead, Christine, but we'll get through it together.' She swivelled round on the stool, resting her foot on her knee while she put on her socks. 'You look tired, Christine. Why don't I book you some time with Stella? Stella Parker. I'm not sure if you've met her. She worked miracles for me during the court case. It would help me to know that my right-hand woman is in peak condition.' She smiled.

'I'm fine, Mina, really.' I didn't want to have anything to do with Stella Parker's black magic.

'Oh, come on, Christine. Let me take care of you for once.' She came over and sat on the arm of my chair. 'It'll reassure me to know that you're being looked after. Oh, it's raining,' she said as if that was the worst thing that had happened that day. The wind was stronger and the branches of the magnolia whipped around like the arms of a drunk dancing at a wedding. 'The police have gone,' she said, and I turned to see the last of them trudging out. 'Those boxes, Christine. From the archive . . .'

'I took them home. I burned—'

She raised her hand.

'I don't need to know the details.' She smiled as she stood up and went back to her dressing table, opening a drawer and taking out a jewellery box. She picked through the items and I thought she was selecting something for herself, her fingers picking through earrings, bangles, looking for a bauble to cheer her up, but she turned and held her hand out to me.

'I'd like you to have this. It was given to me on my twenty-first birthday. It's always been something I've treasured.' She came over to me, her fingers slipping inside my blouse as she pinned on the brooch. Gold with a deep-red stone surrounded by tiny pearls.

'I know you're not one for showy jewellery, but I hope you like it. I want you to have something personal of mine.'

'It's lovely. Really lovely. Thank you.' I discovered later that it was a ruby set in rose-gold and, although I haven't worn it for a while, I still have it in my tin of mementos.

'Thank *you*, Christine. I don't know what I'd do without you, I really don't. Shall we go down?' She waited for me to stand, then slipped her arm through mine, and we walked back along the corridor and down the stairs.

We settled in the study – she at the desk, me in my usual chair by the window. The sound of the rain pouring off the guttering outside and the wind rattling the sash windows made the room feel so snug. From memory, I ran through her engagements for the rest of the week.

'Thursday ten a.m., a meeting with the Ministry for Agriculture, you're going there. Then lunch with Sam from the production company. I've booked The Ivy. In the evening, drinks with the editor of the *News of the World* and then on to a casual supper at Number Ten. I think the new host of that TV talent show will be there. Friday is the press launch for the BBC's spring schedule. You'll need to be there for eleven. The press office say *Mina at Home* is the centrepiece, but you should be able to get away by one, and then there's the board meeting with . . .'

I looked up and saw she was smiling.

'It's as if you go into a kind of trance, Christine. Like you're communicating with the other side. You really do have a phenomenal memory.' I think she may even have laughed and, perhaps, I laughed along with her.

I remember that day as a happy one. The two of us in the tranquillity of the study, working alongside each other – she phoning around the board of directors, reassuring them, back in control, while I set about the practical task of replacing her laptops and phones. We were in synch. A natural rhythm between us.

When Andy put his head around the door at six, having made himself scarce for as long as he could manage, I winced at the way Mina spoke to him, keeping my eyes fixed on my notebook while pretending not to hear.

'Wait in the hall, will you? I'll be with you in a minute. Christine and I are just finishing up.' She came and sat in the window seat by my chair. 'I love this spot,' she said. The sky was clear, the stars out and the lights in the garden twinkled through the shrubs. 'Andy and I will have an early supper at the pub. It'll be full of journalists but I have to face them at some point. Margaret can get you supper before you leave – then Dave can drive you home.' She took my hand. 'Thank you again, Christine.'

The weekend papers and television news were full of images of Mina and Andy walking hand in hand through the village under a clear, evening sky. One broadsheet made reference to the full moon and wolves, but on the whole the coverage was positive. They looked relaxed, walking into the thatched, whitewashed, fairy-tale inn, where they were greeted by the landlord.

There they are, the pair of them smiling and leaning against the bar, looking back at me from the page in my scrapbook. They look so pleased with themselves – no idea what I've pasted on the facing page.

East Harning Gazette, 23 July 2009

Two women out walking their dogs in Swainston Forest came across the body of a seventy-five-year-old man last Thursday morning. A gun was found near the remains. Police believe the man took his own life.

It was a story that, at the time, Mina's press department succeeded in keeping out of the national press, yet I hoped that
someone, somewhere considered the death of that old man
newsworthy. It took me a while to track it down online, but I
found it in the end, a few lines in a local paper. No link to
Mina – they wouldn't have dared – it was right after her victory
in the libel trial and journalists were wary.

An inquest was held, a verdict of suicide recorded, an old man
buried and mourned by his family. Significant, life-changing
events that went unmarked by those responsible, and I include
myself in their number. Local, not national news. Still, it's there
now, in its rightful place in my scrapbook – the filling in the
sandwich between Mina's victory in court and her stroll with her
hubby to the pub. It's part of the pleasure for me – putting order
back into the narrative. Filling in the missing parts.

Which reminds me. I've had a message from Mr Ed Brooks,
chief investigative reporter for the *Business Times*. I'd read that
he was working on a book, so I sent him a message. *Good Luck*,
I texted. And he texted me straight back: *I'd very much appreciate
talking to you. Off the record.* It's good to know I haven't been
forgotten. Now he has my number. He already had my home
address, and I'm sure he'll know, by now, I'm not there. Perhaps he thinks I am in hiding, at a secret address. *I don't feel
safe, yet*, I text back, fertilizing the idea. Then I switch off my
phone. If he knew I was in The Laurels, it might prejudice him
against me. I can't have him thinking I am not of sound mind.

26

It was five a.m. on Sunday when I was woken by banging on my front door. I remember how it felt. Like sharp, bony fingers finding the edges of my skin and peeling it away. One quick movement that left me raw and unprotected. Like a rabbit hanging in a butcher's shop. *Skin the rabbit*, my mother used to say when she undressed me for my bath as a little girl, and I'd raise my arms so she could peel off my vest.

By the time I got out of bed they were already in the house. The frame of my front door splintered when they barged their way in. It was how I spent Sunday afternoon – phoning around to find someone to repair it. They spoke so loudly, booming, masculine voices, though I picked up one female amongst them. There seemed to be so many, although afterwards I found it hard to remember the exact number. Four? Five? Maybe six. Let's say six. Six police officers.

'Christine Butcher?' I nodded. 'Is there anyone else in the house?'

'No,' I managed.

'Get downstairs,' the officer repeated. I was outnumbered – alone, but grateful Angelica wasn't there.

'Do you have a warrant?' I asked.

It was flashed in front of me as I was sent into the sitting room. I had no idea whether it was genuine or not. How would I know what a warrant looked like? I was on my sofa, in my sitting room, yet it was no longer my home. It belonged to them.

'Can I make you tea or coffee?' I asked the officer nearest to me. He was on all fours, crawling around in front of me, running his fingers beneath the edge of the carpet. He turned and smiled, almost apologetically.

'Well. That would be nice. Thank you.'

I took their order: coffees – four white, one black, all with sugar – two teas, one with, one without. Seven then. Now I remember. There were six policemen, one policewoman. I picked my way through the debris, finding one of my slippers at the bottom of the stairs, the other further down the hallway where it had been kicked out of the way. I put them on, clenching and unclenching my toes around the lumpy fleece linings.

I filled the kettle and in the reflection of the kitchen window watched the policeman behind me going through the drawer by the fridge – looking through old receipts, bills, instruction manuals. Things I was too nervous to throw out in case someone, one day, asked to see them. It was a chaotic system I would never have tolerated in the office. I returned with the tray of hot drinks.

'Shouldn't be much longer now,' the female officer said, taking a cup. Tea with two sugars. There were still policemen in the garden, their torches scouring the ground around the incinerator, which I'd never bothered to put away. After all those months, there was nothing left but soggy ash. Still, they fingered through it, picking out bits and pieces and bagging up whatever they could. They took the desktop from the spare room, though I knew there could be nothing on it of interest to them – nothing at all in my house that could possibly help them with their inquiries.

They left at eight a.m., apologizing for the mess and the damage to the door. Not that they offered to help clear up. Still, it gave me something to fill the time before I could phone Mina. It was Sunday morning. I couldn't wake her before nine thirty. I worried, when she picked up, that I'd burst into tears, that her sympathy would tip me over, but she was businesslike.

'I see. Did you say anything?'

'No. I—'

'Good. Don't worry. I'll find you a lawyer.'

'A lawyer?'

She sighed with impatience.

'Yes. They will probably call you in for questioning. I'll talk to Douglas.' A tear trickled down my cheek. 'Christine, are you still there?'

'Yes, I'm still here.'

'Just stay calm. Don't say anything to anyone.'

'No, I won't.'

Mina was arrested first. She told me she was prepared for it.

'Well, maybe *prepared* is the wrong word. *Expecting* is perhaps more like it,' she said. 'Yes, I was expecting it. I just wasn't sure when. I kept waking up in the night, thinking I could hear them downstairs. I got Andy to stay over so he could go down and check for me. I didn't want some awful picture of me in the papers – dragged from my bed, looking guilty.'

When the police did come for her it was not the middle of the night, nor the early hours. It was five o'clock on a Friday afternoon, and she was not prepared. If she had been, I'm sure she wouldn't have chosen to wear a mustard-coloured suit that made her skin look sallow. Blue would have been better – yes, I'm sure she would have chosen something in a light blue that brought out the colour of her eyes.

She came out of the lift straight into the arms of two police officers. The media were waiting – her arrest well timed to make the six o'clock bulletins. There was no one there to protect her and I heard later that Douglas Rockwell was livid and took it as a personal slight that he hadn't been given the heads-up. Even her PR team were in the dark, Mina's friends in the tabloids failing to tip them off. I imagine she must have felt her power slipping away as they read her her rights. Dave was waiting in the car to drive her home, and when he saw her coming out of the building, a police officer on either side, he trailed behind the police car, and sat outside the station for hours in case she came out.

She was questioned, then released on police bail, early on the Saturday morning. There were more pictures in the papers, but at least she was prepared for them this time. She looked tired but someone had brought her a change of clothes – a navy dress with white collar and cuffs. When I saw the picture in the paper I was struck by how childlike she appeared with her hair tied back and her husband's hand holding hers. I looked for a quote from her, anything to tell me how she was feeling, but there was nothing. It was another twenty-four hours before she finally called me.

'So, expected but not really prepared. I won't chat for long, Christine. I just wanted to touch base. I'm going to be at home this week, so clear the diary and take the rest of the week off. Sarah can man the phones.'

'I'll come to Minerva, shall I?'

'Not a good idea. I'll be in touch.'

I couldn't face being at home, and so I set off for work the next morning, as usual. It was the first time I'd disobeyed Mina. As I was walking up the slope at Euston station, on my way to the Underground, I heard the tap, tap, tap of a stick some way ahead of me. It triggered that sixth sense I'd developed for those in need of assistance. I picked up my pace, and, as I worked my way through the throng of commuters, found its source. A blind man, caught in the mob. He was making some progress, but he was in danger of being trampled and so I pushed forward, and slipped my arm through his.

'There. We'll walk together,' I said. He cocked his head, and I felt him stiffen. 'I'm not in a hurry,' I said. 'Don't worry.' I could tell he was proud – unwilling to accept help.

'I'll be fine, from here,' he said, when we reached the station concourse, but I doubted he would and so I reached across and took his white stick away. 'We don't want anyone tripping on that, do we?' I said, and gave his arm a squeeze, as we walked towards the Underground.

'Now, where are you heading?' I asked.

'I do this journey every day,' he said.

'And what journey is that?' His stick was in my left hand, and I wondered whether people might think I was blind, and that he was leading me. I rephrased my question, raising my voice over the announcements on the Tannoy. 'What is your final destination?'

'Goodge Street,' he said, at last. He was a stubborn man.

'Perfect. That's where I'm heading.' Not on my way at all, but I was mindful of his pride and kept my arm tightly linked through his. We must have looked like a two-headed creature, as we stepped on to the escalator.

I managed to deposit him on to his train, though it felt like leading a rather reluctant shire horse. And not even a thank-you, but I was getting used to that. Increasingly, I was finding that not everyone appreciates the kindness of strangers.

When I arrived at work, Sarah was sitting around twiddling her thumbs, so I sent her down to the press department. Their phones were ringing non-stop, ours were not, and as the week went on I felt the silence creep up on me and settle around my desk. A few journalists got through on Mina's direct line, assaulting me with a barrage of questions. I learned more from them, however, than they did from me. I was told my employer was likely to be charged with perjury and perverting the course of justice. They alleged that Mina had lied in her libel suit against the *Business Times* – that what that newspaper had written was very likely true. Nonsense, I thought. I'd read hints of it in other papers, but I can't pretend that hearing it spoken out loud, down the telephone to me when I was alone in the office, was not upsetting. That week was the first time I heard from Mr Ed Brooks. Unlike the others, he didn't offer me money; instead, he said he just wanted to talk. *Off the record.*

'I have nothing to say,' I told him, and, back then, I didn't.

I waited for Mina to call, staying close to my phone like a lovesick teenager – the volume on my mobile set to maximum, just in case.

In the end it was Dave who delivered a note from her. I must have just missed him – the receptionist said he'd dropped it off, then left. When I called him, he was already on his way back to Minerva. I was envious; I would have liked to have been in the car with him, to have been on my way to Minerva too – to feel needed, and busy. I propped the envelope against my desk tidy, delaying the moment of opening it, imagining it might be an invitation to go over at the weekend, or a few words of reassurance from Mina, telling me not to worry, that it was all a silly mistake and that everything would be fine. I stared at my name on the envelope, written by Mina in green biro.

How to describe that handwriting? Small. Neat. With a flourish – the result of her Swiss education, no doubt, where I believe they encourage that French style of adding curls and tails on the letters. Making the words seem grander than they actually are. I peeled back the flap. Inside was a small square of paper, bordered with a William Morris print. I recognized it from the block on her desk in the study. There was no note, as such, only a name and telephone number, with the word *solicitor* underlined. Unsigned, not even initialled. I picked up the phone.

'May I speak to Sandra Tisdale, please? It's Christine Butcher.'

A few days later I was arrested.

27

*Hertfordshire woman arrested at home on suspicion of perverting the
course of justice . . .*

It was in every newspaper, although I read it first in my local
one. I knew it was only a matter of hours before my name came
out, and I phoned Angelica at once.

'Please try not to worry, my love. I'm just so sorry it's happening to you. That it's your mum. But as they say – what
doesn't kill you makes you stronger.' She didn't say anything
for a moment, and when she did, she was very direct.

'Did you do it?'

'Do what, love?'

'Jesus, Mum! Get rid of evidence. Pervert the course of
justice.'

'Of course not. It's a misunderstanding, that's all.' I repeated
to Angelica what I kept telling myself. And at that point I still
believed it. I was finding it increasingly hard to separate fact
from fiction.

When I went off to meet Sandra Tisdale for the first time, no
one would have guessed the smart-looking woman in her navy
suit, stepping confidently out of the Underground station, was

off to meet a criminal litigation solicitor and that soon she would be known as 'the accused'. I barely believed it myself. Ms Tisdale specialized in people like me – white-collar workers who found themselves suspected of doing something criminal.

My difficulty in those days in distinguishing fact from fiction was not helped by the fact that my solicitor's offices looked like a film set for a period drama: a terrace of perfectly restored Georgian houses. It can only have added to my sense of stepping into a world of make-believe. At times it felt like an out-of-body experience – as if I was looking down on events happening to someone else, not me.

Sandra Tisdale was tall and wore a uniform rather like mine, except she had a large diamond on her wedding finger. I wore the brooch Mina had given me on the lapel of my jacket. I thought it might bring me luck, but I wonder whether I was cursed as soon as I allowed her to pin it on my chest.

'How are you?' Sandra Tisdale said, holding her hand out to me. Her smile was warm but brief. She was a busy woman. It showed in her handshake and the way her eyes darted over me, assessing what kind of material she had to work with.

I followed her upstairs, concentrating on her large calves, debating what shade of tights she wore – anything to take my mind off where I was. *Illusion* or *Whisper*? Certainly something on the nude spectrum. Mine were *Plage* – tan rather than nude. My mind darted off in all sorts of directions. I was anywhere but in the moment – a child following a trail of breadcrumbs into a forest, not thinking about what lay ahead.

'Here we are.'

We were in a wood-panelled room capable of holding twenty people. The two of us sat at the end of a long oval table, the wood polished to such a degree that I could see the glint of my brooch reflecting back.

'Coffee?'

The sideboard was set out with a selection of beverages and snacks, and I noticed the thermos jug for the coffee was manufactured by the company Dad had worked for. I picked it up.

'Let me,' Sandra said, reaching for it, but I didn't want to let it go. She probably put my trembling fingers down to nerves, but it was more to do with the sudden need I had for my dad. I wished we could have had one more conversation. Holding that jug made me feel, for a moment, as if he was with me and that, perhaps, he forgave me.

There were notepads and pens set out and I helped myself, writing that day's date in the corner, then taking the file I'd started from my handbag. At that stage all it contained were the papers I'd signed at the police station and a copy of my charge sheet. It was early days, though – plenty of time to fill it up.

'So, describe your job to me, Christine. I know we've been through some of this on the phone, but just so I'm absolutely clear . . .'

'Well, I look after Mina and ensure all secretarial duties are taken care of. That includes her television work too. I am her number-one PA.'

'Number one?'

'Yes. There's a number two who works under me, but everything comes through me. It's easier that way, more straightforward.'

She smiled. Perhaps she picked up the pride in my voice; certainly she wrote something down on her pad. *Loyal? Stupid? Naive? Suggestible?* Any, or all, of the above would have been accurate.

'Good. Now, tell me about your visit to the Appleton's archive. What were the contents of the boxes you signed out? Shorthand notebooks, you said on the phone?'

'Yes.'

'Would you describe the items in those boxes as personal?'

'Yes.'

'Personal to you?'

'Well, yes.'

'You don't sound sure. Did you check through everything in them?'

'There were old notebooks of mine and Angelica's – my daughter. Her drawings were in there too. Ones she did at school when she was little.'

I lied to my own solicitor, though I'm sure she wouldn't have been surprised to hear that. It was expected. As long as I lied well, and didn't tell her I was doing so, there wouldn't be a problem. I understood. Since my arrest, Mina had called me every day – she couldn't have been more attentive. It was like clockwork – she'd call me at six each evening, and we'd go through everything, and I would picture her sitting in the study with a drink in her hand. I'd hear the occasional clink of ice as she swirled the whisky in her glass. I looked forward to those calls, and would pour myself a drink too, as if we were having one together at the end of a working day.

'I see. But the labels on the boxes had Mina Appleton's name on them. Is that correct?'

'Yes, but things got a bit muddled when we moved offices. Most of it was my stuff.'

'Most of it? How can you be sure there wasn't anything belonging to Mina Appleton if you didn't check?'

'Well, I can't be absolutely sure.'

She put down her pen.

'That's a problem, I'm afraid, Christine. You need to be sure. Any sign of doubt will be seized on by the prosecution. So.' She picked up her pen again. 'You didn't check the boxes, but you are clear your daughter's drawings were in there, along with your old shorthand notebooks. Presumably going back a number of years – given the length of time you have worked for Ms

Appleton.' A full stop pressed into the paper. Whenever I was unclear about anything, Sandra never failed to straighten me out. 'You didn't go through the contents of the boxes because there was no need.' She looked up and smiled.

'That's right.' I smiled back.

'Good. It's important you remember that we, *you*, stick to the facts. No speculation. Anything you cannot say with certainty, best not to say at all. So. Why a bonfire?'

'I was clearing out my ex-husband's things. Things he didn't want any more. I thought that would be the best way to dispose of them. It was a way for me to move on.' I'd practised that one in front of the mirror, after one of my calls with Mina.

'Yes. It must have been a painful time for you. Divorce. It's never easy. Why so thoroughly? Why did you decide to destroy everything? Your shorthand notebooks and your husband's things?'

She waited for me to answer, pencil poised.

'It's something that will come up. You need to have an answer.'

'The items from my office were an afterthought. I was clearing out Mike's things, I just added the work things after.'

'And it was your decision to take the boxes home with you from work?'

It was a question, yet I heard it as a statement. All I had to do was nod. A story took shape with minimum effort on my part.

'It must have been a very difficult period for you. Not surprising that you sometimes made mistakes. The mislabelling of the boxes. It's easy to see how you would have, perhaps, not been thinking clearly, that you might have been distracted by the break-up of your marriage.' She gave me a sympathetic smile. It was Mina who suggested I use the break-up of my marriage as a reason for my uncharacteristic inefficiency. It was useful material in constructing our story. Still, I resented

Sandra Tisdale pressing home the point as much as she did. *You were muddled. Distracted. You made mistakes.* It wasn't true – I had never allowed my personal unhappiness to interfere with work – but I sat there and nodded all the same. Biting my tongue was something I'd grown accustomed to over the years. Self-control is vital in my work, and I would advise anyone thinking of entering my profession to bear that in mind. There are many occasions when one is required to hold one's tongue.

'Nearly there now. The diary. Why did you remove entries from Mina Appleton's diary?'

'It was a bit of housekeeping. There was a period when the press were particularly intrusive in Mina's life and so, from time to time, I'd go through the diary and remove entries I worried might be misinterpreted by outsiders.'

'Outsiders? You mean journalists?'

'Yes, but not only journalists. The trips I removed were of a personal nature and I worried that perhaps some people in the company might judge Mina, if they saw her out of the office on personal business, so I changed the entries to a series of meetings.'

'And did she know that you had done this? Removed entries?'

'No. There was no need to bother her with it. It was just housekeeping, as I say.'

'I see. I wasn't entirely clear, when we spoke on the phone, what the nature of Ms Appleton's "personal business" was? You were rather vague.'

'Was I? Sorry, I didn't mean to be. I believe she was visiting her mother.'

'You believe?'

'Yes. Her mother lives in Geneva.'

'But you're not sure that's where she was?'

'Yes, I am sure.'

'You don't sound it.'

'Yes, I am. That is what the diary said. Ms Appleton's flights were booked by my number two, Sarah. She entered Geneva into the diary but I decided to change the entries so they appeared more professional. Meetings, rather than vague trips to Geneva.'

'I see. I'll say again, Christine: if you are not certain about something then it is best not to say it in court. The jury need to be convinced by your testimony – if you're vague then it might seem as if you are being evasive. You do understand that, don't you?'

'Yes, I do.'

I looked away, fascinated for a moment by how clean the windows were. There was no way a building in central London could have windows gleaming like that, without them being cleaned at least twice a week.

'Christine?'

I pulled myself back into the room.

'I was asking whether you'd ever been in a courtroom.'

'No, I haven't.'

'Right. It will be the magistrates' court first. I think it's unlikely we'll enter a plea there.'

'Surely it will be "not guilty"?'

'Most likely, but we won't enter a plea until we see the full case against you.' She stood up. 'I'll meet you at the magistrates' court fifteen minutes before we're due. Mina Appleton and David Santini will be there too, and you will all appear together.'

I was pleased about that. The thought of us standing together, shoulder to shoulder. She sat down again.

'You must understand that your defence is entirely separate from theirs. The three of you have independent defence teams. I am here to represent you, not Mina Appleton.' I smiled; I knew that to be not entirely true. Mina was paying for my defence. It was Douglas Rockwell who'd recommended Sandra Tisdale.

She pressed on: 'Ms Appleton is facing the further charge of perjury. You are not. And it is important for your case that your defence is independent of hers, although, obviously, her defence is important to yours. It is likely that if she is found guilty of the perversion charge, you will be too, as will Mr Santini. You stand or fall together on that count. But it is important you understand that I am representing you alone.'

Yes, we would stand or fall together. I understood that well enough.

'I know you are close – you and Ms Appleton. That you are loyal. And I know she has been a good employer to you – generous and supportive. But I cannot stress enough how important it is for you to understand that she must not be seen to have influence over you in the course of the trial. This is why you have a separate solicitor, me, and why you will have your own barrister.'

I gave her a reassuring smile and she shook my hand and then chat, chat, chat all the way back down the stairs, telling me about her plans for the weekend. Thoughtless, really. I had no plans and, on top of that, there were the eight weeks ahead I had to fill before I appeared in front of the magistrate. It made my skin itch to think of it – I was scratching before I left the building – the eczema I'd suffered as a child choosing that moment to make its re-entry into my life.

I managed to fill those eight weeks. My section of the cul-de-sac had never looked so clean or pretty as it did in that period, the small scraps of earth beneath the trees bursting with flowers I planted.

Sadly, they didn't survive. When the trial was over I went out one night and pulled the lot up, flinging them out into the road. Not one of my neighbours tried to stop me, or even came out to see if I was all right. I imagine them peering through their curtains, watching me crawl around in the dark. Perhaps they were too nervous to approach me, and I suppose I can't really blame them. I wasn't myself.

It wasn't long after that I was pulling up outside the gates of The Laurels. I remember trying to see through to the house and, back then, it seemed such a dark, forbidding place. Not any more. Now I feel right at home.

28

Magistrates' courts have a particular smell – tobacco and alcohol – rather like a pub before the smoking ban. There is, however, no exemption for the accused. No special dispensation that allows us a drink or a cigarette to alleviate stress. Yet the smell of it is there – coming from the bodies sitting on plastic seats or lounging against the walls. Oozing from darkened livers, seeping out through pores, sticking to yellowed fingers and furred tongues. It mingles with the scent of cheap washing powder that clings to hooded tops and tracksuit bottoms. Fetid bodies, clean clothes. I felt, and no doubt looked, out of place. Much thought had been given to my appearance – Mina offering me advice. Photographs from the time show Sandra Tisdale and me walking into the court building together, and you'd be hard-pressed to know which of us was the solicitor and which the accused, if there wasn't a caption to tell you.

'Won't be long,' Sandra Tisdale said, and marched off with her files clasped to her bosom. She behaved as if she were at a cocktail party, chatting and smiling to officials, but I suppose she was doing her job, oiling the wheels. I remember feeling utterly abandoned as I watched her walk away, and relieved when Dave walked in. I would have waved and beckoned him over, but then I saw his wife, Sam, and I realized they were holding hands, and pretended not to have seen them. A short while later, Mina and Andy walked in, and were whisked off into a private room, a privilege I didn't begrudge them.

Mina Appleton. Christine Butcher. David Santini. We were to be top of the bill – our names called first. Dave and I flanked Mina, the three of us in the dock behind glass. When I spoke to confirm my name and address, my mouth was dry, each word accompanied by a clicking sound – my fear audible to everyone. The charges were read out, one apiece for me, the secretary, and Dave, the driver. Two for our employer. When the magistrate pronounced our bail conditions, I was stunned. There was to be no communication, directly or indirectly, between us. I had been cut off from Mina, from my work, and I left the court feeling even more alone than when I had arrived.

A week later, Stella Parker telephoned me. Mina's nutritionist, healer, masseuse – her *lifeline*, during the first trial. Now, she was to be mine. Stella was Mina's way of keeping me close, and the resentment I'd felt when I'd first met her melted away. Stella became our go-between.

It had been a long time since I'd taken off my clothes in front of anyone, and the first few appointments were excruciating. But it didn't take long for me to learn to appreciate the feel of her hands on my skin, and I came to look forward to her visits, to depend on them, even. I would lay myself out on the padded table she brought with her, close my eyes and surrender to her touch.

She'd begin at my feet, pressing her thumbs into the fleshy parts, then working her way slowly up my body, lingering in places she sensed needed attention. When she reached my head, her fingers would stroke and knead my scalp until it seemed they slipped right through my skull. I'd imagine her hands resting on my brain, washing it clean of negative thoughts. I became empty-headed, surrendering to it all, and allowing myself to be taken over.

As the trial drew closer, I became increasingly anxious and found it hard to sleep.

'We can't have that, Christine,' Stella said, in her oh-so-gentle voice. 'Let me see what I can do.' I lay there with my eyes closed, in an almost trance-like state, accepting whatever she offered me. 'Diazepam for your anxiety. Temazepam to help you sleep,' she said, on her next visit, placing the bottles of pills on my bedside table. *Stella Parker was trained in conventional medicine,* I remembered reading on her website. What was good enough for Mina was certainly good enough for me.

29

The night before the trial I fell asleep around ten, still smelling of the oils Stella Parker had massaged into my skin. She'd settled me like a baby, soothing my fretting, rattling the bottles of pills lined up next to my bed.

'Take one of these if you wake in the night, then two of these in the morning.' I watched her write on the labels. 'Mina sends love, by the way. Stay strong, Christine,' she said, before going downstairs and letting herself out. I was touched by her care.

When I walked into the Old Bailey on that first morning, the fear I'd anticipated was not there. I was calm, unnervingly so when I look back. Dosed up like an animal before it's taken to slaughter. I was soothed too by knowing I was returning to a routine of sorts. Perverse perhaps, but having lived the past weeks in a kind of purgatory, now I found I had a reason to get out of bed in the morning.

Within days I was on first-name terms with the security men and women, greeting them rather like I had those at Appleton's. I found it odd at first, when they asked me to remove my coat and place it on a tray with my handbag, as if I was going on a foreign holiday, but that too I got used to. The ritual of the proceedings was a welcome distraction – the ancient dress code, the wigs, so strange, absurd even, at first – it all seemed perfectly normal by the end of the first morning. There was a pleasing clarity to the hierarchy too. In that courtroom, I knew my place and was in no doubt who was in charge.

We were all under the command of Mr Justice Beresford, who led the proceedings with a clear and calm authority. I grew fond of him over the weeks. A slight lisp gave him a touching vulnerability and he was always courteous, humorous at times too, but never inappropriately so.

I was a child in a school play waiting my turn to deliver my lines, but until then all I needed to do was find my mark each day and stay on it. I sat to Mina's right, Dave to her left – the three of us recreating the formation of the magistrates' court. Side by side, jugs of water in front of us, our bags at our feet, Mina with her laptop open, Dave with a packet of Polo mints as his constant, me a notebook and pen. Not that I wrote anything down – unlike Mina, who tapped away on her keyboard at a rate of at least sixty words a minute. She typed out every word, as the prosecutor, James Maitland, set out the case against her.

'We are not here to try Ms Appleton over her business practices, however unscrupulous they are. No, what the prosecution will show is that Mina Appleton lied under oath in a court of law. She sued the *Business Times*, a respected national newspaper, over a story she claimed was a pack of lies. We will show that, in fact, that story was true and Ms Appleton perjured herself in that courtroom. She put her hand on the Bible and swore to tell the truth. Instead she lied, and then tried to cover up her lies, enlisting the help of her two most trusted employees. Her secretary and her driver.'

He paused. Turned and looked at us. And we looked right back at him – pictures of innocence.

'Appleton's supermarkets boast of fairness to suppliers; *a fair deal for all*, says its advertising. Not true, said the *Business Times*. Appleton's, once Mina Appleton was at the helm, broke contracts with long-standing suppliers, cancelled orders at no notice, drove farms that had been in families for generations to the brink of collapse. And when those farms struggled, it was Mina Appleton who offered herself up as their saviour.'

James Maitland was a man of modest height, with insipid-coloured eyes that seemed to bulge in his head as he built up steam.

'Far from being their saviour, Mina Appleton took advantage of those farmers. She offered to lend them money – but only if they used their land as collateral. And when they struggled under the weight of debt forced on them, what did she do? She triggered the purchase of their land.'

He paced back and forth, his gown catching now and then on the back of his trousers.

'She gobbled it up, then sold it on. And who did she sell it to? Shadowy enterprises exposed through the tireless investigation of the *Business Times* as shell companies. Those shell companies then sold the land again. This time for substantial profit. Profit Mina Appleton then deposited into Swiss bank accounts . . .'

He went on and on and on, and I fear the jury found him as tedious as I did.

'Ladies and gentlemen of the jury – I am sure you have all seen Mina Appleton on your television screens. Perhaps you've bought her cookbooks? You might think you know her. But do not be taken in. The *Business Times* exposed Mina Appleton as greedy and dishonest. A hypocrite. That is why she sued them. Greedy and dishonest. That is the true face of Mina Appleton.'

I wonder if the jury had rubbed their hands at the prospect of a celebrity trial – their appetites whetted by the thought of juicy titbits. Rather like me when I crack open a crime novel, anticipating bodies, hopefully more than one. So, faced with the minutiae of a white-collar crime, it's no wonder the jury became jaded in the weeks that followed.

There was in fact a body in that trial, but the jury stepped over it – barely noticing it lying there, buried as it was, so expertly by the defence, under a labyrinthine paper trail.

30

Clifford Fraser was the first farmer called as a witness for the prosecution, a face I recognized. He touched me in a way the other witnesses did not. The way he hid his hands beneath the stand, so no one would notice them shaking.

I learned that the Frasers were the only Appleton's supplier who refused to take a loan from Mina, though it didn't save their farm. Their land has now been turned into flats.

'Mr Fraser, how long did your family supply Appleton's supermarkets?'

'Twenty-five years.' He could hide his hands, but not the tremor in his voice. 'We had rolling contracts with Appleton's. Signed every year.'

'And what was Fraser's Farm contracted to supply to Appleton's supermarkets?'

'Fruit. Pears, apples and plums.'

Mina's fingers flew over her keyboard, her perfect nails clicking softly against the plastic, as she took down his testimony.

'I'd like to refer the jury to document twelve in their bundles. If you would turn to page ten. The contract is signed, as you can see, by Mina Appleton and Clifford Fraser's father, John. It is dated 23 November 2004, the year before Lord Appleton died. The copy in your bundle is Mr John Fraser's copy. The copy of the contract held by Appleton's mysteriously disappeared.'

'Mr Maitland,' said Justice Beresford. 'Can we expect a question?'

'Your Honour. Mr Fraser, what was your understanding of the commitment between yourselves and Appleton's?'

'Before he retired, Lord Appleton came to see us on the farm to give us his word that Appleton's would continue to use our produce. He told us he'd agreed it with his daughter and that she'd given him her promise. And that's what happened for a while – the contracts continued, but they weren't worth the paper they were written on after Lord Appleton retired.'

'Can you explain what you mean by that, Mr Fraser? How things changed when Mina Appleton took over the business from her father?'

'It started off with orders being cut at the last minute – they'd ask for a quantity of fruit and then, with no notice, they'd halve it so we were left with produce we couldn't sell. That went on for months.'

'And what did that mean for your business?'

'We were operating at a loss, so we began to run up debts.'

'And was Appleton's aware of that?'

'Yes. They offered to help us out but they wanted the land as collateral and we, Dad particularly, didn't want to do that.'

'You refused Appleton's offer of a loan?'

'Yes. It was a family decision. We agreed, instead, that we'd take a loan from the bank to keep the farm going. We had our contract with Appleton's, you see, and we still hoped everything would be all right.'

'And can you explain, Mr Fraser, why the copy of your last contract with Appleton's was not produced as evidence in the previous court case? When Ms Appleton sued a newspaper for libel?'

'We only found it after Dad died. It was in his room – locked up in a metal cash box. His room was a real tip and he wouldn't let any of us in to tidy it. We thought it was lost but then, after he died, we went through his things and found it. It was too late by then. She'd already won the court case against the newspaper.'

'And that contract, signed between Appleton's and yourselves. What year was that?'

'Two thousand and four.'

'And did Appleton's honour that contract with you?'

'No. She cancelled it. Two months in. She sent a fax late one night, cancelling the next day's order. They said they'd no longer be using our produce. It was sent at ten o'clock at night. My wife was still up and she ran upstairs to show me. We couldn't believe it. We had an exclusive deal with Appleton's. We had nowhere else to go, so we knew it was the end for our farm.'

'You say, she sent it?'

'Mina Appleton.'

'And what happened to the fruit you were due to supply?'

'We had to dump it. Tonnes of it. It broke our hearts.'

'How many tonnes?'

'Fifty. Enough to fill the shelves of every Appleton's supermarket in the country.'

'Were there no pears, apples or plums in Appleton's stores in that period?'

'Oh, there were plenty. They'd already set up another producer to take our place.'

'And it broke your hearts, you say. Yours and your father's?'

'Yes. All of us. My wife, my boys. It was a family business. I tried to talk to her about it. I thought maybe there'd been a mistake.'

'You tried to speak to Mina Appleton?'

'Yes. Her secretary said I should make an appointment and come and see her.'

'Her secretary?'

'Yes.' He looked over at me and I felt Mina stiffen beside me. She stopped typing, her fingers hovering over the keyboard.

'And what happened then, Mr Fraser?'

'I made an appointment to meet her – I thought if I saw her, face to face, we could work something out – but they cancelled the meeting. I knew it was because we wouldn't take the loan from them.

'Then Dad tried to see her. He went up to London, early one morning, without telling us. He took a box of our pears with him. He'd picked them that morning. He wanted to show her the quality of our produce. He was proud of what we did. He thought if she saw him, saw the pears, she'd understand.'

'And did Mina Appleton understand when she saw your father?'

'She didn't see him. He sat and waited for hours. Then they sent him away. He left the fruit and wrote her a note but we never heard from her. When he got back home he told us where he'd been. He still hoped, even then, that it was all a misunderstanding. That she'd put it right. And when she didn't, it broke him. I'd never seen Dad cry, but he sat in the kitchen and wept when we knew it was over for us. Farming is hard – we'd been through difficult times before – but I'd never seen Dad cry before. Never seen him defeated like that.'

I imagined Clifford Fraser's father sitting at their kitchen table, exhausted, his head in his hands, tears seeping through his fingers, and I tried to tell myself a different story. One where I was kind. One where I stopped to talk to Mr John Fraser when I'd seen him waiting outside the building early that morning in the rain. One where I led him inside and sat him down. I might have fetched him a warm drink. Taken his wet coat. I would have taken the box of fruit from him and admired it – made him a promise that Mina would see it, taste it, and that I would do my best to persuade her to reconsider her decision. I would have ordered him a car home and made sure his expenses for the trip were reimbursed. It was too late now. I hadn't been kind. I had treated that old man with scorn and disdain.

'Mr Fraser. Please tell us what happened when, overnight, Appleton's cancelled their contract with you?'

'We had to sell the farm. We had no choice.'

'So quickly?'

'We'd run up debts from when they'd cut our orders and then when they cancelled the contract altogether, we couldn't go on. We had to sell the land to pay off the money we owed the bank.'

'And who bought your land, Mr Fraser?'

'A company called Lancing.'

'Lancing is an offshore company. A shell company,' the prosecutor explained to the jury. 'And how long had your family been in farming, Mr Fraser?'

'Seventy years.'

'Seventy years. And, Mr Fraser, why did you only agree to speak to a newspaper if they withheld your name?'

'I was frightened. If the other supermarkets found out, then we'd have been blacklisted. No one else would take our fruit. That's how it works. We'd be labelled troublemakers. As it turned out, we lost everything anyway. After she won in court, well, I had nothing left to lose.'

'Mr Fraser, it was soon after the court case that your father died, wasn't it?'

'Yes.'

'I know this is painful for you, Mr Fraser, but can you tell the court how he died?'

'He shot himself.'

I began to shiver. Mina must have felt the cold too, because she reached down and took her pashmina from her bag, unfolding it with care, making sure the delicate fabric didn't catch on her rings as she wrapped it around her shoulders. The image sketched of her by the courtroom artist made her look like a nineteenth-century governess. Plain, dull colours, skin clear of make-up, her abundant hair pulled back from her face, one curl straying.

'He went into Swainston Forest one morning, before any of us were up. He took one of the guns we kept on the farm and killed himself.'

Bile seeped into my mouth. I remembered how I'd opened a letter to Mina from John Fraser. Handwritten, it had been mistakenly put in with her fan mail. I always answered her fan mail. This letter, though, I read as a begging letter. It was during the libel trial and I made an executive decision. I tore it up. Mina never saw it. It must have been written a few days before John Fraser shot himself.

'Dad loved Swainston Forest. He used to take me there as a boy. Two women out walking their dogs found his body.'

'And when was this exactly, Mr Fraser?'

'I'll never forget it. It was the day after Mina Appleton won the case against the newspaper.'

I was with Mina that day. We were at Minerva and I remember a call coming in from her communications director. *Kill the story, Paul*, she'd said. She was heady with her victory in court – we all were. John Fraser's death was never covered in a national newspaper. Her press department saw to that.

'Thank you, Mr Fraser. No further questions.'

I wondered whether John Fraser's suicide had crossed Mina's mind when we all sat and drank champagne at her celebratory lunch. My fingers were numb with cold and I clasped my hands on my lap. And then, beneath the desk, hidden from the eyes of others, Mina rested her hand on mine. I remember how warm it was, how she squeezed my fingers to stop them trembling.

31

Clifford Fraser was in the stand again after lunch, this time questioned by Douglas Rockwell. I hardly recognized Mina's barrister in court – the softly spoken man who'd been such a calming presence in her office, the one who always declined the offer of a drink with a smile and shake of his head. *Just water for me please, Christine.*

'Mr Fraser, how old was your father when he died?'

'Seventy-five.'

'Seventy-five. It doesn't matter how old they are, does it, or how old you are. It is a terrible thing, the loss of a father.'

I looked up to the public gallery, almost expecting to see my own father staring down at me. I know what I would have read in his eyes. *Shame on you, Christine.*

'And for you, for your father to have taken his own life, it is difficult to imagine what pain that must have caused.'

Clifford Fraser nodded, accepting the sympathy.

'From what you have said it sounds as if he, your father, Mr John Fraser, was living in a state of chaos – "a real tip" is how you put it. Is that right?'

'Well, I'm not sure—'

'He was hoarding things, refusing to let you or your wife into his room to help him. Didn't he trust you?' He gave Clifford Fraser no time to reply. 'A room crammed full of papers, boxes. The chaotic way in which he was living reflected his state of mind, perhaps?'

'No. No, it didn't. He was old, that's all.'

'John Fraser, your father, was a man who worked on the land his whole life. He must have seen many changes in that time, a new way of working, new technology. It was a new world, wasn't it? It must have been very difficult for someone of his generation to cope with. Your father had a history, in his later years, didn't he, of mental health problems, anxiety. He was on antidepressants, had been for some time before he took his life.' He looked down at his notes. 'All that came out at the inquest, didn't it?'

'Dad was depressed because of them lying to us. She lied to us. And once Lord Appleton was no longer there—'

'Mr Fraser. The fax you spoke of. The one you received from Appleton's which you say was sent by Mina Appleton, and in which *she* cancelled the contract with you. Do you have a copy of it?' He smiled, as if his question was benign, and I watched Clifford Fraser squirm in confusion. There was a sprinkle of dandruff on the shoulders of his jacket and I wanted to rush over and brush it away, comb his hair, straighten his tie.

'No.'

'No?' Feigned surprise. 'And yet you say it was from *her* – from Mina Appleton.'

'Yes.'

'She signed it, then.'

'I think so . . .'

'You think so? Fortunately, we do have a copy of that fax. I refer the jury to bundle twenty-six in their folders.' Papers rustled. Douglas Rockwell passed a copy to Clifford Fraser.

'Mr Fraser, can you read the signature at the bottom of the fax for me?'

His response was inaudible.

'Mr Fraser, please speak up so the court can hear you.'

'Dominic Taylor.'

'Dominic Taylor. Do you know who Dominic Taylor is, Mr Fraser?'

'Yes . . .'

'For the jury's benefit – Dominic Taylor is a junior buyer for Appleton's. It is unlikely, given how junior he is, that Mina Appleton would even have seen that fax, although you claim it was from her.'

'It would have come from her, she would have known about it. Nobody did anything without her say-so.'

The backs of my knees sweated inside their nylon skin.

'And that contract, Mr Fraser, that you produced as evidence.' He held it up. 'Two scrappy pieces of A4 paper, folded so many times the signatures are barely legible. This is not a contract. This is a wish list, Mr Fraser. My eight-year-old son could have knocked it up on his computer. Ms Appleton's signature would be easy to forge – you need only get your hands on a signed copy of one of her cookbooks. It is rather convenient too, is it not, that this copy turned up after your father had died, when he was no longer able to confirm it as genuine. We have only your word for that, Mr Fraser.'

There was an unpleasant sing-song in Douglas Rockwell's voice. The cocky confidence of the playground bully.

'The truth, Mr Fraser, is that there is no evidence to suggest Mina Appleton had anything to do with that fax, or that she ever signed a contract with you. There is no copy, other than the illegible scrap you produced as evidence.'

'She knew, all right – it was her decision. You're just twisting it . . .'

I dug a fingernail into the fleshy pad of my thumb, as words failed Clifford Fraser. I couldn't watch, and looked down at the perfect half-moon I'd carved into my skin.

'Mr Fraser, you have never actually met Mina Appleton in a professional capacity, have you? The only time you came into contact with her was at her father's memorial service, isn't that right?'

He nodded.

'Please answer the question, Mr Fraser.' Judge Beresford showed a rare flicker of impatience.

'Yes. Lord Appleton used to visit his suppliers. She never bothered.'

'So you met her at her father's memorial. You hadn't been invited though, had you? It was your father, John, who was on the guest list. Yet you turned up anyway, uninvited and drunk, to the memorial of a man, you would have us believe, you respected. You were so drunk, in fact, that you had to be escorted from the building after you became abusive and violent. Isn't that right?'

'No.'

'You didn't have to be escorted out?'

'I was upset.'

'You were upset. It was Mina Appleton's father's memorial and yet you were so upset that you became aggressive and had to be restrained by Mr Andrew Webster, Ms Appleton's husband. There are witness statements from members of the museum staff present during the evening. All of whom were willing to come to court to testify, should prosecution counsel have asked them to appear. They have not. I'd like to read an extract from one of those statements.' He turned to face the jury. 'This is from Mr Angus Cathcart, keeper of pictures at the Wallace Collection, and I think it gives a flavour of Mr Fraser's behaviour that evening.

'"... Ms Appleton's husband, Andy Webster, had to protect his wife when he [Clifford Fraser] tried to grab and push her. He was very drunk and we asked him to leave, but he refused. Ms Appleton's PA called him a taxi and we had to help her get him out of the building."

'Thankfully, you made it home safely that night, didn't you, Mr Fraser. All the way to Kent in a taxi paid for by Ms Appleton. In fact the last thing Ms Appleton did before she left her father's memorial was to ask that her secretary ensure you made it safely home. Isn't that right, Mr Fraser?'

He was so persuasive, Mr Rockwell, that – had I not been at the memorial myself – I might have believed the picture he drew.

'No. That's not how it was.'

'Perhaps your memory is hazy. Have you had a drink this morning, Mr Fraser?'

Who knows whether Clifford Fraser had had a drink that morning? His face reddened at the question, and that was all it took for the jury to consider it a possibility. I wouldn't have blamed him if he had – I had taken two pills with my lunch-time sandwich to ease my own anxiety and the medication allowed a pleasant mist to re-enter my head, as if everything I heard and saw came from a distant place.

'What we can agree on, Mr Fraser, is that you were angry with Mina Appleton. You felt you had a score to settle. You'd run your business into the ground and had to sell up, so you were looking around for someone to blame. When a newspaper approached you, you were more than happy to say whatever they wanted to hear. Isn't that right, Mr Fraser?'

'No.'

'Mina Appleton did not break any contract with you, because no contract with you existed.' I had seen what looked like con-tracts in the box I'd taken from the archive. Yet Douglas

Rockwell was such a convincing storyteller, I allowed myself to believe him.

'Since taking over her family business, Mina Appleton has succeeded in making Appleton's one of the leading supermarkets in this country, something her late father would be proud of. It would be entirely understandable, Mr Fraser, if your father – a man who had run a successful farm for many years – had concerns about his own family business, but I suggest they had more to do with your running of that business than they did with Mina Appleton. No further questions, Your Honour.'

Mina's fingers floated over her keyboard, as elegant as a pianist's. I don't know why she took it all down. There was no need. The court reporter was there for that. Yet, she snatched up the words like a greedy frog catching flies on its tongue – feeding them into her laptop and savouring the flavour of Clifford Fraser's destruction.

32

Even the most innocent of actions can appear suspicious on footage extracted from CCTV cameras. Shady images in black and white with grainy outlines. Skulking, lurking figures who look all the more guilty because they are secretly observed, moments frozen on the screen and then replayed over and over. The prosecuting barrister, Mr James Maitland, made sure the jury missed nothing.

The black Audi – *Mina Appleton's business car, driven by Mr Santini* – pulls into the petrol station. David Santini gets out of the car and takes a pair of disposable gloves from the dispenser and fills the tank, his head turned away from the camera. He returns the nozzle to its holder, removes the gloves, drops them into a bin, gets back into the car.

'Mr Santini, we see you then re-park the car and walk the length of the forecourt to go inside the shop. The interior cameras show you buying sweets, I think. Then you queue up and pay. And here you are leaving the shop. You return your wallet to your back pocket, walk over to a pump and take a second pair of disposable gloves. You then return to the car, crossing the forecourt once more. Yet you don't get into the car. Instead you walk around to the back and open the boot. And here we see you putting on that second pair of latex gloves.'

I watched the images too, seeing what I hadn't seen when I had been sitting in the car at the time. I tried to remember what I'd been thinking, what I'd been doing as I looked at the dark smudge that was me on the footage. I remembered that, while Dave was paying for the petrol, I had been texting Angelica, and I watched myself on the monitor, saw how my shape changed when I leaned down to find the thermos of coffee I'd prepared for our trip to Fincham.

'We have the advantage of three cameras at this point and we can see quite clearly why you chose that particular space to park, Mr Santini. It was a puzzle at first, but now it becomes clear. You moved the car so it was up against the refuse bins. Three of them. Here you are, opening the boot of Ms Appleton's car. You chose to wear gloves to protect your hands. We can see too that you were accompanied on this trip by Mrs Butcher, Mina Appleton's PA. There she is in the passenger seat.'

The mention of my name made my hands sweat and I clasped them in front of me. I remember how on edge Dave had seemed that evening. I'd thought it was embarrassment in accepting Mina's gift of her father's car.

The footage played on. I watched Dave take a box from the boot and tip its contents into one of the bins. Three times the images played – three times frozen on screen. It looked as if he'd been caught red-handed and I felt a familiar burn inside my elbow.

'You have already told the court, Mr Santini, that your employer, Mina Appleton, asked you to make that trip to her late father's home. That she instructed you to go. You claim that Mrs Butcher just "came along for the ride". The purpose of that trip, however, was not to check over the house, as you claim, was it? It was to dispose of documents for Ms Appleton. She asked you to get rid of papers that would incriminate her if they were found. She knew by then there might be a police investigation into her business affairs after new information came to light following that first trial.'

Mina's eyes locked on Dave. I couldn't bear to watch him lie, so I looked away.

'I don't know anything about any documents. That box was full of rubbish from the car. You know, old newspapers, food wrappers that were left under the seats. I always kept a box in the boot for rubbish – stuff I cleared out so the car was always clean for Ms Appleton. I emptied it whenever I stopped to refuel.'

'If you expect us to believe that, Mr Santini, then you expect us to believe Ms Appleton's car was awash with rubbish. What a lot of food and newspapers Ms Appleton must consume on her journeys to have filled that box. It was full to the brim with papers.' He replayed the shot again, froze it, then zoomed in, and it seemed clear to me the papers were A4 typed sheets.

'It is difficult, I grant you, to read any detail on the papers on screen, but what we can see is that they are not newspapers, nor do I see anything that resembles sweet wrappers or indeed any kind of food packaging. What we see are official-looking documents.'

'Objection, Your Honour. The quality of the CCTV, zoomed in, is too poor to offer any clarity. It is impossible to read a single word on the screen. Mr Maitland is leading the jury.'

'Sustained.'

'Your Honour. Mr Santini – I see no food wrappers or newspapers in that box.'

'They were at the bottom – like I said. It was all rubbish I found shoved under the seats. A lot of it was Christine's – she often left stuff she didn't need in the car. So I used to clear it up for her.'

He didn't flinch in this lie and I did my best to hide my surprise. I told myself, he had no choice. We were in this together. We would stand or fall together. Mr Maitland played the tape on, and I listened out for the sound of the boot closing, willing it to happen, but it didn't. Not until Dave had taken something else from the boot. The image froze, zoomed in again, and this time there was no doubt what it was. A laptop. Unmistakably, a laptop. Dave dropped that too into the bin, pushing it down with his gloved hands.

'You're making some effort there, Mr Santini. To ensure you conceal the laptop and the "rubbish" you disposed of. You are burying them as deep as you can under the rubbish already in the bin. No wonder you chose to wear gloves for the job. You need to hide the laptop in case someone comes along and sees it and decides to remove it. And that would not do, would it, Mr Santini? That laptop belonged to Ms Appleton, didn't it? She asked you to get rid of it because it too contained information that could incriminate her.'

I'd replaced a number of laptops for Mina over the years, and I'd always believed her when she told me she'd lost them.

'The laptop, Mr Santini. Do you expect the jury to believe that you periodically cleared laptops from the boot of Ms Appleton's car as well?'

'It was my laptop.'

'Your laptop? Really, Mr Santini. The car you were driving was Ms Appleton's company car, you were, by your own admission, instructed by her to make the journey to her late father's home. You were working. She'd given you instructions, and one of those instructions was to get rid of papers and her laptop, wasn't it, Mr Santini?'

'No. It was my laptop.'

'She rewarded you, didn't she – for getting rid of those papers and her laptop? She gave you a very valuable car that had belonged to her father. A Jaguar. Do you deny that too, Mr Santini?'

'No. She did give me the car. That was one of the reasons I drove up that weekend. To collect it. She's generous like that, is Mina. She's generous with all her employees.'

'Is that so? Not all, I'd say. Certainly generous to you and Mrs Butcher. She gave you the car in payment, didn't she? For disposing of papers and her laptop. I remind you, you are under oath and stand accused of perverting the course of justice.'

'It was my laptop. I got rid of it because I didn't want my wife finding it. She'd caught me before.' He glanced up at the public gallery where his wife sat.

'Sam, my wife, she told me if she found porn on my laptop again she'd leave me. And there was porn on it. I wanted it out of the house – I wanted to get rid of it in case she found it. I promised myself I'd stop after that.'

I felt Mina shift in her seat and saw her look up at Dave's wife, and her sympathy seemed genuine to me, and I wondered whether, perhaps, he was telling the truth. That perhaps we were not in this together, after all. That he was innocent and I, alone, was guilty. It was the first, though not the last, time I felt like I'd slipped between the cracks and was falling into a world where nothing was as I had believed it to be, leaving me flailing around, trying to catch hold of something solid, but as soon as I reached for it, it melted away.

33

At the end of the day, when court was over, I used to slip out and walk around the corner to change my shoes, crouching in a doorway to take off my high heels and put on my trainers, unnoticed by anyone. A few moments later I'd hear the sound of journalists shouting, the clicking of cameras, and I'd know Mina had come out and was giving the press a moment – standing with her husband and children for photos before getting into their cars and driving away.

They'd take minicabs to and from court, as if they were an ordinary family. Mina did her best to look ordinary too – simple dresses with Peter Pan collars – a tip, I imagine, from her stylist. I'd witnessed a few of these 'consultations' in the past – Mina trying on outfits before settling on the 'right look'. They went for the puritan-style at the Old Bailey. Not everyone was fooled, though. I read one comment later in a broadsheet that made me smile: *Mina Appleton, celebrity royalty, had no chauffeured car waiting for her outside court but a Ford estate from her local minicab firm and her clothes too were simple, almost Quaker-like – but then one of her greatest skills has always been her acute eye for detail, ever mindful of her image.*

I got into the habit of walking every day from the Old Bailey to Euston station to catch my train home – it helped clear my head and remove some of the garbage I heard spoken in court. I saw the case against Mina as a conspiracy whipped up by rival supermarkets to damage her reputation. It was a line I'd heard so often repeated by the PR team that I believed it was true. All those times I'd hung around, making myself invisible while I poured drinks, served food, sucking up their words like a thirsty sponge.

Stella kept me on a strict regimen throughout the trial – certain foods encouraged, alcohol limited, absolutely no newspapers or television and radio news. Drama yes, comedy absolutely, but news or current affairs? *Verboten*.

'Not until it's over, Christine. Protect yourself. Mina is. She'd love to know you're following the same advice.'

I suggested that the comfort I drew from the routine of being in court each day was perverse and I think that is right. The need for order in my life became almost manic – I suppose some might call it an obsessive compulsion. On my way from the station to home at the end of a day in court, I'd stop and blow my nose beside a sycamore tree on the edge of the green, four hundred yards up from the station. I would blow my nose then inspect the tissue, darkly smeared from the polluted London air. I'd then walk on, holding the tissue in my hand before dropping it into the third bin I passed between the sycamore and home. I was frightened that if I broke this routine something terrible might happen, as if I wasn't already trapped in a nightmare.

Once home I took off my court clothes, hanging them up for the following day, then put on my dressing gown. I made myself supper from the list of foods prescribed by Stella, and ate it in front of the television, flipping through the channels to avoid news or current affairs, settling on something soft and unchallenging.

Stella was a great support to me and, as the trial progressed, her visits became more frequent. She would pick up my prescriptions for me, leaving the pills by my bed when she left.

'Sleep well,' she'd say.

'Like the dead,' I told Sandra Tisdale, when she asked me how I'd slept the morning I was to take the stand for the first time. We met early for a short conference in the Old Bailey canteen – a breakfast of pastries and coffee.

'Sorry I'm late,' said my barrister, Henry Anderson, sweeping his gown beneath him and placing his wig down on the table. I worried he might get crumbs on it from my Danish pastry, and pushed the plate away.

'Now, Christine, how are you?' he said, studying me.

'Fine,' I said, and I think he thought I was.

'Good. The prosecution will try to plant the idea that by removing the boxes from the archive you were covering up for Ms Appleton. Mr Maitland will try and rattle you – confuse you – so try and stay calm, but it's important, too, that you don't appear too distant. Let the jury see who you are – a working woman, a mother. Someone of good character who would never dream of breaking the law.' He gave my hand the briefest of pats then picked up his wig. 'I'll see you in there.'

I sometimes wonder now what Mr Anderson would have thought if he'd run into me when the trial was over. Would his conscience have pricked him? Might he have told himself he would have handled things differently, if he'd known my state of mind? Or perhaps not taken me on at all. I was unreadable though, cloaked as I was in prescription drugs. Or perhaps he did realize that, and it suited him. I was being managed well by someone – that's what mattered. My medication had been adjusted, so I was perfectly able to perform in the stand. Calm, yet present and alert.

As we walked to the courtroom, Sandra Tisdale kept up her usual small talk – the weather, holidays – but it was the sound of her heels clicking on the marble floor I focused on. Click-clack, click-clack. When I slipped into my seat, Mina whispered good morning and Dave, as he passed behind me, brushed his hand against my back. It was a small thing, yet it meant a lot.

We all rose when Justice Beresford came in and I stood as if I was in church, hands clasped in front of me. I looked up to the public gallery, and it was Mina's family who smiled back at me with encouragement, not my own. It was how I wanted it. Mike and I had agreed that it would not be right for Angelica to be there. He'd offered to come, but was quick to understand when I said I'd rather he didn't.

It was only when we sat down again that it hit me – the enormity of what I was about to do. Walk across the courtroom and take the stand and deliver the lines I had rehearsed so often. My hands trembled. I began to sweat. I was frightened. I might have appeared calm but I wasn't. Mina created a distraction by knocking the pile of papers in front of her on to the floor. When I bent down to help pick them up she seized the opportunity to take my hand – a few seconds of contact, that's all, but it helped me understand that, even though I had to cross the courtroom alone, take the stand by myself, she would be with me in spirit.

It was the first time the jury had had a good look at me. A woman of five feet seven, not so tall, but a giant compared to my employer. Chestnut-brown hair cut to my jawline. Good skin, though slightly red on the cheeks, thanks to an outbreak of rosacea that flared up over the weeks, but I did a good job of covering it under make-up. Brown eyes. Strong brows. No beauty, but I like to think I have always made the best of myself. I wore a primrose-yellow silk blouse, navy skirt and jacket. No wedding ring, no earrings, just the brooch Mina had given me, pinned to the lapel of my jacket.

'Mrs Butcher. You have worked as personal assistant to Mina Appleton for nearly eighteen years, is that right?'

'Yes, I started working for Appleton's in 1995. It will be eighteen years next April.'

'And would you describe for us your duties as Ms Appleton's PA?'

'The job has changed over the years. When I started, I looked after her correspondence, but nowadays, with emails and suchlike, that's less important . . .' It was my chosen subject and I was fluent and articulate, my confidence growing with every word.

'I imagine, from what you've said, that even with changes in technology, even if Ms Appleton handles more of her correspondence through emails you are still across most communication that comes in and out of her office. Would that be correct?'

'Yes, and I do have access to her emails. She has so many, you see. I help her stay on top of them.'

'And, presumably, your job involves managing other aspects of her life too. Personal engagements, the more private side of things. Is that right?'

'Yes. There is an overlap with her personal and public engagements. Part of my job is to make sure she has enough time to meet all the demands on her. Anything she doesn't need to do herself, I take on to free her up.'

'So, for instance, when her children were younger, you might be involved in hiring nannies for them? That sort of thing?'

'Yes, that's right.'

'So you were intimate with her children and her husband.

One might say you were like one of the family. That you were trusted like a member of the family. Would you agree?'

'Well, I'm not sure I'd put it like that. I certainly don't see myself as one of the family, although of course I am fond of her children and I believe I am trusted.' I couldn't resist looking up to the public gallery; I received a reassuring nod from Lottie and the boys.

'Trust is crucial in a job like yours, isn't it, when you're working for such a public figure? Mina Appleton must trust you perhaps even more than she does her most senior executives.'

'Well, I'm not sure . . .' Know your place, Christine, know your place.

'Really? You were, you are, across both Ms Appleton's professional *and* her private life. You, more than anyone else, are privy to details that others are not. That's right, isn't it?'

'In a way, I suppose it is.'

'Mina Appleton depends on you. She knows you to be loyal and trustworthy. Even now, as you stand here in the witness box giving evidence in court, she trusts you.' He paused. 'So, in your view, Mrs Butcher, Mina Appleton was, forgive me, *is* a good employer?'

'Yes, absolutely.'

'Fair?'

'Yes.'

'And generous too, it seems. You are paid a salary of' – he looked down at his notes, raising an eyebrow – 'seventy-five thousand pounds a year, are you not?'

The figure, said out loud, did sound a lot. Certainly the jury seemed surprised. It is a fair salary though, for a high-ranking secretary.

'Yes.'

'That's a lot of money for a secretarial position, isn't it? Above average, wouldn't you say?'

'My job is more than secretarial – the responsibility is greater and the hours longer. These days some like to call themselves executive assistants, but, to be honest, I don't feel the need for such a grand title. I'm happy with secretary.'

He smiled.

'Indeed. And I don't doubt for a moment that you earn every penny of your salary as a secretary, Mrs Butcher. Would you consider Ms Appleton a *reasonable* employer?'

'Yes, I would.'

'She never makes unfair demands? Expects an unreasonable level of commitment from you?'

'Absolutely not.'

'I'd like to direct the jury to document fifteen in bundle five, page twenty-six.'

I remember thinking what a silly word it was – *bundle*. As if it had been deliberately chosen to make the jury's task of wading through mounds of paper somehow seem less arduous.

'In front of you is a record of the phone calls on Mrs Butcher's mobile telephone. You will see from that document that Mina Appleton telephoned Mrs Butcher, her secretary, on average twenty times a day over a period of a month. Some of these calls were in office hours, but many were early in the morning or in the evenings at a time when, one might assume, Mrs Butcher, you were at home. The highlighted calls are ones made to you at weekends by your employer. Often as many as nine. That seems an awful lot. Would you call that "reasonable behaviour", Mrs Butcher? To be disturbed nine times by your employer over a weekend?'

'It comes with the territory. Mina doesn't keep nine-to-five hours, that would be impossible. She would never get through her schedule if she did so. As her assistant, my hours are irregular too. That's not unusual for someone in my position. It's often so busy in the day, the evenings or weekends are the only chance we have to catch up. I don't mind.'

'You don't mind. Your idea of what is *"reasonable"*, Mrs Butcher, is what many of us might consider *un*reasonable. And these little catch-ups were so urgent to your employer, Ms Appleton, they couldn't wait until the following day?'

'As I said, there was not always time to catch up during the day. Mina was often in meetings or out of the office.'

'Mrs Butcher – I say "Mrs" because that is the title you choose to give yourself although you are divorced from Mr Butcher, I believe.'

'Yes.'

'Given the intrusion into your private life, your home life, by Mina Appleton, it's not surprising your marriage suffered. That's quite a sacrifice to make, isn't it? Your marriage for your job.'

'Objection, Your Honour. My client's marital status has no bearing on this trial.'

'Sustained. Mr Maitland, it is not uncommon for marriages to fail due to pressures of work, as I am sure you yourself would agree. In fact the legal profession, I believe, has one of the highest divorce rates, does it not, Mr Maitland?'

'That may well be true, Your Honour.'

'Move on, Mr Maitland.'

'Your Honour.'

That day, I gave an outstanding performance – delivering my lies with ease, steaming on, feeling rather pleased with myself.

No, I was not asked to take the boxes from the archive. Not by Mina Appleton, not by anyone. It was my own decision – something I'd been meaning to do since the office move, but hadn't got round to. The items in the boxes belonged to me. They'd been mislabelled. A silly mistake, entirely my own. All part of the general chaos of moving offices.

Mr Maitland must have hoped my lies would be exposed when he cross-examined the archivist, Rachel Farrer, a few days later, but Douglas Rockwell succeeded in presenting her as a rather tedious pedant, and the jury's eyes glazed over in boredom during her testimony. I, in contrast, came across as calm and reasonable, my lies coming thick and fast, yet I didn't consider them lies. I considered myself on the right side – the whole case still, in my mind, a witch-hunt against a woman I'd served for longer than I'd been married.

'Fire is an efficient form of destroying evidence, Mrs Butcher.'

'Objection.'

'Sustained. Mr Maitland, please.'

'Your Honour. Mrs Butcher, please tell us why you chose to burn the contents of the boxes you retrieved from the Appleton's archive? It is odd, given that you considered the paperwork important enough to archive in the first place, that you then chose to set fire to it.'

'To be honest, most of it was not important, except for my daughter's drawings. I put everything in the archive because I didn't want to clutter up my new office. The top floor was designed in the minimalist style, you know, everything hidden away.'

'A bonfire in the middle of the night seems a very thorough way of disposing of a bit of clutter, Mrs Butcher.'

'It was an afterthought to burn my bits and pieces from the office. My intention, at first, was only to get rid of the things my husband had left in the garage. He'd told me he didn't want them, and so I burned them. Everything was in a bin liner in the garage and I wanted to get rid of it all, you know, to be thorough. I suppose it was a way for me to move on after my divorce.' I was word-perfect. 'Once I started, I thought I might as well clear the rest of the garage too, and that included my boxes from work.'

'A bonfire. Late at night. Not just late at night. At three in the morning. A time when you might have thought no one would notice. It certainly would appear that you were trying to destroy material, if I can put it like that, in secret. When no one would see.'

'Not at all. I thought it would be less annoying for my neighbours if I had the fire at night. Besides, I wasn't sleeping well then. It was a difficult time for me.'

'Really? And yet if it had not been for one of your neighbours – up at that time with a new baby, looking from her window, wondering who on earth was having a fire – no one would have known, would they? That is what you hoped, Mrs Butcher, isn't it? That no one would find out that you destroyed those documents. You wanted to keep it a secret.'

'No, that's not right. As I say, it was a difficult time for me and I wasn't sleeping well. I was often awake at three in the morning.'

'You destroyed contracts that night, didn't you, Mrs Butcher? The contracts with suppliers that Ms Appleton claims never existed.'

'No, I didn't.'

'Would you not agree that it is very fortunate for Ms Appleton that you decided to take those particular boxes home? Boxes that were clearly labelled *Mina Appleton Personal*? Boxes that contained documents that could have been used in evidence against Ms Appleton in this trial if you had not destroyed them.'

'Objection, Your Honour. Mr Maitland claims knowledge of evidence in the boxes when there is no proof it existed.'

'Sustained.'

'Mrs Butcher, do you remember ever saying "no" to your employer?'

'I'm not sure what you mean.'

'It's a straightforward question. Do you remember ever, in the eighteen years you have been in her employ, saying "no" to Mina Appleton?'

'Not quite eighteen years. I don't remember Ms Appleton ever asking me to do anything that seemed unreasonable, so, no, I haven't.'

'In all the time you have worked for Mina Appleton, not once have you refused to do anything she asked of you?'

'I don't recall so, no.'

'So one could describe you, Mrs Butcher, as Mina Appleton's "yes" woman. Someone who is prepared to do anything she asks.'

'That's not how I would describe myself. Mina has never asked me to do anything that I did not feel comfortable with.'

'Mrs Butcher, part of your job is to accompany Ms Appleton on business trips, of which, I imagine, there are many. I'd like to take you back to one in particular. You accompanied Mina Appleton on a visit to New York in 2003. Do you recall that?'

I glanced at my barrister. I wasn't sure where this was going. He gave the briefest of shrugs; he didn't appear concerned.

'Yes.'

'You were not the only secretary working for Ms Appleton at that time. There were two others working there too, weren't there? You have described them as number two and number three – secretaries who worked beneath you. You being number one. Is that correct?'

'Yes.'

'On that particular trip, it was secretary number three, Lucy Beacham, who was supposed to travel to New York with Ms Appleton. Her ticket had been bought and paid for.'

'Yes, I believe so.'

'She may not have had the title of personal, or even executive, assistant, but certainly she was not new to the job. She was an experienced secretary, was she not? Although this would have been her first trip abroad with Ms Appleton. There was a last-minute change, though, wasn't there? You accompanied Ms Appleton on that trip, instead of Miss Beacham, didn't you? Why was that?'

'I believe Mina was worried that Lucy wasn't up to it. She was right, in fact. It wasn't long after that that we had to let Lucy go . . .'

'Really? Your employer must have thought Ms Beacham was "*up to it*" when her ticket was purchased and a visa organized. Yet with two days' notice, Mina Appleton made it clear she wasn't happy. She said she wanted you to accompany her instead. Is that right?'

'Well, yes.'

'At not inconsiderable cost. Ms Beacham's business-class ticket went to waste and a new, first-class ticket was purchased for you – although Appleton's would have picked up the bill for that. You paid a price too, though, didn't you, Mrs Butcher, for that trip? You agreed to go at great personal cost to yourself. Your father was ill. That, I assume, is why Ms Beacham was originally asked to accompany Ms Appleton. I understand your father had been taken into hospital earlier that week. He was still in hospital when Mina Appleton asked you to accompany her to New York. Your father was over eighty years old and suffering from pneumonia.'

'Yes.'

'Were you close to your father, Mrs Butcher?'

All I could manage was a nod of my head.

'Your mother died when you were young and you have no siblings. I have no doubt you and your father were close.'

I looked down.

'Forgive me, Mrs Butcher, I know this must be difficult for you. Do you need to stop for a moment? I am sure the court will understand.'

'No. I'd like to carry on.'

'Thank you, I appreciate that. Did Mina Appleton know your father had been rushed into hospital when she asked you to accompany her?'

'I'm not sure.'

'Really? You're not sure? You had worked together for many years and yet you are not sure whether she knew your father was seriously ill?'

'Well, yes. She did know. I had taken the day off earlier in the week when he was admitted to hospital.'

'I see. So she'd given you one day off to go to the hospital. In fact, my understanding is that in all the time you've worked for Ms Appleton, this is the only day that you have taken off. Apart from annual holiday. Quite a record, Mrs Butcher.'

'Well . . .'

'So, Ms Appleton knew your father was gravely ill and yet she still asked you to accompany her?'

'Well, I'm not sure . . .'

'Yes or no, please, Mrs Butcher.'

He took a step towards me.

'Yes, she did.'

'Your father died while you were on that trip, didn't he? It is hard to imagine how you felt, not being there.'

'Objection, Your Honour.'

'Mr Maitland, I need to hear a question or I will ask you to move on.'

'Yes, Your Honour. Mrs Butcher, did you consider Mina Appleton's request for you to accompany her on that trip as a reasonable one?'

'Yes.'

'Even though she knew your elderly father was seriously ill? Even though it was likely he might die while you were away? Most people would view Mina Appleton's request as not only *un*reasonable, but positively cruel and manipulative. And yet you do not. Mina Appleton made you choose between your father and her, didn't she? One cannot help wonder, Mrs Butcher, whether spending so many years in the service of Mina Appleton has blinded you to what is fair, what is reasonable. What is legal, even.'

Nonsense, I wanted to say, but the word dried up in my mouth. I looked up and saw Angelica in the public gallery. She shouldn't have been there. We'd agreed. I wondered when she'd slipped in. How much had she heard? She was looking right at me.

'Mrs Butcher.'

I turned away, and looked at Mr Maitland.

'Do you need a break, Mrs Butcher?'

I shook my head.

'You have told the court that in all the time you have worked for Ms Appleton, you have never said no to her because she never asked you to do anything that made you uncomfortable or that you considered unreasonable. Do you stand by that?'

'Yes.'

'Did you not feel just a little discomfort, Mrs Butcher, in choosing to leave your dying father in hospital alone so you could accompany Ms Appleton to New York?' Angelica had been a child. She loved her grandfather. She was hearing this for the first time.

'It was a short trip. I was sure he'd be OK.'

'How could you be sure?'

'I hoped . . .'

'You hoped. Your father died, didn't he? While you were away. Do you still consider your employer's demand as reasonable?'

'Yes. She needed me to go. Her schedule was such that only I could manage it.' Mr Maitland looked flabbergasted. The jury disgusted. I knew Angelica would be sickened too.

'It's a question of judgement, is it not? It depends on what you are used to. One person's *reasonable* behaviour would be considered cruel and manipulative by another. I think we are left in no doubt how strong the ties are between you and Mina Appleton. How much influence she exerts over you. You would do anything for her, wouldn't you, Mrs Butcher? No wonder, when you were asked to help cover up her lies, you didn't think twice.'

'Objection.'

'Sustained.'

There was a glass of water in front of me, but I didn't dare reach for it.

'It was my job to accompany her. She needed me. Lucy Beacham wasn't up to it.' I looked up at Angelica, saw her shaking her head.

'It was your job? Is there nothing you would consider beyond the remit of your job, Mrs Butcher?'

I looked down, and the tears I'd been holding in fell. The judge called lunch fifteen minutes early, and I managed to walk back to the dock, but then my legs buckled.

It was Mina who caught me, Mina who put her arm around me, and I imagined Angelica watching as I allowed her to help me from the courtroom.

The Old Bailey matron had been called, and I sat with her for a while, and then she sent me home. When I walked from the building, I looked for Angelica, hoping she'd be waiting. I wanted to explain myself to her.

She wasn't there, though, and when I called her, she didn't pick up. In that courtroom, she saw me for who I was.

34

Home was the last place I wanted to be. This break in my routine meant more empty hours ahead, and they hung before me like a loose fold in the tightly bound skin of my existence. I hung my coat, put my handbag under the hall table, took off my shoes, put on my slippers. I filled, then switched on the kettle, went to the back door, unlocked and opened it, then stepped out on to the pitted, slimy paving and looked towards the garden. It had been raining and puddles filled the uneven surface. I stepped around them, taking small shuffling steps like an old woman. I was scared of falling. The soles of my slippers had no grip. Mike used to power-hose the path every spring, removing the green slick that built up over the winter.

I'd left two small bowls out that morning. One was empty and I picked it up but there was no sign of the black-and-white cat that had appeared at my back door a few mornings before, mewing its little heart out to be let in. I took the empty bowl inside and put it in the sink, made tea, took it upstairs, showered, then put on my dressing gown and went back down to prepare supper.

Fat congealed in a yellow skin on the frozen mince I tipped

from a Tupperware into the pan. I thought of my father and the meals we'd eaten together before I left home, before I was married. The dishes I used to prepare at weekends, then freeze, for us to eat during the week – a routine I took with me into my marriage.

I turned on the gas and stirred the mush with a wooden spoon. It hissed against the hot metal. I left it to thaw and refilled the kettle for spaghetti, moving from stove to counter to sink and back again. Not even a radio playing in the background. I poured the boiled water from the kettle into the pan, put on the lid and watched it until it shook, ready for the pasta. I pressed down the strands with a spoon until they were submerged and replaced the lid, then found Sellotape to reseal the packet of spaghetti.

While my back was turned, the water boiled over, glutinous slop flooding the stove and extinguishing the flame. The smell of gas was strong but I didn't turn it off. I relished its odour, inhaling deep breaths of it while I dabbed at the pool of water with kitchen roll, tearing off more sheets and laying them down, watching them soak up the water, leaning in towards the gas. It was feeble and half-hearted. I knew it wouldn't kill me – it was only later I seriously thought about taking my life.

I ate from a tray on my lap in front of the television, thinking of Angelica. I imagined her eating supper with her father and stepmother in their new home. We'd spoken the day before, and I'd told her the trial was going well. Now, she'd seen it for herself. I waited for her to call that evening. I tried her several times. In the end, I sent a text. *I'm so sorry.* She didn't reply.

My father died while I was in New York for work. That was not a crime. It was shameful though and, however hard I tried that evening, I could not keep thoughts of Dad at bay. Even the documentary I watched on television tormented me. I struggled to hear the commentary over the soundtrack – something Dad used to complain of when we lived together. I took the tray back to the kitchen and scraped my uneaten meal into the bin.

I hadn't wanted to go to New York. When I'd visited Dad in hospital, that week, I knew how ill he was. I'd prepped Lucy and got her ready to take my place with Mina. I wanted to be with Dad at the end. It was my last chance to talk to him, about Mum. For me to tell him the truth and for him to listen, and, I'd hoped, forgive me. Mina knew that, and yet, ultimately, it was my decision. I could have said no. Perhaps I feared that Dad, even on his deathbed, could never say the words that would give me peace.

I remember his body, the waxy skin, those milky eyes, and how I sat holding his hand. He passed away in the early hours while I slept in my first-class seat next to Mina. Mike drove me straight to the hospital and walked with me to the room where Dad's body lay, then he waited outside to take me home again. He was kind. And I should have listened to him. I shouldn't have gone on that trip and left my father to die alone.

It must be the loneliest place on earth. To be alone at your death. After Dad died, I made a promise to myself that if I am fortunate enough to be in the right place at the right time, I will make sure I hold the hand of whoever lies dying. I will be the one to comfort them in their last moments.

Dearest Christine,

I will never forget the strength and loyalty you showed me during a time of such heartbreak. In you, your father had a daughter he could be proud of. I am sure he would have been in no doubt of your devotion to him over the years.

Do not blame yourself for not being with him when he died. He would not have needed to see you, for I am sure you were a constant presence in his heart, as he was in yours. You were there in spirit, dear Christine. With him at the end.

With all my love, Mina xxxx

That letter had comforted me and I took it out that evening and read it again. I tried to convince myself that Dad would have respected my commitment to work – that he understood the pull of duty. He'd lived through the war. Never put himself first. It was what I admired most in him – something I tried hard to emulate. What had been noble in him, however, was a failing in me. I was a coward. Mina Appleton's yes-woman.

I don't remember hearing Stella, but she must have let herself in with her key, for the next moment she was by my side. She took the letter from me and put it away, then drew the curtains, lit the candles and turned off the lights. I stood up and let her take off my dressing gown, then lay on the table. She pulled a blanket over me. Her hands stroked and kneaded my skin.

'She wants you to know how proud she was of you today,' she whispered. 'She thought you showed such dignity. It will have done the prosecution no favours to be seen bullying you like that.'

When she finished, she wrapped me in my dressing gown again, then led me up to bed.

I woke later to the sound of the cat mewing outside the back door and I went down and let him in. He followed me upstairs and sniffed around in the bathroom while I sat on the loo, then followed me to bed, fitting his small, warm body into the space behind my bent legs.

35

I brushed a cat hair from the waistband of my skirt. I was determined to do better on my second day.

'Mrs Butcher, you say you are not in the habit of losing things but your employer is, isn't she? How many times has Mina Appleton lost her mobile telephone or laptop over the last two years?'

'I have no idea.'

'Surely you must know. It was your job to replace them, wasn't it?'

'Yes.'

'So how many times did you have to call the IT department to arrange for replacements for Ms Appleton's mobile telephones and laptops? Let's say, in the last year?'

'A few times – I don't remember exactly.'

'A few times. I have a record of the number of times you called the IT department to replace mobile telephones or laptops that Ms Appleton had apparently mislaid. I refer to pages forty-four and forty-five in bundle eight. This covers a period of three years. It is quite a list, isn't it? In the first year, four mobile phones lost and replaced. Along with – if you look further down the page – five laptops. Five. The next year, three mobiles and three laptops vanished. And in the third year, the most recent year, the same number. Three mobiles and three laptops. That is more than carelessness. Emails, telephone calls that could be used as evidence in this trial, all lost. How do you explain the disappearance of these devices, Mrs Bucher?'

I took a moment – I'd got up early that morning to practise my answers in front of the mirror, even trying on a wry smile.

'It is infuriating, to be honest. Mina is always losing things. And I'm always having to chase round trying to find them. Mina is scatty.' Exasperated yet fond – that's what I was going for. 'I can't lie. It does drive me mad. And it wasn't only during those three years, Mr Maitland. Mina has always been in the habit of losing things. A lot of my time is spent retrieving or replacing things she's lost or left somewhere. She's famous for it in the IT department. One time she even left her laptop in the kitchen of Downing Street and walked out with the PM's instead. They'd been having supper. It was embarrassing. Potentially very serious. Luckily, I spotted it as soon as she got in the car. It was fortunate I was there. I'd been working late and Dave was giving me a lift home. Anyway, I managed to sort it out before there was a major security alert.'

'That's quite a story, Mrs Butcher. You're telling us that Mina Appleton went off with the prime minister's personal laptop? And that you managed to sort it out, averting a major breach in the country's security?'

'Yes. It does sound strange when you put it like that. But it's about trust, you see. If it had been someone other than Mina, perhaps it might have been different, but the PM's secretary, Vera, knows us well and she and I sorted it without the PM ever finding out. To be honest, everyone who knows Mina knows she's a bit of a Dozy Doris when it comes to things like that. She's always losing her credit cards and her car keys. It's not just

IT that know me well, it's her bank and the garage too. I'm always having to organize replacements.' I heard laughter and wondered for a moment whether I'd gone too far. 'The incident. With the laptop. It was a few years ago. I hope it's OK for me to speak about it now?'

Mina shrugged but I could see she was amused, pleased even. I was told by Stella that a few of the papers described the moment as '. . . *an indication of the affection between the two women, a shrug that said*, It's too late now. *It was a moment of blessed light relief in what had been a tedious morning.*' I felt as if I'd received a positive review by a theatre critic.

'I think you're probably safe, Mrs Butcher, to speak up now.' Judge Beresford smiled at me over his glasses.

I did well that day. I was invited to Mr Anderson's chambers for tea afterwards and, for the first time, Sandra Tisdale remembered how I took it. Milk, no sugar. Their confidence in me had been restored. Perhaps I was forgiven a little by the jury too, for abandoning my sick father. I'd treated them to a glimpse into a world of private suppers at Number Ten, shown them the human side of a TV celebrity who ran a multimillion-pound business, but, like some of them, was in the habit of losing her keys and her credit cards. My testimony that day lightened the mood.

On the walk to Euston I held my head high. A bit too confident, perhaps. It wasn't over yet and I knew the next day would be a difficult one, but I set aside time that evening to rehearse myself. It was the truth that seemed to catch me out. Lies, I managed with fluency.

36

'Mrs Butcher. You were, you are, the keeper of Mina Appleton's diary.'

'Yes. I manage all her appointments. My number two, Sarah, has access to the diary, but I am the only one able to make amendments. Everything comes through me. I am always kept informed.'

'Indeed, you are always kept informed. It is your job to know where Mina Appleton is at all times, isn't it?'

'Yes.'

'So if she were out of the office for any reason, you would know where she was and what she was doing, is that correct?'

'Yes.'

'I'd like to refer the jury to the printouts from the diary covering three years – 2009, 2010 and 2011. On the dates before you, you will see highlighted entries that show Mina Appleton at meetings out of the office. The highlighted entries are all at the start of the months of February, May, August and November. Four times a year over a period of three years. Did you make those entries, Mrs Butcher?'

'Yes.'

'Yet as I understand it, you are not responsible for making

Ms Appleton's travel arrangements. That falls to your number two, as you call her. Is that right?'

'Yes, Sarah looks after Mina's travel arrangements – something Mina and I decided on to free me up. You see, it's rather tedious—'

'Yes, thank you, Mrs Butcher. Can you tell us where Mina Appleton was on those dates?'

'Well, I can certainly tell you what she told me to say. She was visiting her mother. She went as often as she could. They're very close. I didn't believe her, though. You see, Mina and her mother are not close. Not at all. The truth is, I doubt very much Mina was in Geneva doing her daughterly duty on those days.'

'And yet you still say it was you who removed the entries from the diary and inserted false ones?'

'Yes. But it was Mina Appleton, my employer, who asked me to do it. I helped her. In good faith. I trusted her. I didn't think twice.'

I like to think there was a moment when I considered telling the truth, but there wasn't, and I didn't.

'Can you tell us where Mina Appleton was on those dates, Mrs Butcher?'

'She was visiting her mother. She went as often as she could. They're very close.' Christine told such dreadful lies.

'She was visiting her mother? You're sure of that?'

'Yes.'

'Then why, Mrs Butcher, were those "visits to her mother" deleted from the diary and other entries put in? Entries that covered up the fact that Mina Appleton was in Geneva?'

'Aah, well, that was my mistake, I'm afraid.'

'Your mistake?'

'Yes, I changed the entries at a later date.'

'You changed the entries? You're saying that you falsified the diaries to cover up the fact she was in Geneva?'

'No, I'm not saying that. What I'm saying is that I altered the entries, that's all. She was visiting her mother, as I say. It's what I like to call housekeeping.'

'Housekeeping? Removing entries from the diary and putting in false ones? I'd like to draw the jury's attention to pages thirty-three to thirty-eight in their bundles. The printouts reveal the original diary entries. Can you read them out for us please, Mrs Butcher?'

I glanced down at the paper, though I knew the words already.

'Mina to Geneva. Mina to Geneva. Mina to Geneva . . .'

'That's right. Mina to Geneva. Yet, those entries were deleted and false entries put in. Unfortunately for Ms Appleton, the original entries were found on her computer's hard drive. An attempt was made to delete them from the record but that attempt failed because, there they are: *Mina to Geneva*. Plain for us to see. Mina Appleton asked you to remove the original entries, didn't she, and put in false ones to hide the fact that she had been visiting her bank in Geneva on those dates. Isn't that right, Mrs Butcher?'

'No, that's not true. It was my decision to take those entries out. Mina didn't know anything about it.'

'You're saying that Mina Appleton did not know you removed those entries?'

'Yes, that's exactly what I'm saying.'

He turned to the jury and although I couldn't see his face I can imagine the look of incredulity on it.

'Mrs Butcher, do you make a habit of going behind your boss's back to falsify her diary?'

'It's housekeeping, as I said. It's something I do now and again if Mina is out of the office on personal business. You see, some members of the board resent it – the men, primarily. They don't like it if she's away from the office for a whole day on something that's not about them. They can get a bit whingey about it, so it's easier if they don't know.'

'I'm sorry, let me get this clear. You falsify Ms Appleton's diary so that members of the board don't know where she is? So if she is in Geneva at her bank, for instance, they wouldn't know?'

'She was in Geneva visiting her mother, not a bank. As I say, she went as often as she could. They're very close.'

He shook his head. He didn't believe a word of it, yet I pressed on.

'It wasn't the first time I've changed entries in the diary, though I try not to make a habit of it. There's rarely any reason to. Mina is hard-working – always putting the business above everything else. From time to time, however, there have been periods when she's been out of the office on matters that have nothing to do with Appleton's. For instance, there was a period when she was having cosmetic treatments so I took those out too and replaced them with meetings at one of her charities – The Haven, I think it was.'

This revelation was not one I'd cleared with Mina, but it worked, I think. Gave the jury a juicy gobbet and pleased certain members of the press.

'Let me remind you, Mrs Butcher, that you are under oath. I will put it to you again: Mina Appleton asked you to delete those trips to Geneva because they flagged up the dates she was visiting her Swiss bank to deposit profits from the sale of land. Isn't that right, Mrs Butcher?'

'I don't know anything about bank deposits. I changed the diary – Mina didn't know anything about it.'

'How convenient, Mrs Butcher – given the reason we are here in court – that you should take it upon yourself to strip the word *Geneva* from the diary. How helpful to Ms Appleton. Geneva is well known for secret banking, a place where money can be moved about in numbered accounts, a place where the authorities have no jurisdiction to investigate. Once again, Mrs Butcher, it seems you were unable to say no to your employer when she asked you to cover up for her. She told you to falsify the diary, didn't she? To delete those entries and write in false ones. She wanted you to help her cover up those visits to Swiss banks.'

'No. That's not true.'

'There is a very good reason why Ms Appleton would have wanted evidence of her trips to Geneva to disappear. The entries were deleted when inquiries began into the shell companies that had purchased the land from Appleton's.'

'I'm sorry, I really don't know anything about that.'

'I believe you, Mrs Butcher. I am sure you didn't know the reason behind Ms Appleton's demand for those entries to be deleted, but you did it anyway, didn't you? As you have always done everything she's asked of you without questioning it.'

'When I did it, I had no idea the police would investigate Mina. I see now it was a mistake and that what I've done has complicated things. It was silly, I see that now.'

'Mrs Butcher, the truth is you exist in a myopic state, concerning yourself only with the detail of your boss's wishes. Not the bigger picture. You are a small cog but you are an important one, vital to Ms Appleton. You follow orders, never wavering in your mission to take care of the woman who, after all, takes care of you. She is accused of lying under oath, of perjuring herself, and you are accused of covering up her lies. That is why you are here, standing in the dock of the Old Bailey. You are prepared to do anything for Mina Appleton, aren't you? So if she asked you to remove entries from her diary, to destroy paperwork for her, you wouldn't think twice. How much more are you prepared to sacrifice for Mina Appleton, Mrs Butcher? Your freedom? No more questions, Your Honour.'

37

Mina walked across to the witness box with the dignity of a young Tudor queen about to lay her head on the executioner's block. All eyes on her as she climbed the steps, head held high, slender, pale neck rising from the white collar of her dress. She was not young though, she was a woman of fifty-six, yet there was barely a line on her face, nor a single grey hair on her head.

The jury were seeing her close-up, in the flesh for the first time, and they were fascinated. Stripped of make-up, she looked a more fragile version of the person they'd seen on their television screens. For someone who was used to appearing in the public eye, she appeared nervous – touchingly so.

'You're fond of quoting Thomas Paine, are you not, Ms Appleton?'

'Actually, that was my father – he was very taken with Paine.'

'Your father, yes. An honest man. A man of integrity, trusted by his employees, his customers and suppliers too. He held strong views about the industry he worked in and he was not afraid to express them. Would you say that's fair?'

'Yes, I would.'

'He practised what he preached. He was no hypocrite. Is that fair too, Ms Appleton?'

'Absolutely.'

' "*A long habit of not thinking a thing wrong, gives it a superficial appearance of being right* . . . " Thomas Paine. Your father used that quote in a piece he wrote for *Farmers' Weekly*. He was referring, was he not, to what he saw as the unfair practices of large supermarket chains. He called for legislation to make the position of suppliers – fruit growers, farmers – more secure. He wanted contracts between suppliers and supermarkets to have safeguards built in, so orders could not be cancelled at the last moment – so mountains of perfectly good produce did not go to waste. The point he was making was that, just because these legal practices had been going on for years, it did not make them right. Is that a fair interpretation, Ms Appleton?'

'Yes, it is.'

'The image of Appleton's as a business with a conscience was built on your father's reputation. You have capitalized on it in advertising campaigns: "*Appleton's. Fine food. Right price. We make it our business to be fair.*" That image of treating your suppliers with "fairness" is what makes the brand stand out, is it not? Today Appleton's is among the top three supermarkets in this country. Something, one suspects, that may not have been possible under your father. But then, perhaps it was never your father's intention to grow a monster.

'When a newspaper article detailed how Appleton's, under your leadership, bore no resemblance to the image you cynically exploited, you sued that newspaper and you won. Why did you sue? Because you knew it would destroy your own image if the truth came out. And the truth, Ms Appleton, is that you are a hypocrite. Greedy and dishonest was how the *Business Times* described you. That is the real Mina Appleton, is it not?'

She parted her lips, perhaps considering whether to protest, then closed them again.

'Appleton's, with you at the helm, *did* break contracts with long-standing suppliers, and the result was to push them into bankruptcy so you could grab their land, buying it up through a series of shell companies. Far from being a business with a conscience, you turned Appleton's into a monster. Can you explain, Ms Appleton, why every copy of the contracts signed with those suppliers disappeared from Appleton's archive?'

I imagined, beneath her composure, Mina was seething. Yet her voice, when she spoke, was gentle and patient. She might have been taking us through the recipe for her surprisingly delicious beetroot brownies.

'My father, as you say, was a man of integrity. When he gave his word to someone he kept it. In turn, he trusted the word of those he did business with.' She hesitated, then gave a regretful sigh. 'For all his qualities, my father did not have an eye or indeed the patience for detail, and I am afraid there were those who took advantage of him in later years.' She was the picture of a concerned daughter.

'When I took over the business, I was shocked to see how bad things had got. The produce from some of the suppliers my father favoured was not of high enough quality – it was a problem brought to me by my buyers. I rely on their advice, you see, and I trust them to do their jobs. I try not to interfere. For example, with Fraser's. My fruit buyer was beside himself with frustration – he told me Fraser's had become unreliable, their produce inconsistent. I accepted my buyer's word for it. I trust and respect my staff.'

'You haven't answered the question, Ms Appleton. There were signed contracts with those suppliers, but you cancelled them. Then you ensured that the copies of those contracts, held by Appleton's, disappeared. You got rid of the proof of their existence.'

'I never signed a contract with John Fraser – there was no contract. The Frasers supplied Appleton's when my father was in charge and, in good faith, we continued to use them for a period after. As I said, it was on my buyer's advice that we stopped using them. All I ever wanted was to do the best for the company, to keep its integrity as a supplier of quality food. And to save my family business from collapse.'

I wanted to believe her, even though I knew I had burned those contracts, even though I could feel the flames licking my cheeks. I needed Mina to convince me that the years of service I'd given her were worthwhile – that she was a woman who deserved my loyalty.

Mina's family sat in solidarity, right at the front of the public gallery. I noticed, behind them, in the back row, Jenny Haddow, sitting alone. She was not one of them. I can only imagine how she must have felt, watching Mina scrape her claws along Lord Appleton's dead flesh with a regretful smile on her face.

'And what of those other "family businesses", Ms Appleton? The ones that were forced to sell up because of your unfair practices? Can you explain why they too – all of them with exclusive deals to supply Appleton's, all of them considered good enough by your father – went out of business when you took over control of the company?'

She shook her head. As if it was utterly baffling to her.

'I can't explain it, but I can make an educated guess. Those suppliers, like Fraser's, were already struggling. That is why my buyers decided to no longer use them. Their businesses were already in trouble.'

'Is that so? Easy pickings then, for someone who knew that and who wanted to grab their land.'

'I am not interested in grabbing anyone's land.'

'Really? Yet you ended up using their land as collateral for the money you loaned them. Money you knew they would not be able to repay. You took their land and then you sold it on.'

'Appleton's loaned them money – not me. And yes, that land was sold, but not for profit.'

'Not then, at least. That came later, didn't it, Ms Appleton? You sold the land – at no profit, as you say – to six different purchasers: Brownlow, Percival, Simpson, Lancing, Hogarth and McTally. Those were the names of the six shell companies you set up. It was those shell companies that then sold the land on for profit. Profit which you kept.'

If only he had not named the shell companies. Then I might have been able to hold on to my faith a while longer. But hearing them listed together like that was the moment when I began to see daylight – a glimpse of the bigger picture.

Brownlow, Percival, Simpson, Lancing, Hogarth and McTally – a family of woodland creatures – names plucked from Mina's childhood memory. I could see her sitting at her desk at Minerva, a pencil in her hand, doodling on a scrap of paper. Beside the Frasers' name, I saw the sketch of a fawn: Lancing. I remembered then, it was the company Clifford Fraser said had bought his farm. Jenny Haddow heard it too, though she wouldn't have been able to make the connection I could. I should have stood up at that moment and spoken out. Instead, I closed my ears and said nothing. I preferred not to know, clinging to my role as Mina's faithful servant.

The prosecutor pointed his finger at Mina, taking a step towards her, which was unwise. He became a pantomime villain, and she, with her exquisite femininity, the fragile princess. She looked down for a moment, then blinked her blue eyes, waiting stoically for him to finish.

'Then you, Ms Appleton, deposited that profit into Swiss bank accounts – cash you carried by hand. Untraceable. You made those trips to Geneva to deposit cash into numbered Swiss accounts – accounts beyond the reach of the authorities. That is the truth, isn't it, Ms Appleton?'

'No. That is not the truth. I travelled to Geneva to visit my mother.'

Mina told such dreadful lies. And she made them sound like the simplest of truths.

'Really? Then why attempt to cover up those visits if they were innocent? Why ask your secretary to delete the original entries and replace them with false ones?'

'My secretary told you the truth. I knew nothing about it. When I discovered what Christine had done, I was, to say the least, surprised.'

'When you *discovered*? Really, Ms Appleton. It beggars belief that you would not have known they'd been removed from your diary. That you yourself had not ordered your secretary to delete them.'

'It's the truth.'

'It served your interests to hide those trips to Switzerland, to cover your tracks, not your secretary's. You had motive, Ms Appleton. Your secretary did not. Unless she was told to by you.'

She tucked a strand of hair behind her ear, and I knew she was having to resist the urge to pull at it.

'I had no reason to "cover my tracks", as you put it. Why would I? My mother has lived in Switzerland for many years and I go as often as I can to see her. The first I knew about Christine altering the diary was when the police questioned me. When I asked her about it, and she told me what she had done, frankly, I was shocked. Of course she was horrified when she realized the police thought it was me, and she was very apologetic, but there was nothing sinister about it. It was a stupid thing done by someone who . . . what can I say – well, Christine was not herself at the time.'

204

This was not the story we'd agreed on. *Christine looked after the diary. It wasn't unusual for her to tidy it up when she saw fit. We called it housekeeping. There was no need for her to consult me. I trust her.* That was what I'd expected her to say. I looked across the courtroom and saw Mina standing on terra firma, while I clung to a leaky raft – a murky grey ocean opening up between us.

'Oh, come now, Ms Appleton. Your secretary has shown herself to be someone who will do anything for you. She has put you before her own family. Even when her father lay gravely ill in hospital, her allegiance was to you. Mrs Butcher seems incapable of making any decision without consulting you first. The idea that she would go behind your back and tamper with your diary seems utterly implausible.

'I see your difficulty though. If only the original entries had not been discovered on the hard drive of your computer, then no one would have known, would they? But those entries were found. You had a problem, but one that seemed easy to solve. Simply ask the obedient Mrs Butcher to lie for you. Why not blame her? And then get her to lie in court? I doubt she would have needed much persuading.'

How right he was. I fiddled with the button on the cuff of my blouse, undid it, slipped my fingers under the sleeve into the crook of my elbow and scratched, digging in my nails and enjoying the feel of the flakes of skin. Mina sighed, looking down at her hands.

'It's difficult for me to try and explain Christine's behaviour. Even for her, it was odd.' She smiled with affection. 'Christine is known around the office for her eccentricity. So when she confessed to me about the diary, I admit, I was worried about how it would look to the police, but I was concerned too for Christine. Colleagues had come to me in the past with tales of her unpredictable, sometimes high-handed, behaviour and I'd always dismissed it, but this was different.'

I was naked in the courtroom. The room cast an amused eye over me. Mina had whet their appetite. They were curious about this odd creature – Mrs Christine Butcher. I tried to picture my colleagues slipping into Mina's office when I wasn't around, whispering tales of my *unpredictable behaviour*. Mina sitting behind her desk, smiling with understanding – speaking out as my loyal defender. I couldn't picture it, because I knew it wasn't true, yet the jury lapped it up.

'Christine and I have worked together a long time, but the impression you have given of our relationship is not one I recognize. You described her as a "yes-woman" – well, I can tell you, that is far from the truth.' She chuckled. 'We all stand to attention when Christine comes into the room. She's known as the Gatekeeper around the office.' She turned to the jury, gracing them with a smile.

'I mean, this business of number-one, number-two, number-three secretary – it's nonsense. I've heard Christine describe herself on the phone as my "Number One"' – she delivered these last two words in a prim tone – 'but that's not actually how it is. I don't believe in, or encourage, that kind of hierarchy – it can be divisive – but I'm very fond of Christine and so I choose to overlook her eccentricities, including that one. To be fair, she is my longest-serving secretary, so yes, in that sense, she is the most senior.' I noticed an unpleasant smirk on the faces of several members of the jury, and even Dave seemed to find the description of me amusing.

'This business with the diary – Christine was only telling half the truth. Yes, she removed those entries because I was out of the office on personal reasons, but it was not because *others* might frown on it. It was Christine herself who frowned on it. Her own work ethic is rigid, and she can be rather unforgiving when the rest of us take time off for personal reasons.'

I don't remember whether Mr Maitland asked a question at

this point, because all I could hear was Mina's voice drilling into my head, her eyes bright and playful as she entertained the court.

'The reason I asked Sarah to take on my travel arrangements was so she could book my flights to Geneva without Christine getting involved. She's never bothered to hide her disapproval of my mother and I know it's because Mummy chose to live in Geneva rather than near me, and Christine considers that disloyal. The truth is, my mother and I are very close. She moved abroad years ago – when my father started having an affair with his secretary.' I felt myself wither under Mina's words, yet she delivered them with a lightness tinged with compassion, as if she spoke of me with fondness.

I looked at the clock – a digital timepiece, anachronistic in that ancient place – a red-eyed devil that taunted me, seeming to grind to a halt while Mina told tales of her pitiful secretary.

'And yet you have employed this woman for eighteen years – a woman who, in so many words, you have described as dishonest and delusional.'

'No, that's not what I meant at all,' she protested with wide-eyed innocence. 'At the time of the incident with the diary, Christine was unhappy. She is a very private person – something I have always respected.' She bit her lip, then carried on. 'But it's important the court knows her state of mind in that period and why she behaved so erratically. When I finally got it out of her, I understood. Her daughter had just told her she didn't want to live with her any more and was moving out to be with her father and his new partner. I can only imagine how painful that was, and I think it tipped Christine over.'

She didn't look at me once and I felt as if I'd stepped out of the room and was listening from the other side of the door to a conversation I wished I wasn't hearing.

'Christine relied on her job, and me, I suppose, to fill a hole in her life. Her marriage was over, her daughter had gone – work was everything to her. If I was out of the office, particularly for personal reasons – she didn't like it. I think it made her feel . . .' She stopped and looked over to the jury as if they might throw out some suggestions. 'Not jealous exactly, but certainly insecure. As I said, she was not herself.'

Mr Maitland failed to hide his impatience and I began to see him as my defender. I wanted him to trip her up and expose her.

'You present yourself, Ms Appleton, as the picture of compassion. It's not true though, is it? It's why we are here in court: because you are prepared to lie – to do anything – to protect the false image of yourself. It covers up who you really are, doesn't it? Greedy, dishonest. A hypocrite. Where was your compassion when Christine Butcher's father was dying? One wonders whether you even allowed her a day off to attend his funeral?'

She put back her shoulders, looked him in the eye.

'I told Christine to take off as much time as she needed. If I'd known how ill her father was, I would have insisted on it. I told Christine many times that her family should be her priority.' I watched her with bewildered pain. She *had* known how ill Dad was. It was why I had asked Lucy to go in my place. I remembered the scene in her office before that New York trip. *You've made your priorities clear,* she'd snapped. The scorn in her voice when she'd said, *Run home to your family.* In the end, however, it had been my decision. I'd been a coward not to stand up to her.

'Really?' Mr Maitland didn't believe a word. 'Yet it seems she ignored your advice. That doesn't sound like the Mrs Butcher we have seen in court, the woman who has never said no to you.'

She nodded, as if she agreed with him.

'I've wondered why she made that decision to come with me and not be with her father, and I think it's because she was frightened. It would have been too painful.'

I watched her look over at the jury, and then back at me. Her expression seemed one of genuine concern. Now I realize that, in fact, she was selecting her next weapon, cleaning it off, then slipping it into my ribs with cold-blooded precision.

'I wish I'd reached out to Christine sooner – perhaps I might have been able to persuade her to get help. Beneath that no-nonsense exterior, she is very fragile. I had a glimpse of it once when she was talking about her mother's death. It was soon after my own father had died, and a moment of rare intimacy between us. Christine's mother died in an accident when she was a child. She felt responsible. It's not appropriate for me to go into the detail, but what I will say is that it haunted her. So, yes, perhaps I failed in my duty of care to her, Mr Maitland, but I did not insist she accompany me on that trip to New York – in fact, quite the contrary.'

I slipped out of my body, looking down at myself, and wondered who she was, this woman in the pale yellow blouse, her hands clasped on her lap. I could see a line of grey along her parting where the hair was growing out, its true colour coming through. So many things I'd heard in court over the weeks had taken me by surprise, yet none more so than Mina's portrayal of me. Delusional. Desperate. Unstable. At times, even a source of amusement. I understood then what I hadn't before: a vital aspect of Mina Appleton's defence relied on the assassination of my character. She must have always known it. And I had allowed myself to be used. I had played right into her hands.

'I can see, Ms Appleton, how someone with such extreme devotion, such a profound sense of loyalty – such a "fragile" woman – could be very useful to you. Someone who would be easily persuaded to do whatever you asked of them. Dispose of material that might incriminate you – remove entries in your diary – then lie on oath in court for you.'

'No, no, no. Christine has a mind of her own. She sees herself as indispensable, and is committed to her job one hundred per cent. I will not fault her for that, Mr Maitland. But Christine would never lie for me – or anyone else, for that matter. It is simply not in her nature. And removing entries from my diary – well, odd, yes, but dishonest? No. She was not herself, as I said. It was a blip. An unhappy period in her life. We all have times like that, don't we? Christine is not a dishonest or deceitful person. However misguided her actions may seem, I do know her intentions would have been pure. She is honest and kind. She would not knowingly hurt anyone.'

'You paint a picture of a rather desperate woman, Ms Appleton. Someone who'd do anything to please you.'

'No. That's not fair on Christine. She is a dedicated, hard-working woman who takes great pride in her job.'

'Dedicated and hard-working? Or unpredictable and paranoid? Which is it, Ms Appleton? You describe Mrs Butcher's actions as a blip – a blip that proved extremely convenient for you. If she really is as "unpredictable" as you say, it seems hard to believe you would have continued to employ her for as long as you have.'

'I would trust Christine with my life. With the lives of my children. But over that period she was erratic. It wasn't just the muddle over the boxes in the archive or the diary, there were quite a few mistakes around that time and my other secretary, Sarah, had to pick up a lot of the slack. I am very fond of Christine. She made some mistakes, that's all. We all make mistakes.'

Yes, we all make mistakes, Mina.

To everyone there, I looked like the woman she'd described. A sad, lonely creature who relied on her job to fill her empty

life. Unreliable, inefficient, deceitful. Even a little creepy, sneak-
ing around behind her back with a deluded sense of my own
status. I gave one hundred per cent to my job, yet still, it wasn't
enough for her.

And how did Mina come across? This woman who claimed
to be fond of me? A generous, fair employer – a woman prepared to overlook my shortcomings. A person who had
remained loyal to me where other, less understanding employers might have dismissed me long ago.

What fun the press had in writing about me.

Not so much Miss Moneypenny as Mrs Danvers. An isolated, middle-
aged woman, verging on the unstable, who clung to her employer as if
her life depended on it . . .

While Mina Appleton's family has been in court every day, sitting in
the front row of the public gallery and, behind them, the wife of her
driver, David Santini, listening to testimony that, at times, must have
been painful to her, there has been only one sighting of Christine
Butcher's family: her daughter attending court on just one occasion.
Throughout Mina Appleton's evidence her assistant remained impas-
sive, apart from one moment, when she smiled at the description of
herself as the Gatekeeper.

I cannot fault Mina's performance. She bore herself with
humility and kept her voice steady throughout the cross-
examination. The untruths that came from her lips floated up
and away, as lies do in a courtroom, spectres hovering just out
of reach. You know they are there, but unless you can see them,
touch them, they remain intangible, not real. Mr Maitland
knew they were there and tried his best to make others see
them too, but he failed. He didn't stand a chance.

Stripped bare of all the trappings of money and success, with
her simple clothes, her hair pulled back, her skin clear of

make-up, it was near impossible for the jury to believe Mina was capable of the deceit he accused her of. How could this petite, softly spoken woman have ruined the lives of those poor farmers and their families? It was beyond their imaginations to believe she had snatched their land and squirrelled away the profits, and driven an old man to put a gun to his head. Mr Maitland was not able to produce a shred of hard evidence, thanks to me, her secretary, and Dave, her driver.

When Mina returned to the dock she reached for my hand and gave it a squeeze. She must have felt how cold and clammy it was. And when I turned and looked into her eyes I saw then how black her soul was. In that moment I knew she was guilty of all the crimes of which she was accused.

And what did Mina see when she looked back at me? Nothing, I suspect. A blank. No danger at all.

38

'The defence calls Lady Appleton.'

Before Mina had taken the stand, I'd worried her mother would not be a convincing witness, and that she might let Mina down. Now, I hoped she would. That she would prove to be as cold-hearted as Mina had described her. I hoped for the truth. That Mina's mother would stand up and deny she and her daughter had ever been close. That Mina's alibi would be exposed as a lie. I wanted to see her humiliated and exposed, as I had been.

The old lady who walked across the courtroom bore no resemblance to the indulged, selfish woman I had imagined. She did not fit at all with the image I'd carried with me over the years. A mother who, Mina had claimed, always put herself first.

Lady Appleton was approaching ninety, and appeared frail. She walked with two sticks, the deformity of her spine visible beneath the thin brushed cotton of her check shirt. She was not grand, yet she carried herself with dignity in her tailored trousers and flat shoes with their Velcro fastenings. They gave her a common touch – made the jury, I am sure, think of their own grandmothers. Her white hair was neatly cut, two tortoiseshell combs pulling it back from her face – blue eyes like her daughter's, a fine nose, determined mouth.

'Blasted things.'

She may have appeared frail, but her voice carried across the courtroom and sympathy and admiration spread across the faces of everyone there as they watched her do battle with her walking sticks, as she made her way to the stand.

'May I assist you, Lady Appleton?'

'No, I'm perfectly fine, thank you.'

Her testimony was brief – it was painful for her to stand for too long but she refused the offer of a chair.

'My daughter has a very busy life and yet she still finds the time to come and see me. I used to return to England when I could, but in the last few years it's been hard for me to travel. We've always been close, though. Mina has so many commitments – the business, naturally, but her charitable work too – so it isn't easy for her to travel to Geneva and yet she manages it. She always has time for her old mother.

'I chose to move abroad – well, I say chose, but the circumstances were not of my making. Anyway, Switzerland is my home and has been for many years. The air is better there. The climate suits me. My doctor tells me my lung capacity has doubled since settling there.'

She rested a veined hand on her chest, her wedding ring visible. It said so much to the jury, that narrow band of platinum. It spoke of promises broken, of a woman betrayed by a man who was, perhaps, not as honourable as the prosecution would like the jury to believe. Lady Appleton living in exile while her husband carried on his affair with his secretary.

Jenny Haddow looked down from the public gallery. Elegant as always. To me, she looked more suited to the title of Lady Appleton than the plainly dressed woman in the stand.

'Lady Appleton, can you confirm your daughter was with you on the dates she claimed?'

'Yes, I can. It's absolute nonsense to suggest otherwise. She was with me on every one of those visits to Geneva. I'm cross with her secretary for causing such confusion, but then she's never been the most reliable. I have my own girl who looks after my affairs and she would never take the liberties that my daughter's secretary does. Mina won't hear a word against her, despite having admitted to me she's a maddening creature – but then my daughter is too trusting. Loyal to a fault, in fact. The truth is, there is no earthly reason why Mina would seek to cover up the fact that she was visiting me.'

'To be clear, Lady Appleton – you can confirm that your daughter was with you on those dates.'

'Yes, I absolutely can. I have sworn on the Bible to tell the truth, and that is what I am doing. Mina came straight to me from the airport and then left in the evening to travel back to London. She remained with me all day. If she had disappeared to get up to some shenanigans at a bank, I would have known about it. She is a good daughter. She always has been.'

Before she left the stand, I saw Lady Appleton turn to Mina and the look that passed between them sent a chill through me.

As usual, I tried to slip out at the end of the day without being noticed, but Sandra Tisdale caught me.

'Are you all right, Christine?'

I could see she thought I was not – her eyes flicking back and forth over my face, desperate to know what was going on beneath.

'Just need the loo, that's all. I'll see you tomorrow,' I said, turning away, but she took hold of my arm.

'Try not to worry. Everyone understands, you know. The pressures of standing up in court. Juries can be surprisingly sympathetic – particularly to someone like you, who's not used to being in the public eye.' She leaned in closer, her breath hot in my ear. 'We're feeling confident.'

I hurried away to the Ladies, pushed through the door, grateful to see there was no one there, and locked myself in a cubicle. My heart was pounding, and I burrowed into my bag for my pills. I had become dependent on them, relying on them to slow down my heart and wrap me in a blanket of calm so I could carry on. I waited a moment, then flushed the chain, an old-fashioned cistern, so loud it echoed off the tiles. Perhaps that's why I didn't hear the door open and someone come in.

When I opened the cubicle door, Lady Appleton was standing in front of a basin looking at herself in the mirror, her sticks lounging nearby. I was struck by her posture – upright, sturdy – her back ramrod straight. She looked back at me, through the reflection – studying me as I studied her.

'I wondered where that had gone. It's a ruby, you know.' I wasn't sure what she meant, and her eyes flicked with impatience. 'The stone in the brooch you're wearing. Eighteen-carat gold, a seed-pearl surround. Must be valuable now. I take it Mina gave it to you, and you didn't just help yourself.'

There was no point in replying.

'I only ask because it was a gift I gave her. She told me she'd lost it, but there it is. Pinned to your chest. How sweet. Mina's always been a terrible fibber – even as a child. She has a cold little heart, you know.'

I saw her now, the Lady Appleton I'd pictured over the years. Imperious, cold. I remembered the photograph I'd found on Mina's dressing table at Fincham. Mina as a child sitting at her mother's feet, posed in imitation – a teacup held like a cocktail glass, a pencil as a cigarette. Mirror images of each other. Mina must have learned at a very young age that people like her can get away with anything.

Lady Appleton unclipped her bag and took out a lipstick, twisted it up, opened her mouth a fraction and leaned into the mirror. Her pale, bare lips turned red, the colour bleeding into the lines around her mouth. She turned her face one way, then the other, studying the effect.

'Perhaps not,' she said. She reached out her hand. 'Would you fetch me some tissue?' She spoke to me through the mirror, not bothering to turn round, and I could see it didn't cross her mind I might refuse to do as I was told. I ripped some toilet paper from the roll and gave it to her. She rubbed off the lipstick until only a faint purple stain was left. 'I think I went down rather well, don't you?' She examined her face. 'Right. I'm ready for my close-up.' She held out the tissue for me to dispose of, and as I took it, I knocked against her sticks. We both watched them clatter to the floor.

I stooped down and picked them up, though I suspect she was perfectly capable of doing it herself.

'Door?' I held it open for her, and heard it sigh as it closed behind her. I looked at the tissue in my hand, stained red from her lips, and was disgusted with myself.

I'd hoped they would have left by the time I came out, but they were still there. It was quite a circus, Mina and her mother surrounded by journalists. *Lady Appleton, Lady Appleton.* What a game old bird she was. How they loved her. She smiled, lifting her chin and facing the cameras. 'What do you think your husband would have made of this court case, Lady Appleton?'

'My husband, John, was always proud of our daughter. I know he would have stood by her. As I am doing.' She patted Mina's hand.

'What are your plans now, Lady Appleton? Will you stay in the country for the rest of the trial?'

'Of course. My priority is this one,' she said, patting her daughter's hand again, then leaning against her as they walked down the steps. 'A daughter needs her mother in times like this. Now, if you'll excuse us . . .' She gripped her sticks and waved one in front of her in a playful gesture, the journalists and photographers parting before her as she and Mina processed through to join the rest of the family at the kerbside.

I was transfixed by them – Mina helping her mother into the front seat, then taking the back, her husband slipping in beside her. The three grandchildren followed on in a second minicab. I had stepped through a looking-glass into a world where nothing was as I had believed it to be. Including, it seemed, myself.

39

In the final weeks of the trial, witness after witness appeared for the prosecution and defence, but their evidence washed over me. I was present, but not quite there. I do remember Rupert French, Mina's finance director, taking the stand and giving a convincing performance, insisting that he knew nothing of Swiss bank accounts or shell companies. As he laid out the structure of loans made to the various suppliers, in painstaking detail, I looked up at the ceiling and it seemed as if a flurry of white paper floated down, swaddling the courtroom like newly fallen snow, burying me, along with the jury, beneath it.

It must have been Stella who alerted Mina, who then, I imagine, consulted with Douglas Rockwell, who, in turn, had a private word with Sandra Tisdale. I was vulnerable, or fragile, or perhaps *failing* was the word they used. Whichever it was, there was clearly concern that I had lost some of my resilience. Not standing up as well as they'd all hoped.

Stella could not have been more solicitous – taking care of me each evening, making sure I ate properly, comforting me if

I was weepy, and relaying constant messages of encouragement and support from Mina.

I no longer took the train to court. Stella told me, *Mina insists you have a car at your disposal*, so I was picked up each morning, and driven home at the end of the day.

My barrister, Mr Anderson, spoke to Judge Beresford: *The trial has taken its toll on my client*, or something like that, and I was permitted to sit outside the dock, in the well of the court, for the remainder of the trial. Separated from Mina and Dave, I felt myself become invisible. In the well of the court I disappeared from view. Even the judge, in his summing up, got my name wrong. Christine Baker, he said, but then corrected himself with an apology and a look that seemed sincere.

Fear the worst but hope for the best, my barrister said when the time came for the jury to retire and consider their verdicts. He warned me the wait would be stressful, and that I must not stray too far from the court.

'No more than fifteen minutes away, Christine.'

Sandra Tisdale wanted to keep me with her, but I needed to get away and did my best to assure her I was fine. I wanted air, to be outside, and yet, once I was, I didn't know where to go. I remember wandering the streets around the Old Bailey in what felt like ever-decreasing circles, but then I looked up and saw I was standing outside St Paul's, and took sanctuary there.

I sank to my knees, resting my forehead on the pew in front, relishing the feel of the wood, hard against my skull. Around me, I heard the murmur of tourists coming in and out. I closed my eyes in the hope that something might seep into me and give me strength. When my phone rang, I snatched it from my bag with trembling fingers.

'Mum, where are you?' I hadn't seen or heard from Angelica since the day she'd come to court. She was leaving that day to go travelling with friends – a gap year, post university.

'Mum?'

'Yes. I'm here.' My eyes burned with tears.

'Where?' Angelica repeated.

'St Paul's Cathedral. Are you at the airport?'

'Not yet. I wanted to see you before I left, so I came to the court. I thought you'd be there. I'll come to you. Stay where you are.' She sounded frantic. I sat back on the pew and wept. I thought Angelica had given up on me.

I wiped my eyes, stood up and made my way out of the cathedral. I could feel my phone, heavy in my pocket, and decided, if the call came before Angelica arrived, I would ignore it. I switched it off, refusing to give up this moment with my daughter.

The weather forecast that morning was rain in the southeast, and the sky had darkened, poised for a downpour. Not yet, though. I could see the tiniest glimpse of sun behind a cloud. I waited on the steps, searching through the faces in the crowd for Angelica.

And then I saw her running towards me, felt her fall into my arms. I held her tight. Something I'd never expected to do again. Neither of us could speak for a moment, and I stroked her back, like I used to when she was a child.

'I needed to see you before I went away. In case . . .' she said. In case I was found guilty. In case I was sent to prison.

'Where's your rucksack, love?' I suddenly worried she'd changed her mind about going away, because of me.

'Dad and Ursula have it. They're driving me to the airport. When I told them this morning I wanted to see you, they said they'd drive me up to court first, but then you weren't there . . .' She began to cry, and I took her hand and led her around the corner, and we found a bench and sat down.

'So, what time's your flight?'

'Not 'til five.'

'It was good of Dad and Ursula to do that. Dad hates driving in London.'

She smiled. 'God, Mum. He drove around for ages in a right flap, not knowing where to park, and then he put the car in a multistorey miles from the court, so we had to get a cab to the court, and then I got another one here . . .'

'Poor Dad.' I held on to her hand – I didn't want to let it go. 'I'm so happy you're here. Just to see you . . .' Her fingers were trembling and I felt a fury inside me at the pain I'd caused her. 'I am so sorry, Angie,' I said. 'For everything that's happened. For putting you through all this – seeing me in court. I've failed you on every level.'

'Don't, Mum. I couldn't bear not seeing you before I left. I didn't want you to think I was still angry. Or that I didn't care.'

'Sweetheart.' I pulled her closer. 'I wish I could go back and undo it all, but I can't. I love you so much. I know I haven't been very good at showing it – but I love you more than anything.' She rested her head on my shoulder, and I breathed in her smell. 'I remember that perfume,' I said. 'Didn't I bring it back for you after a trip away? You must have been about fourteen. Chanel No. 19?'

'Yes. I only wear it on special occasions.' She took her hand away, but then slipped her fingers between mine, so we were joined together. 'Do you remember I used to keep that scrapbook, Mum?'

'Yes, I remember.'

'You thought I did it because of Mina, didn't you? Because she was famous.'

'Yes, I suppose I did.'

'That wasn't why. I found it the other day, when I came back from court, and I looked through it. I remembered it's what I used to do, when I was little, and you were away or late home from work. When I was missing you. I'd look at pictures of her in the newspapers I'd cut out, and tell myself she was important – that's why you had to be with her and not me. You had a job to do.'

It's what I'd told myself for years. 'I'm so sorry, Angie. I've let you down.'

'No. *She* let *you* down, Mum. Why did you let her treat you like that?'

I looked away in shame.

'I don't know.'

'It's weird, but when I was in court watching you, it was like you had Stockholm Syndrome or something. Like she'd been holding you captive for years, and you'd been brainwashed.'

I laughed. 'Well, I'm free now. And, you know, I'm not scared, Angie. I'm prepared for whatever the jury decide. I want you to know that. So, when you're away – you mustn't worry about me. I'll be fine. I really will.'

'I know she's guilty, Mum, but I want her to get away with it. I don't want you to go to prison.'

I put my arm around her and pulled her closer. 'The strange thing is, love, I don't mind going to prison. It really doesn't frighten me. There have been so many lies told in court. I want the truth now.' I took her face in my hands and kissed her. 'Now, I should put you in a cab back to Dad or he'll be panicking. Will you thank him and Ursula for me?' She nodded. 'I understand, Angie – why you wanted to live with them. Ursula's a kind woman. Dad's much happier and, actually, it helps me to know you have a loving home with them. Never feel bad about that.'

We held hands as we walked to the road, and when I saw a cab, I stuck my fingers in my mouth and whistled for it. It made Angie laugh, and it was a nice way to say our goodbyes. One more hug, one more kiss, and then I waved her off, waiting until the cab was out of sight before switching my phone back on.

I hadn't missed the call – it was another hour before it came. I was eating a sandwich in a café, and my voice was steady when I answered. I felt strangely calm. The truth is, I was looking forward to seeing Mina sent to jail. When I walked back, the threatened rain began to fall, and I put up my umbrella, and emptied my mind.

40

Sandra Tisdale was waiting at the entrance for me, and we walked together to the courtroom. Plastic yellow signs had been set out along the route, warning of the wet, slippery surface, and I remember thinking the cartoon man, with his slapstick tumble, looked so out of place amongst the sculptures and the columns. My shoes squeaked from the wet that squeezed out through their leather soles on to the marble floor. If I was found innocent, this would be the last time I walked those corridors, and I looked around, appreciating their classic style.

Dave was already there, his hands in constant motion, tiny shreds of silver paper from the Polo mints he'd eaten littering the floor. For a moment it was just the two of us and I looked over to him, but he kept his eyes down, and then Mina arrived. I remember she brushed her hand against my back as she passed behind me and took her seat.

My heart raced so much that I pressed my fingers against my wrist, checking my pulse, feeling it beating away at record speed. Mina sat motionless, her slim fingers at rest on the desk in front. There was more colour in her cheeks than usual, but I cannot say whether it was natural or cosmetic. I saw her look up to the public gallery where her family were gathered – her mother, husband and three children.

Mina's two verdicts were read out first – one count of perjury, one of perverting the course of justice – and I closed my eyes and prayed they'd find her guilty. *You will stand or fall together*, the phrase that had been drilled into me, repeated itself over and over in my head. I wanted us to fall.

When I heard them say, *Not guilty on both counts*, I was sickened. My knees buckled. I leaned against the desk, kept my eyes shut. Didn't even hear my own and Dave's verdicts. I didn't need to. *You will stand or fall together.* When I opened my eyes the three defence teams were already shaking hands and congratulating each other. A job well done.

I turned to look at Mr James Maitland, the prosecuting barrister, busying himself, gathering up papers, delaying for as long as possible the moment he'd have to shake hands with the opposing counsel. The prosecution team seemed diminished – as if their gowns were suddenly too big for them.

Waves of gratitude wafted down from the public gallery to the jury. Did they really believe justice had been done? Jenny Haddow was the only one not on her feet and I looked up at her and shook my head – sorry – and hoped she'd understand. And then Mina pulled me towards her into an embrace.

A newspaper described that moment as *the two women clinging to each other*. It wasn't like that. Her eyes sought mine, but I wouldn't let her have them. I had wanted confinement. For us to be locked away. A fresh start, some order imposed. Justice done. But now I found myself cast out into freedom.

'A good result. Well done. I hope you're going to celebrate.' My barrister and solicitor shook my hand, beaming with congratulations, though surely they noticed there was no one there for me to celebrate with. I suspect it made them uneasy – worried that they might be obliged to drink a glass of fizz with me.

'Later, perhaps. All I want now is to go home and sleep. Thank you,' I said, as if they had offered to whisk me off and toast our victory with champagne. I felt their relief as they left me and said goodbye.

I stepped outside, sheltering in the portico from the rain, to wait for my car. Mina swept past, cocooned within her family, Andy holding an umbrella over her. I watched as photographers and journalists crowded around them. She gave them what they wanted. A few choice phrases – ... *time with my family ... the support of good friends ... maybe a glass or two of champagne* ... The Appleton clan then piled into their cars, water spraying up from the road as they sped away.

I stayed where I was, unnoticed by Dave as he ran down to the kerbside and flagged a taxi. He turned and beckoned to his wife, opened the cab door, then scooted in after her, and I kept my eyes on their silhouetted heads in the back window until they were out of sight. They must have been happy and relieved. Poor things. They had no clue Dave's heart was about to give up on them.

I stood there alone. It was raining hard now, and I'd left my umbrella somewhere. I wondered whether there was a lost property office at the Old Bailey, and if my umbrella would be added to the pile of forgotten items there, and I imagined myself joining it, curling up on a shelf, waiting for someone to come and retrieve me.

I made my way down the steps, and walked along the road, searching for my car. Perhaps the rain had delayed it. I wasn't sure who to call – the car had always just been there – organized *for* me, not *by* me. I tried Stella Parker, but her phone went straight to voicemail. I waited for half an hour, until I accepted that a car would no longer be at my disposal. It began to gnaw at me then – a disgusting self-pity that chewed on my gut and swallowed down what little was left of my self-respect.

I retreated into a doorway, crouching to change my shoes, relieved to take off my heels. When I tried to lace up my trainers, though, the loop kept slithering away. It seemed I was incapable of even that small thing. I wanted someone to scoop me up, deliver me into a car and drive me home, then put me to bed and sit with me until I fell asleep.

My phone buzzed in my bag, and I saw I'd missed a text from Mike, another from Angelica, both of them happy for me, and I fumbled back replies – *Relieved. Off to celebrate with my legal team, xxx*, then switched it off. I could have hailed my own taxi, but the effort it would have taken – to raise my hand, tell the driver where I wanted to go, reach into my bag for my purse and pay him – felt too much. I set off on foot to Euston, dumping my smart shoes – specially bought for the trial, one hundred and fifty pounds' worth – in a bin on the way. I must have looked a sight – the rain plastering my hair to my scalp, soaking through my clothes. Yet it was a relief too, cooling my hot skin.

When I finally made it on to the train, I closed my eyes and pretended to sleep, avoiding the eyes of my fellow passengers – not that any of them would have guessed who I was, or where I'd come from. The rough cloth of the seat irritated my skin through my damp clothes, and I couldn't wait to get home and peel off my outer layers.

I closed the front door behind me and stood for a moment. The cat was mewing outside the back door, and I walked through and let him in. He was pleased to see me, running in as he always did. I put down a bowl of food, filled another with milk.

I remember little of the first twenty-four hours after the trial – it is more a feeling I still hold inside me. I do remember stripping off my wet clothes and standing naked in front of the hall mirror, and how revolted I was by the sight of myself. There were red, scabbed patches on my skin, and I clawed at my neck, my wrists, the inside of my elbows. The more I attacked myself, the more those thirsty mouths seemed to open up on my skin – parched and screaming for relief.

I remember the cat brushing up against the back of my legs, then running to the stairs, waiting for me to follow him up, but it was the pills on my bedside that drew me up there. I wanted to disappear into sleep. When I got into bed, his purring and craving for affection only irritated me, and I kicked him off. I took four pills, closed my eyes and waited for release.

I was woken by the sound of the dustmen outside, and knew it was Thursday morning. I'd slept for a long time, but I didn't feel refreshed. Downstairs I found my bag and switched on my phone, sitting on the bottom stair as I waited for it to come to life. No one had tried to reach me. Not a single text or missed call. A wave of misery swept through me. Hard on its heels, that bite of self-loathing.

I smelled it then, a stench that turned my stomach. For a moment I wondered if it came from me, but eventually I realized it was the cat. It must have been crying for hours, to be let out. He'd dirtied himself. There were faeces on the mat by the back door, urine on the floor, and I remember thinking, how quickly things fall apart. It wasn't his fault but still, I punished him. I rattled his bowl and he came running out from wherever he'd been hiding. I grabbed the scruff of his neck and rubbed his face in his mess, opened the back door and threw him out. I stood at the window and watched him scurry off into the dark. He never came back, and I can't say I blame him.

I was glad there was no one to witness my decline in the following weeks. I allowed my home, my body, my mind to deteriorate into squalor, a thick fog descending around me, until I was unable to see the path ahead, and too frightened to look back.

It's strange to recall it now, but it was Mina who guided me out of the darkness. A few words she wrote, in a note she sent to me after the trial. *A change of scene would do you good, Christine.* She was right. A change of scene was what I needed. And so I came to The Laurels.

41

And here I am. Sitting in my usual chair, with a cup of tea, looking out at the gardens. Quite content. The night is clear, the moon bright, so I can see beyond the silver birch trees, planted to shield my neighbour from prying eyes. From here, I have a bird's-eye view, particularly now, in the winter. I put down my cup, pick up my binoculars, and notice a light on in the pink room – the bedroom I used to sleep in, when I worked late at Minerva. *Christine's bedroom*, they used to call it. Or maybe it was just Margaret. Yes, I spend a lot of time at the window, just sitting, watching, waiting.

When I first walked through the front door at The Laurels, I can't say I was bowled over. It's not exactly cosy. Like so many rental properties, it lacks the personal touch, though I've done my best to make it feel like home. I have not met the owners – they live abroad – but I am sure they will receive good reports of me from the letting agency. I am a good tenant. Quiet, tidy, prepared to pay a little more for my privacy. My landlords may be strangers to me, but I have a quiet admiration for them. I know them to be stubborn, principled even, and I like them for that. It is good to know there are people out there who are prepared to say no to Mina Appleton. They refused to sell any of their land, and that has allowed me the space to roam freely.

Looking back, those early days at The Laurels seem like a dream – suspended between the past and the present. I drifted from room to room, not knowing where, or how, to settle. I needed to establish a routine, and so I began to rise early and take a walk before breakfast. I have always loved that time of day. A quiet space between home and work. At The Laurels, my early-morning walks restore me, help clear my head after sleepless nights. I refuse to take any more pills, but it hasn't been easy to wean myself off them.

Being so close to Minerva has inevitably stirred up memories. The sound of the clock on the mantelpiece in the study, the smell of Mina's perfume, the taste of whisky – just the thought of these things leaves me sickened. I am haunted too by that sound of my wet shoes on the marble corridors of the Old Bailey, and the verdict. They were wrong. Mina Appleton is not innocent, but then, neither am I. And though I am no longer dependent on prescription pills, I still suffer an addiction of sorts.

I brought with me my mementos from my days at Appleton's. I keep them in a cake-tin Mina once gave me, and I look through them more than is, perhaps, healthy. Christmas and birthday cards she sent, notes she wrote, even her very first, offering me the job. *I do hope you say yes. Very best wishes, M.* Some are torn from pads, others on Post-it notes – scraps of hurried words signed off with the flourish of an *M* and, occasionally, a kiss. Amongst them is the letter of condolence after my father died, still folded in its envelope.

Dearest Christine,

I will never forget the strength and loyalty you showed me during a time of such heartbreak. In you, your father had a

daughter he could be proud of. I am sure he would have been
in no doubt of your devotion to him over the years.
*   Do not blame yourself for not being with him when he*
died. He would not have needed to see you, for I am sure
you were a constant presence in his heart, as he was in
yours. You were there in spirit, dear Christine. With him
at the end.

With all my love, Mina xxxx

I would like to believe those sentiments were genuine, but the
truth is, I wrote that letter to myself. It was one I would have
liked to have received from Mina. Still, the act of writing it out
in her elaborate hand, and then reading it back, gave me some
comfort at the time.

Mina is known for her cards and thoughtful notes. It is one
of the things people admire in her. How Mina Appleton always
remembers the little things. Her way of making people feel better about themselves in a few, carefully chosen words. Words
that were often mine. I wrote so many letters on Mina's behalf
over the years, why not send one to myself? When Dad died, I
received a text from her. *Thinking of you, M xx.* I remember
being grateful for the two kisses.

The last letter I received from Mina was after the trial and,
when I read it, I had no doubt every word was hers. I recognized her handwriting on the envelope as soon as it landed on
my doormat. It took several readings before I understood what
it meant, and, when I did, I thought, this is not a letter I would
have allowed to go out – not without some fine-tuning first. It
lacked finesse.

That letter bears the signs of my fury – sticky tape criss-
crossing the joins where I pieced it back together, having ripped
it to tiny shreds.

Dear Christine,

I have decided to take a back seat from Appleton's, for the time being. Consequently, I will not be needing your services for the foreseeable future. I advise you to take yourself off on a well-earned holiday. I am certain a change of scene would do you good, Christine.

In appreciation of your years of service, I have arranged for a one-off payment into your account which, I am sure you will agree, should be more than sufficient for you to take as long as you like to consider your future. I wish you well with it.

Kind regards,
Mina

The sum was, indeed, more than sufficient – generous, even. If I was careful, I might never need to work again, though that was not a life I could bear to contemplate. I tore up the letter in anger – a flash of strength that drained away in seconds, leaving a dark hole where my future had once been. I thought of John Fraser, and the despair that had overtaken him – how death might be a relief for me too.

I am still wounded by the missing parts of that letter. The words that aren't there. No w*ith love,* or *fondest regards.* Not even a *thank you.* I have been severed, no doubt about that, yet now I am able to see my severance as a kind of freedom. To come and go as I please, to keep my own hours, no longer confined by the demands of another.

The fence that used to separate The Laurels from Minerva is no more. It has fallen into a terrible state of disrepair. Not something I will trouble my landlord with, though. It was a feeble construction anyway. These days, I need only step over it to extend my walks. Twice daily now. I've added a late-night stroll to my routine. I find it helps me sleep, if I stretch my legs before bed.

42

This morning I have struck gold. A photograph of Mina Appleton on the inside page of a broadsheet. She is at a fundraising event and stands right next to the Minister for Health. Their shoulders are touching and Mina's head is cocked to one side. She looks coquettish, which, when you think about it, is rather grotesque for a woman her age. It seems she's been invited to join a government campaign to improve the diet of our nation's children. It is the first real evidence I have found of her intention to thrust herself back into public life.

For a brief period, after the trial, she almost disappeared from the papers. I picked her up in a couple of diary columns – no photos, only her name. Her television show is still off air, but her agent is no doubt beavering away behind the scenes to get *Mina at Home* back on our screens. She will have been advised to take a softly-softly approach, I imagine. It would not look good if Mina bounced back too quickly. After all, there are a few cynical folk out there – Mr Ed Brooks of the *Business Times* amongst them – who do not believe Mina Appleton is innocent of the crimes of which she was acquitted. They have no proof, though, and I am not yet ready to speak out.

As I cut around her photograph and paste her on to the page, I see her slinking back as if she has never been away. As if everything will be forgotten and re-versioned to suit her new manifestation. Not so much a businesswoman now, more a philanthropist. It wouldn't surprise me, looking at this photograph, if she has her eye on a career in politics too. How cosy she seems, snuggling up beside a government minister. Not a member of the cabinet, but still he'll do for now, she'll be thinking. I know the signs when Mina is feeling confident. I see it in that cock of her head, and I sense it too when I venture out beyond the confines of The Laurels and walk through the silver birch trees to look out towards Minerva. I can smell it in the air. Entitlement. Complacency.

She has allowed her security to become lax. There was a time when she had three men patrolling the grounds, but now there is only one, and he's a lazy so-and-so. He takes himself off to the summer house between two and four in the morning to have a sleep. I've seen him, zonked out, earbuds in, absolutely useless – deaf to the sound of someone prowling around outside. There are still cameras up on the perimeter wall, and I suppose they might catch an intruder ignorant of their location. The alarm no longer works; it has been a week since I snipped the wire and nobody seems to have noticed. Mice have always been a problem at Minerva. It won't be the first time one has chewed through a cable. In my time, I made sure the system was tested on a regular basis, but I'm not there any more to call up the security company – *as a matter of urgency* – and get it fixed within the day.

Poor Margaret must be tearing her hair out. I am pleased to see there's no change to her routine. Every other Sunday off, and on the weekends she works there are the usual guests to cater for, though, I've noted, not as many as there once were. Still, it is early days – only two months have passed since the trial. Mina is just getting into her stride. Softly-softly.

She had a small gathering last Sunday. I heard the cars arrive at twelve, and it wasn't difficult for me to conjure up the scene in my mind. On arrival, the guests would be taken through for drinks in the sunroom. At one, lunch would be served in the dining room, and then, at three, Margaret would take them through for coffee in the drawing room. At three thirty, I went out for a walk – keeping to my side of the silver birches – curious to see whether my predictions were correct.

They were. It was like clockwork. At three forty-five, I heard voices through the trees. Mina, as I knew she would, was giving her guests the usual post-lunch tour of the grounds. She laughed, at one point, and the sound of it shot through the trees, right at me. That laugh. I'd never realized before just how piercing it is. It set my teeth on edge, and made me retreat, as quickly as I could, back to the quiet of The Laurels.

So, yes, I am familiar with the routine at Minerva, though it has taken some adjustment to get used to seeing a new driver behind the wheel of Mina's car. Poor Dave is still critically ill in hospital, so I shouldn't have been surprised to discover he had been replaced. And yet, I was. Since then, I have made a point of listening out for the car leaving in the morning and returning in the evening.

I was surprised to discover Mina hadn't changed the password for her computer, but then I am not there to look after the little things any more. I keep abreast of her diary from my laptop, logging in and watching appointments appear, and disappear. Over the past few weeks, I see there have been trips to the theatre, lunches, meetings with her agent, one with her publisher, still the regular monthlies at The Haven, and now with the new charity, too. No television work, though, and I imagine how she must miss being in front of a camera – still, it might give her some sense of what it feels like to disappear from view.

It was inevitable that I, like Dave, would be replaced, and I am constantly on the lookout for the new girl. Once or twice I think I have heard her voice, in the gardens. She sounds so young – yet perhaps she is the age I was when I first started working for Mina. I thought I saw her once, standing in the window of the pink bedroom. She was looking out through the trees, towards The Laurels. It took me years to earn that privilege, yet there she was, within weeks, making herself at home. My hands shook as I picked up the binoculars.

When I looked through them, there was no one there. I had imagined it. It's happened several times since then, and I understand, now, that it is me I see. The memory of being there, in that time, playing back to me, over and over.

It's nearly lunchtime. Time for a break. When I hear Mina's car driving off and the hum of the gates closing behind it, I decide to take advantage of her absence and go for a stroll in the gardens. And this is when I set eyes on my replacement. Instead of the resentment and envy I expected to feel, there is only pity. There she is. Like a little bird, perched on the bench outside the kitchen door, eating a sandwich she's obviously brought in from home. Beside her, a sandwich-sized Tupperware box. I stay for some time, screened by the pleached hornbeams that run along that stretch of garden, watching her. She has no idea I am here, yet she seems nervous. If I clap my hands, I am sure she will fly away. This girl, surely, cannot be the one to fill my shoes. Even with Sarah muddling along in the office, Mina needs someone more capable to take over from me. This snip of a girl is no more than twenty – far too inexperienced. In fact, I wouldn't be at all surprised to discover she's a temp from the agency we used to use.

Note to self. Phone agency and find out.

43

It has started to rain and I watch it come down, listen to it pour from the guttering, enjoying the cosy feeling of being tucked up safe inside, at my desk. I have set it up nicely, with everything needed to run an efficient office. A landline, my laptop, stationery. I enjoyed choosing that, it's always been an indulgence of mine – decent pens, fine paper. Once a secretary, always a secretary. As I look around my study, I realize it is not unlike the one at Minerva. Business, cloaked in domesticity. This morning, I found another gem.

Mina Appleton signs six-figure sum for the rights to her memoir.

The idea of Mina writing her own memoir seems so absurd, it almost makes me smile. The written word has never been her strong point, and I doubt the temp will be much help in that department.

I close the curtains and settle back down at my desk. Evening is drawing in and, before I finish for the day, I turn my attention to a task I have been putting off. I run my finger down my to-do list. *Check bank accounts.* She will have changed those passwords, I am sure, and, if she has, I'm wondering if I have the courage to call the bank in the morning. I've written myself out a few sentences, so when I do, I won't falter. *Yes, I know we've only just changed them, but what with everything that's been going on, Mina's become very mindful of her security. We don't want to take any risks. I'm afraid I'll probably have to bother you again, in the next few days. You really are very patient with us, Mr Oakshott.* I type in the customer number – that will not have changed – take a breath, and then put in the four-digit password. The page opens, and a knot of resentment tightens in my stomach. There would have been some satisfaction if I had been locked out. At least then I would have known she considered me a risk. The kind of person who would abuse a position of trust. Instead it turns out that she hasn't given me a second thought. She believes I'm harmless, and the insult takes the edge off the pleasure of having access to her bank accounts. I try to look on the bright side. At least I am still able to enjoy the privilege of being Mina Appleton's number-one PA, even if I am no longer employed as such. She trusts me. I strike the phone call to the bank from tomorrow's to-do list, and get to work.

I run through her personal accounts, re-familiarizing myself with the standing orders. Here is Stella Parker. How well she did with all that extra time spent with me during the trial – her payments went up considerably. I wonder how she'd feel if they suddenly stopped, and for a moment I think about cutting her off, but then she is just another employee. She was only doing her job.

I am surprised to see my name on Mina's personal bank statement. I assumed the money paid to me came from Appleton's, but no, there I am. Perhaps Mina wants to keep it secret. Dave's name is there too, but she hasn't been fair. He has been paid less than me, and I am tempted to correct the injustice by sending him another substantial sum. It is the least Mina can do. I cannot risk it yet, though.

The payments I am most interested in, however, are those to

Elizabeth Appleton. Lady Appleton. Mina's mother. I used to feel aggrieved on Mina's behalf that she paid so much money into her mother's account each month. I knew Lord Appleton had given his ex-wife a substantial allowance when he was alive, and that he'd left her a large sum and property in his will. Mina always shrugged it off. *Mummy has expensive tastes. She's always been a terribly vain woman.* I suspect that, at least, was true. It must have taken some effort for Lady Appleton to look so dreary and harmless in court.

I scroll down, tracking the payments, and notice how they went up before the trial, and then again, right after. Considerably so. Elizabeth Appleton's share, no doubt, of the profit – or perhaps simply payment for playing such a convincing role at the trial. I suspect both are true. It is tempting to stop them, but the bank would alert Mina with a text and that wouldn't do. I log off and feel a familiar glow, recognizing it as the feeling I used to have at the end of a satisfying day at work.

I make myself some supper – humble tinned fare, from the hoard I brought with me. My opportunity to shop for fresh produce is limited; I have to wait until I can be sure Mina is out, then nip off in my car to stock up. Sometimes I am forced to go late at night, driving miles to the superstore, open twenty-four hours. Not Appleton's. I rather enjoy bringing enemy brands into my kitchen.

I settle down in the sitting room to telephone Angelica. The last picture she sent me is of her and two girlfriends, standing on a white beach, turquoise sea behind them, smiling. It looks like paradise. I don't expect her to pick up, and when I hear her voice it takes my breath away.

'Mum, how are you?' I hear music in the background.

'I'm really well, darling. Are you still in Sydney?' I look at the picture of her on my phone, smiling, happy, getting on with her life.

'Yes, our last night here. We're driving down the coast tomorrow.' She has to shout above the noise. Farewell drinks in a bar, and then tomorrow she and her friends will set off in the camper van they have bought.

'Exciting. Well, I just wanted to say goodbye.'

'What?'

It is hard for her to hear me.

'I just wanted to say goodbye, love. Before you set off. Have a wonderful time. That's all I wanted to say . . .' It is all I want to say.

'Thanks, Mum. How's the new job going?' She thinks I am working for a small firm in Hertfordshire. It's only a white lie. I am working. I am in Hertfordshire. And I want her to think I am busy. She knows I'm at my happiest when I'm busy.

'Busy. That's partly why I'm calling. I'm not sure when I'll next get the chance.'

'Well, as long as you're enjoying it, Mum. Listen, I'd better go. I'll text you when we get to Melbourne. Love you.' She is in a rush to get back to her friends. I'm glad. That is how it should be. Perhaps I have not been a complete failure as a mother, after all.

'Have a wonderful time. Goodbye, my darling. I love you.' I didn't tell her I missed her, because it wouldn't have been true. I love Angelica more than I have loved anyone, but I don't miss her and I take comfort in knowing she doesn't miss me either. My daughter and I got used to living without each other years ago.

I hear the sound of Mina's car pulling into the drive. I check the time, one a.m., and then look out at the night. The conditions are perfect for a walk. It has rained all day and the ground will be soft underfoot.

I close the back door and step outside. There is still a light drizzle, and I raise my face up to it, then take a torch from my pocket and make my way through the garden, shining the beam at my feet as I step on the damp grass, and then over the fence. On through the silver birches until I am on the other side and can see the gardens of Minerva.

I switch off the torch, keeping to the edges of the trees, and look across the lawns to the house. The curtains are drawn but there are lights on in two of the rooms: the study and the kitchen. The security man doesn't like the rain and has retreated to the summer house, as I was confident he would. Still, I am careful as I walk to my usual bench with its uninterrupted view of the house. For a while I am content to sit, breathing in the damp air. The light goes off in the study and, a short while later, the kitchen too. I wait and watch the dozing house open an eye upstairs.

I get up from my bench and approach it, avoiding the shingle paths, the sound of my footsteps absorbed by the wet grass. Round to Mina's window, and then I look up. It still feels strange to think of her on the other side, cleaning her face, getting ready for bed, no idea that I am down here. It still feels strange, even though this is not the first time I have stood beneath her window, hiding in the shadows of the magnolia tree.

She is alone in the house. Margaret has left for the evening, and the temp went at lunchtime. It was her last day. An inexperienced girl, I discovered, when I chatted to the agency earlier. *She was fine*, I told them, and made all sorts of encouraging noises, not wanting to be unfair, *but we won't be needing her after today. Why doesn't she leave at lunchtime? It is Friday, after all.* Mina has been out since late morning and when Monday comes around, the absence of her temp will be the last thing on her mind.

It is three a.m. when she finally switches off her light. I imagine she must be tired. Her driver dropped her off at one, then she sat for two hours in the study – working on her memoir, perhaps. Then off to the kitchen and, finally, up to bed.

It's bedtime for me too. I turn to head back to The Laurels. As I reach the silver birches I hear the door of the summer house open and turn to see the security man emerge. He shines his torch across the lawns, then begins his circuit of the gardens. I can see his heart isn't in it. Always taking the same route, oblivious to me as I make my way back through the woods, the ground nice and damp, no dry twigs to snap underfoot.

44

Monday morning and I am up and ready, butterflies in my stomach at the thought of the day ahead. I check myself in the mirror. My face is clean of make-up, no sign on my skin of eczema, and my hair, at last, returning to its natural colour, silver streaks giving it a sheen I rather like. Distinguished and elegant. I twist it up into a clip, not unlike the way Jenny Haddow wore her hair.

As I walk across the lawn, my heels sink into the turf. I had wondered about wearing flats, but wanted to look my best for the first day, and settled on an elegant court shoe. I wipe off the mud and dewy grass, then turn the handle of the French doors, hoping Margaret has remembered to leave them unlocked.

When I enter the study I recognize that same prickle of energy I felt when I walked into Minerva for the first time. Everything looks so familiar, and yet I feel as if I'm seeing it for the first time. I take a moment to look around before settling down at the desk.

I am pleased to see the old-fashioned desk diary is still there. I open it to today's date. Nothing until lunchtime. That tallies with the office diary I checked this morning. *Paul Green.* He's taking her to lunch, by the looks of it. The driver – Keith, I see he is called – is due to pick Mina up at eleven. I look through the days ahead, trying not to be distracted by the temp's handwriting or the fact she's used blue biro instead of the black fountain pen I preferred.

Next to the telephone is a neatly stacked pile of papers and I flick through and find the contract with the publisher for her memoir. She is supposed to deliver a draft by the end of the year and I wonder how she's getting on with it – there's no sign of progress amongst the pile on the desk. I open the drawer and take out her laptop, then close my eyes as I tap in the password and when I open them I see I am in. She hasn't thought to change that either. How sloppy.

I am still at the desk when I hear the door open behind me an hour or so later. I turn around and the look on her face has been worth the wait. She is dressed, make-up on, her familiar perfume floating towards me but, like the house itself, I feel as if I am seeing her for the first time. She is almost fifteen years my senior, and yet anyone walking in now would assume I was the elder. It's uncanny, the way I seem to have overtaken her. Perhaps it has something to do with all the minutes and hours I have found, and saved, for her over the years. All that time I conjured up. I have aged while Mina appears to have stayed the same. Petite, brunette, youthful.

And yet, when I look closely I see she is a cheat. There is a smoothness to her skin, and a sheen I once saw as a healthy glow but now recognize as the result of too much interference in the natural process of ageing. It makes me think of a waxwork.

It has been a long time since we have been together and I give her a moment to gather herself. She looks tired and I smile.

'Coffee?'

45

'Margaret?' She takes a step back, her hand still on the door, and calls for her again. I watch her face as she realizes there's no one there to answer.

'Margaret's having the day off. I can get you coffee. No trouble.' I smile, wanting to put her at ease, but she really is agitated.

'What the hell do you think you're doing? Where's Becky?'

'Becky? The temp?' I stay calm, though the way she raised her voice is an affront. 'She finished on Friday. I telephoned the agency to let them know we wouldn't be needing her any more.'

She doesn't like me sitting in her chair, I can see. Her eyes are darting all over the place, no doubt wondering whether I've been having a snoop.

'Why don't you close the door and sit down,' I say, and something in my tone makes her do as I say. At least, she closes the door, but then looks around, wondering where she should sit. Expecting me, no doubt, to vacate her chair. I don't; instead I nod towards the chair I used to sit in.

She looks at me, her eyes scampering over my face, my hair, my clothes. Even my shoes seem to interest her.

'You don't look well, Christine,' she says at last.

'Don't I? I've never felt better. You were right, Mina, a change of scene has done me the power of good.' She's curious about my outfit. I knew it would surprise her. 'Don't you like it? I spent a long time deciding what to wear.' Perhaps that's what bothers her. The pale pink silk blouse with tiny gold buttons. Identical to one she used to wear. The grey suit with white stitching – an old favourite, too. Armani. No, she won't like me in Armani. The shoes, too, are similar to the standbys she used to keep in the office. Numerous pairs, in various colours. She is trying hard to hide her anger, but I see it there, beneath the surface. She crosses her legs and smiles at me.

'Forgive me, Christine. It took me by surprise, walking in and finding you here.' I smile back at her. 'How are you? Really,' she asks, as if she cares. She is buying time. She thinks her driver will be here soon to pick her up.

'Fine, thank you, Mina, though I must say, you look rather tired.'

'Yes, I am. I got in late last night. And actually I have a busy day ahead, so . . . why don't we have a quick coffee, catch up, and then I can arrange for a car to take you home.'

'You *were* late, weren't you? It was after midnight when you were dropped off. And you stayed up working in the study for a while before going upstairs. It must have been after three by the time you finally turned your light out. So, I'm not surprised you're tired this morning. Did you take a pill? They used to leave me feeling rather sluggish too.'

I sense the cold finger running down her spine as she realizes I have been watching her. She opens her mouth to speak, but all I need do is raise a finger to my lips, and she closes it again.

'Do you remember my barrister? Mr Anderson? He was very good. You chose well for me. "*The pursuit of self-interest is all too apparent in the age we live in."* Do you remember his closing speech in my defence? I do.

' *"How easy then to forget there are people among us who live their lives without putting themselves first. Christine Butcher is one of those people. She is an ordinary woman from a modest background who, with quiet humility, conducts her life in an exemplary way. It is a tragedy . . . a tragedy that such a decent, kind woman has found herself in this court. That is a perversion of justice." '*

She takes a breath to interrupt, but I shake my head and she swallows. I go on:

' *"If only there were more Christine Butchers in the world. She is a decent woman who has found herself at the centre of a storm of accusations and false allegations, simply for doing her job."* It really wasn't fair of you, Mina, to put me in that position. You exploited my loyalty.'

I watch her closely. She wets her lips. Her mouth is dry. She is waiting for me to tell her what I want, but I remember the power of silence. How she'd use it to make people, myself included, attempt to fill it, jabbering away, making fools of ourselves, while she sat and watched. I say nothing, instead I look her up and down, in the way she did me when she first saw me this morning. She is, perhaps, not frightened yet, but unnerved at least.

Both of us listen to the clock ticking away, the seconds and minutes, counting down the silence. She turns her head to check the time. And then I see it. Her fear. I have seen it once before, but not like this. I wonder, if I go over to her and lean down, will I smell it on her breath, that same acidic tang I smelled before?

Perhaps she is frightened that I will do to her what I have done to the clock face. Cover it, bind it with tape. It's a possibility, I suppose.

'It must be around ten thirty,' I say. 'I can tell by the way the shadows fall in the room, although it's a bit gloomy today so, ten thirty or thereabouts. It's not important. Time. You mustn't be a slave to it. I'm not, any more. I've given up wearing a watch. It's so liberating. Of course, it's different for you, isn't it? You've never really had to worry about time. I always made sure you had plenty of it.' Is she scared that, now, hers is running out? I smile and walk over to her and hold out my hand. 'I'd better take that. You know how careless you are with them.' She hesitates, but only for a moment, then gives me her phone. She thought I couldn't see her elegant fingers fidgeting around in her pocket, trying to call for help. When I check, I see she failed, her hand not steady enough. I change the password. Her phone is useless to her now.

'Now. How about that coffee?' I say.

'How did you get in?'

I am struck again by the tone she uses – imperious, indignant. Unwise. I ignore her question and put her phone in my pocket.

'I've put an out-of-office on your emails and cancelled your lunch. I told them we'd call later in the week to rearrange. Let's have coffee in the kitchen. It'll be warmer there.' I notice she has to use both hands to push herself up from the chair. Yes, her hands are trembling.

'Where is Margaret?' she asks again and I wonder whether she is worried for her housekeeper's safety, or whether it is herself she's thinking of. The latter, no doubt.

'She's at home, I expect. We spoke last night. She was very relieved to hear I was coming back. You know how she hates change. To be honest with you, she thought the temp was a wet rag, so she was happy to hear my "extended leave" had come to an end. After you,' I say, and follow her to the door.

I walk behind her as she heads to the kitchen, looking around as I go. Nothing seems to have changed since I was last here. We pass the sunroom and I remember how Dave and I used to sit there having our lunch, looking out at the gardens.

'Did you know Dave was in hospital?' I ask.

She turns her head, and I see the familiar curve of her cheekbone.

'Of course.'

'It was the trial. The strain of having to lie for you in court.'

'Oh, Christine. That's simply not true. Dave's father had a heart attack at exactly the same age. I'm surprised you didn't know that.' I want to slap her. 'It's sad, yes, but nothing to do with the court case.'

'I'll arrange flowers and a note from you. You should let the family know you're thinking of them.'

'That's thoughtful of you, but we've taken care of it already.'

I move in closer, so I am right behind her. She really is too thin. Shoulder blades sliding around beneath her sweater – those devilish wings.

The kitchen is gloomy when we walk in and I switch on the lights and sit down at the table.

'You don't mind making coffee, do you? I have a few calls to make.'

She takes the kettle to the sink and fills it and I keep my eyes on her. I don't trust her. It's sad, that. When you lose trust in someone. I notice how she lingers around the Aga when she places the kettle on the ring. She is cold then. Good. I wonder for a moment whether she even knows where her coffee is kept, but eventually she tears herself away from the Aga and takes the coffee from a cupboard and puts three scoops into the small cafetière. She seems to be making an effort for me – putting sugar in a bowl, finding the silver tongs, her favourite milk jug. She's always had such pretty things, and I notice the fruit knife with the mother-of-pearl handle that I'd first seen in her Notting Hill kitchen. I wonder whether she'll cut up some fruit for us to share.

I take out her phone. Driver – Keith. Here he is.

'Good morning, Keith.' She turns at the sound of my voice and rushes forward, but there is so little of her she stumbles when I put my hand out to stop her. She is as surprised as I am, when I touch her.

'It's Christine Butcher here. Mina's assistant.' He's never heard of me. I put him right. 'Goodness no. I'm not new. Mina and I have worked together for many years – I've been on leave, that's all. Becky was filling in while I was away. Anyway, Keith, just ringing to let you know that Mina has decided to work from home today – sorry not to have called earlier but she's only just told me.' He's already on his way. 'Sorry about that. If I were you, I'd turn round right away and go home, before she changes her mind. You know what she's like.'

How quickly my old, efficient self has returned. That quiet authority. Just hearing my voice, speaking on the phone, makes me wonder how I could ever have doubted my position.

'I look forward to meeting you too. Until then. Bye for now.'

I see her hand is shaking as she pours the boiling water into the cafetière.

'Careful,' I say. 'You don't want to burn yourself.' She carries the tray to the table.

'What is it you want, Christine?'

'What is it you want, Christine?' I echo.

She is so unbelievably vain. As I watch her move around the kitchen, I notice how she looks at herself in every reflective surface she passes – anything chrome and shiny. She can't help herself.

'Do you remember, Mina? When you interviewed me for the job? It was in your kitchen in London. You made me coffee and

I sat at the table and watched you. I was so impressed. I'd never been anywhere like that before – in a room where everything was, well, just so. It was lovely. And you were very kind. You made me feel so welcome and at home. I was terribly nervous, you know, but you put me at ease.'

'I do remember,' she says, and pours the coffee. She hesitates and I see she's forgotten how I take it.

'Milk, no sugar.'

'Of course,' she says. *Of course.* I like the sound of those words in her mouth. She adds milk and passes me a cup. 'Were you nervous, Christine? I didn't notice that, but I remember thinking you were rather reserved, if you don't mind me saying. I liked that about you. I saw it as a kind of integrity. That you didn't gush.' She picks up her coffee and looks at me over the cup. Those blue eyes. I look away. She is trying to charm me.

'Don't you get lonely here?' It's so liberating to be able to ask all the questions I never dared before. All the things I've wondered about over the years. 'I mean, we're not going to hear your husband's key in the door, are we? I saw in your diary that you have friends staying next weekend, so I suppose he'll be here then.'

'We have an arrangement. It suits us both. It's not so unusual. He has his life and I have mine.'

I remember her mother describing her cold little heart.

'An arrangement? Like an employee, I suppose. Disposable. And the children? Do you have an arrangement with them too?'

Her hands rest on the table and I am taken back to court for a moment, remembering how I used to watch her long fingers tapping on her keyboard, or resting in her lap. It calmed me, to see how calm she was. How controlled. Now they twitch, her nails tapping on the table. I find it irritating and I put my hand over hers and still her fingers.

'May I speak, Christine?' she asks, pulling her hand from beneath mine.

'Please do.'

'I was found innocent by the jury and so were you. I am not a criminal, Christine. And nor are you. Neither you, Dave, nor I were found guilty. But what you are doing now is criminal. You have broken into my house. You are holding me against my will.' Her eyes glisten. Are those tears? Certainly she sounds desperate. '"I would trust Christine with my life. With my children's lives too. I am very fond of her – she is someone I trust." I meant every word of it, Christine.'

She's rushed it.

'But you've missed a bit, Mina. You said more. "She started to make a lot of mistakes with little things around the office. Sarah, the other secretary, had to pick up a lot of the slack. It was not unusual for Christine to get things wrong."'

'But surely you understand, I didn't mean that. I was told to say it by Douglas Rockwell. I had no choice. I have always trusted you, Christine – but what you're doing now – it's a mistake. We could pretend it never happened. You're not a criminal. This isn't you.'

Oh, but it is.

46

She is hungry, poor thing. She hasn't had breakfast yet and coffee on an empty stomach has never been good for Mina. Her body is so finely tuned.

I, on the other hand, began my day with tea, toast, a boiled egg and half a grapefruit. I can see she is suffering – light-headed, a niggle at her temples that she's trying to massage away with the tips of her fingers. If she doesn't eat soon, she will begin to feel nauseous. I used to bring a plate of fruit to her desk to keep her blood sugar up, and my fingers itch to pick up her pretty little fruit knife. I don't. Instead, I watch and wait. Then, finally, she gives in.

'Christine, I wonder whether I could make myself some toast? I haven't eaten anything this morning.' She pushes back her chair.

'Oh, let me,' I say, rising to my feet, and walking over to the bread board. She is quick to allow me, assuming, I suppose, that I am still unable to resist the urge to be helpful.

I pull the bread knife from its holder, cut two slices of sourdough, then place them on the toasting rack on the Aga. When the toast is done, I butter it and sprinkle on some salt, just how she likes it, then bring it to the table.

'Thank you, Christine,' she says, taking a bite and wiping a drip of butter from the corner of her mouth with a finger. She takes her time. Chew. Swallow. 'Thank you,' she repeats, almost choking on the words.

Perhaps it is the knife in my hand. It unsettles her. It is only a bread knife – a kitchen utensil. I rest it on my lap, beneath the table, so she can make believe it isn't there. What a topsy-turvy world she has found herself in. Her dependable secretary – a woman she never dreamed would lay a finger on her – sitting in her kitchen with a knife in her hand.

'You're right, Christine. It can be lonely, but work compensates.' Bravo, Mina. I can't help but admire the effort she's making to hide her nerves. She thinks it will be a mistake if she shows weakness. I see it nonetheless, and I hear that coaxing tone she uses when she is trying to win over a stubborn opponent. It has always worked a treat for her with members of the board. Perhaps I should be flattered she's trying it on with me. 'I suspect you understand that more than anyone, Christine. You and I – we are both hard-working professional women. And my children? Perhaps there was an element of self-concern in their presence in court, but I don't blame them for that.'

She waits for me to respond, and I do – with the tap of the knife on the underside of the table. She goes on.

'You know, the children were there in court for you, too. Lottie in particular. She's always been so fond of you. From that very first time. Do you remember? How she came into the kitchen and sat on my lap and listened to us talking. Afterwards, she told me how nice she thought you were. It was one of the reasons I offered you the job. It was important to me that the children liked you.'

'Of course they liked me,' I say. 'I did so much for them when they were young. When you sent them off to boarding school, I was the one who wrote to them. Letters I signed as if you'd sent them. Little parcels, too – things I made at weekends – cakes, biscuits. I covered up for your absences – made them believe you cared about them. You have no idea how much I did for you.' I sound defensive, and I feel the heat rising under my skin, and know she can see it. She shakes her head, and graces me with a sad smile.

'I knew that, Christine. The children thanked me sometimes when I phoned them. Of course it was you they should have been thanking, not me. But you wouldn't have wanted me to tell them, would you? It would have spoiled it, wouldn't it? All the effort you put into keeping it secret. Surely the point was to make them feel loved and cherished, and you succeeded in that. You filled in the gaps of my absences. And yes, I was grateful, but perhaps I didn't show it enough. I'm sorry for that. I know what a difference it made to them, and how conscientious you were.'

I can't help it. Hearing her say this affects me. I have waited a long time to hear those words.

'And I'm sorry too, Christine, for the things I said in court. I had no choice. It was for all of us – you and Dave, as well as for me. We all understood, didn't we? The three of us. We would stand or fall together.'

'You should have told me the truth from the start.'

'But I did.'

'No. You weren't visiting your mother in Geneva.'

'But I was.'

I hold the handle of the knife firm as I bring it out from under the table. No pretending it's not there now. She flinches.

'Lie number one,' I say, and carve a notch into the wood. 'You paid your mother to lie for you in court. Her monthly allowance doubled after she appeared as a witness in your defence. The amount into Elizabeth Appleton's account went up considerably after the trial.'

Tick, tick, tick. She is working out how on earth I could know this. And then she gets it. Of course she does. She trusted me with everything – never gave it a second thought. Why would she? It never occurred to her that I, her secretary, Christine Butcher, might one day be a threat. Now she understands how complacent she has been.

I worked for her for eighteen years, yet she has no idea who I am. I wonder whether she even bothered to read the snippets about me in the papers. *Mina Appleton's secretary cut a lonely figure in court.* When the trial was over, whole paragraphs were devoted to Dave and me. The histories of our lives told in one hundred and fifty words.

The Driver – David Santini: Former security guard David Santini could never have dreamed, when Mina Appleton first sat in the back of his London taxi, that he would one day . . . etc. etc.

The Secretary – Christine Butcher: When police raided the home of Christine Butcher at five a.m. on a Sunday morning, she apparently showed no outrage or fear, as most people would, but instead greeted the officers with a tray of hot beverages . . .

Mrs Butcher stood shoulder to shoulder with her employer throughout the trial . . .

She was always more than just a secretary – trusted with the most intimate details of Mina Appleton's life, from her bank accounts to the welfare of her three children . . .

No, Mina would have skimmed over us, more interested in the double-page spreads about herself – her celebrated career, her triumph at the end.

I can see the knife is really bothering her now. Her pupils

have shrunk to tiny dots. I take out her phone, the edge of my hand brushing against the knife as my thumbs work over the keys. Within seconds, a text comes in. I turn the phone around, so she can read it. It's from her bank. *The regular payment to Elizabeth Appleton from your account ending . . . 165 has been amended as requested.*

'She won't discover her payments have been stopped until next week. But perhaps she has access to those numbered Swiss accounts. Can she just help herself? I don't know how these things work.'

'Oh, Christine. There are no numbered accounts.'

Lie number two. I score another notch in the table.

'You can't stop yourself lying, can you? Even now.'

She watches as I take a piece of paper from my pocket. Seeing the scrappy little square, she seems to dismiss it. Appearances can be deceptive, though, and I smooth out the creases with the heel of my hand. Now she sees what's written on it. A list of names she will recognize as former Appleton's suppliers. Long gone now – casualties of her greed. Next to each name a doodle. I wonder whether she even remembers drawing those creatures – assigning a symbolic animal to each of her doomed suppliers.

'A squirrel, a rabbit, a badger, a fawn, a hedgehog and a weasel.' I run my finger down each one. 'I slept in your old bed-room at Fincham. I saw the china animals on your dressing table. And how you named them all, so carefully: Brownlow, Percival, Simpson, Lancing, Hogarth and McTally. The same names you used for the shell companies. Hardly a coincidence. They were there, all the time, in your head – plucked from your memory.'

She shakes her head, as if she's disappointed. 'Is that it? Your smoking gun? It's a meaningless piece of paper, Christine. There's not even a date on it. Who's to say when it was written?'

I catch a roll of her eyes as she watches me refold the paper and put it back in my pocket.

'It is proof.'

'Of what? Oh, Christine. That's not proof of anything. A list of suppliers and some scribbled drawings – nothing more than doodles.' She uses the voice of reason, but I know how her mind works. She thinks it would be her word against mine and who would believe me? Irrational, troubled, fragile. 'Don't tell me you have the whimsies in your pocket too?' She actually smiles. 'Please. Let's just stop this, now. I can get you help. Come on, let me look after you.' She speaks to me as if I am a child of six.

'If it's so meaningless, then why did you ask me to get rid of it? It was in the box from the archive, amongst the papers you asked me to burn.'

She is still smiling, though now she must wonder – if I kept that scrap, what else did I hold on to?

'I didn't ask you to burn anything, Christine.'

'You asked me to get rid of the boxes, not to burn them, that's true. Your suggestion was that I dump them on my way home. Just as you asked Dave to dump your laptop and other incriminating evidence at a service station.'

The smile slides from her face, and I see utter hatred replace it, and I wonder whether she has ever, really, liked me. I put her phone back in my pocket. I count to fifteen in my head before I speak again.

'I kept a memory stick too. There's plenty of proof on that – from one of the laptops you so carelessly mislaid.'

'I have no idea what you're talking about.' She does, but I say nothing and she can't stop herself falling into the silence. 'You gave it to me. I remember. There was only one memory stick, and you put it in my hand. You told me there weren't any others. I've always trusted you, Christine – I doubt very much you

260

would have lied to me about that.' Even as she says it, I see her uncertainty.

' *"Emails, paperwork – there is always a trail. Even with shell companies. Computers, telephones – their contents would all lead back to you. So you instructed your driver and your secretary to get rid of that evidence."* '

It used to amuse her – the way I could quote back minutes of meetings from memory, pluck telephone numbers from my head, recite pages from her diary going back months and months. She doesn't seem to find my powers of recall entertaining now, though. And I can see, too, she is worrying about what else I might hold in my head. Overheard telephone calls. Meetings I was present at yet ignored.

There I was, at the heart of events, quiet as a mouse.

'Christine, we have worked together for eighteen years. You wouldn't betray me now, would you?' She takes a risk and reaches for my hand. A brief touch of skin against skin. I leave mine beneath hers for a moment – just long enough to feel the sweat on her palm.

'Mina, you know very well how conscientious I am. I wouldn't have been doing my job if I didn't back everything up. We all heard in court how careless you are – forever losing things. I worried you might mislay the memory stick too, so I backed it up on this one.' I open my hand and show it to her, and, once again, she looks at it as if it is some kind of strange insect. 'I thought that, one day, you might need to retrieve something from your missing laptops, so I kept this safe for you. As it turns out, it is me, not you, who has a use for it.'

47

I close my fist around the memory stick and watch her open her mouth to speak. I raise my hand and she stops. It is so much easier than I had anticipated. There is nothing on this memory stick – no hard evidence – but Mina has no idea what I look like when I lie, and I have become expert in deceit. I have learned from the best. She was right in one respect: back then, I would not have dreamed of keeping anything from her. Back then, I was honest to a fault.

'Can I get you some water?' She is pale and I worry she is about to faint. The nail of her thumb scrapes against the skin of her index finger. In a moment, no doubt, she'll start pulling at her hair.

'What do you want, Christine?'

The knife in my hand surely gives her a clue. It's a bread knife, yet lethally sharp. German. Top of the range. Professional. She used one like this on her show. Sometimes even joked about how it could take your finger off. I find it fascinating, watching her. She's trying so hard to work me out. To find out what is going on in my head. She has no idea. Not a clue.

Yet I see her as clearly as I ever did. I have no problem in reading *her*. I've spent a career doing it. Tuning myself in to her every twitch and quiver, a shift in her tone to pick up her moods, responding to her needs. There they go. Her fingers pulling at a few strands of hair until several come away. One sits on her shoulder, the others float to the floor.

Her phone vibrates in my pocket and I take it out and check the screen. *Sarah*. I wondered about Sarah.

'Good morning, Sarah, how are you? It's Christine.'

I hear the surprise in her voice. The blade of the knife glints in my other hand, and Mina shifts in her seat.

'Extended leave, yes. The doctor said it was exhaustion. Anyway, I'm absolutely fine now. Thank you for asking.'

The agency emailed Sarah about the temp. They want confirmation she's no longer needed.

'Becky, yes. I spoke to her myself on Friday. I think she found it all rather daunting – she was quite relieved when I told her.' I watch Mina as I listen to Sarah. 'I'm sorry, Sarah. Mina said she'd talk to you. You know what she's like. She and I spoke about it at least a week ago.' I see Mina tense. She seems to have lost her admiration for dishonesty. 'Anyway, how are you?' I speak to Sarah for the first time as an ally – my co-worker. Two employees on the same side. 'You must be off on maternity leave soon. How are the other two? They must be excited by the idea of a new baby.' She loves talking about her children, but I was never interested before. 'I'm so pleased to hear that. Yes, it's perfect timing. You know, after everything, I wasn't sure I wanted to come back, but Mina talked me round.'

Sarah understands – she knows as well as I how persuasive Mina can be. We stay on the phone for a minute more. She passes on some messages and I tell her Mina wants to work from Minerva for the rest of the week. 'I'd hoped to see you all in the office, but I suppose she's not there as often these days, is she. Would you like to speak to her? She's only upstairs.

I can easily take the phone to her . . . no? I understand. Bye then, speak soon.'

I put down her phone and smile. Mina is discovering just how good I am at shielding her from unwanted intrusion.

'Shall we work from the study?' I say, and stand up. I wait for her to move, then follow, leaving the bread knife behind. In passing, I pick up the fruit knife. It slides easily into my pocket.

We walk along the corridor, and I glance through the window at the end of the hallway and see the sun has come out – the gardens glisten from the weekend of rain. There is a gardener working on the far side and I wonder whether she has seen him too. Whether she has thought about trying to get out there – to ask for help. I am sure she has. I haven't finished with her yet though. She and I have a busy afternoon ahead.

I close the door of the study and watch to see where she goes. Will she sit at the desk? Or perhaps the window seat – my old favourite spot. How comfortable I used to be in that nook.

She goes straight to the desk and sits down. I don't mind – it is still hers, after all. I pull my chair up close.

At last she notices my scrapbook sitting there. It's been there since first thing. Handsome, leather-bound.

'Take a look. I was putting it together for myself – but actually I think it'll be useful for your memoir. A bit of background research. In case you've forgotten anything.'

She pulls it towards her and opens it. A picture of her and her father looks back. *Mina Appleton and her father, Lord John Appleton*, the caption reads. In the background is a smudgy figure that is me, my face circled in red pen. She pushes the scrapbook away. As if she's afraid the pages are dipped in poison – that the merest touch of the paper will be lethal.

'Perhaps you'll look at it later. I've left some empty pages at

the back. I am counting on there being some sensational head-
lines in the coming days.' She goes deathly pale.

'Anyway, while I was waiting for you this morning I took the
liberty of reading what you've written so far and, if you don't
mind my saying, I think your memoir could do with a bit of
editing. Why don't we make a start? You do have a deadline,
after all.' I put her laptop in front of her. 'You know, I think
there'll be a lot of interest when your book comes out. Demands
on your time for interviews. I wouldn't be surprised if someone
snaps up the film rights too.' She isn't in the mood for jokes. I
watch her type in her password. It's rejected. She tries again
then eventually turns to me with a helpless look, and I smile
and reach over to help her. She's always been hopeless with
technology.

While she was still lounging in bed this morning, I was busy
resetting her password and reading her book. She hasn't got
very far with it – two and a half thousand words, and not very
good ones at that. Still, it's only a first draft.

'I typed up a few thoughts.' I pass her the pages I printed out
earlier and watch her read through them. Her memory has
never been as good as mine, and I see I have reminded her of
some things she'd forgotten.

'Why don't you type the corrections in?' She does, and I
remember how surprised I was in court at the speed of her fingers as she typed. How quickly they pitter-pattered over the
keyboard. I stay close enough to watch the words appear on the
screen, making sure there are no typos and making sure, too,
there's no attempt to send out an SOS via email.

'Why have you stopped?' I ask. But I know why. 'Isn't that a
fair description?' I peer at my notes on the desk, as if I don't
already know what they say. 'Have I got something wrong? I am
sure that's how you described Lady Appleton. *My mother is terribly vain*, you told me once. And another time – I think it was

just after your father died – you said: *"We're not close, Christine. My mother's a cold-hearted woman. She's never been there when I've needed her – even as a child."* It's important to give a true picture, don't you think? It's part of what makes you you, isn't it, Mina? Here, let me help.' I nudge her aside and put my hands over hers, our fingers dancing together over the keyboard, reading the words aloud as I type: *I owe much to my mother. Even as a child, I learnt how important it was to always put oneself first. And perhaps I should credit my mother too, with the discovery, so early on, that people like us can get away with anything.* 'There, all yours,' I say, and move aside again.

'I thought it would be a shame too, not to include a description of the whimsies you kept on your dressing table. How you named them all – those little labels you wrote out, in tiny writing. It's that kind of detail that readers lap up.' She carries on, copying from my notes. Whenever she hesitates, I tap the memory stick against my teeth, like I might a pen. Casual, as if I am thinking about the next entry on my to-do list. It works a treat – giddy up and off her fingers go again: *Brownlow, Percival, Simpson, Lancing, Hogarth and McTally.*

I asked Margaret to leave us lunch in the fridge and we eat it at the desk. Dear Margaret, she was so pleased to hear from me yesterday evening. She had no idea I was coming back to work and I told her what I had told Sarah. That I had taken some persuading.

I've been looking forward to this afternoon, and have spent some time preparing for it. I have typed up, and printed out, the phone call I want her to make to her finance director. She reads it through, then puts down the sheet, and I wait for her to pick up the phone, but instead she turns to me and smiles.

'I'm afraid this won't work, Christine.'

48

I feel the power shift between us – slipping away from me to her. That particular smile of hers has always made me feel small. Once I would have looked away, tried to fathom out what it was I had done wrong. It is the smile given to someone who is rather out of their depth. Condescending. That's what it is. I try to keep my face neutral but she has detected a weakness and her confidence returns.

'I no longer have the power to give that instruction. I have agreed to take a back seat at Appleton's, as I thought you were aware. So, as well-meaning as your plan is, it won't work. Rupert French will simply laugh in my face if I put in your request.'

It is such a small thing I've asked of her. The very least she could do. I have written it out with great care – an instruction to pay compensation to the suppliers she ruined. Money into their accounts from Appleton's. I have worked out all the amounts, to the last penny – figures given to me by Mr Ed Brooks. I understand now that a deal has been done. She's relinquished power on the board in exchange for her financial director's compliance in court. I so wanted that money to come from Appleton's itself – for it to be seen as public acknowledgement of their unscrupulous practices. It is disappointing, and yet I manage to return her smile.

'Then you must make the same call to your Swiss bank. That money doesn't belong to you.'

She doesn't move, looks at me incredulously, and when she shakes her head I see it in slow motion – her hair flying out around her shoulders, her eyes closing. That cat-like smile – and then a tiny pout that transforms it to pity. For me. For poor old, stupid Christine.

'I can see you don't understand how these things work, Christine. It's simply not possible for me to carry out transactions with my Swiss bank over the phone. I would have to go there in person. It would mean me travelling to Geneva.' I feel myself flush – my skin, as ever, giving me away. She is right, of course. I don't understand how these things work.

Her eyes flick down to the memory stick in my hand. I am afraid she might see through that too. Understand that there is nothing on it. I put it in my pocket and it clicks against the blade of the fruit knife. As my confidence flags, I watch hers inflate. She picks up the piece of paper again.

'Morning, Rupert . . .' There's a false cheeriness to her voice. 'I've been thinking about our former suppliers. I'm not happy about the way we treated them . . . blah, blah, blah . . .' She screws up my words, and drops them in the bin. 'Really, Christine. Did you seriously think I'd say that? Follow your instructions? It would be a public admission of guilt – that's never going to happen.'

I say nothing, and she looks at me as if I am a half-wit.

'It's business. That's how it works. Yes, I drove those farms out of business – and yes, I bought their land. It was a good deal. It produced a healthy profit. No tax either. That's not illegal – nothing about my business practice was illegal.'

'You lied in court. You perjured yourself. That newspaper wrote the truth.'

She leans towards me and looks into my eyes and I see in hers the shaft of steel grey that cuts through the blue.

'Yes. But then you lied too, didn't you?' She crosses her legs, makes herself comfortable. 'Do you really see yourself as innocent? The poor secretary who was just doing her job? Who on earth do you think you are? Robin fucking Hood?' She thumps her fist down on the desk. 'You have hacked into my personal bank account – God knows how much money you've helped yourself to. So don't pretend this is about you doing the right thing. Just leave. If you go now, I'm prepared to pretend that none of this has happened.'

She swivels round in her chair, so her back is almost, but not quite, towards me. It is what she has always done when I am dismissed – her signal for me to leave the room. I see how she watches my reflection in the window, waiting for me to get up and go.

I stand up and walk to the door, and hear the swoosh of the chair as she turns to watch me. She has no idea of the contempt I feel. For her lack of imagination and her loss of control. I lock the door and take the key, then turn and smile.

'Let's have a drink. It's about that time.' I tap the blade of the fruit knife against a glass, as if I'm about to give a toast.

49

It is dark outside. It could be any time – from four thirty to nine o'clock. She has no idea. It must be disorientating for her, though I have given her a massive clue. Drinks time. Surely, she can work out that it's around six o'clock.

'Christine, just tell me what you want.' She sounds exhausted. I don't reply, instead I pour her a whisky on ice. I am a little tired myself – and stifle a yawn. It's going to be a long night.

I take over her drink, and she swallows back a mouthful. I watch it travel down her unnaturally smooth throat. She looks away, uncomfortable perhaps under my scrutiny, then slumps down into a chair. I take the window seat, kicking off my shoes and curling my feet up under me. I think I see tears in her eyes again, though she tries to hide them, staring down into her glass, swirling the ice around. I must be careful. I was always susceptible to Mina's rare moments of fragility. Especially when she tries to put on a brave face, as she is now. She looks across at me, her blue eyes swimming, yet I don't feel as much pity for her as perhaps I should. Some, but not a lot.

'Aren't you having one?' she asks.

'Thank you, yes, why not?' I don't move, and it takes her a minute to understand that I want her to serve me. When the penny finally drops, she walks, with some dignity, to the cabinet, choosing a crystal glass that matches hers. She fills it with not quite enough ice and much too much whisky. She's trying to get me drunk, but then I notice she pours an equally generous measure for herself. She turns around and comes towards me, holding out my drink, but she doesn't touch her glass against mine, as she used to. She doesn't say 'cheers'. So, I say it for her, and touch mine against hers. I shan't drink a drop, though I doubt she will notice. The fruit knife nestles in my lap and she sits back down.

'I'm sorry, Christine,' she says after a while. Poor Mina, it's all guesswork. She is lost for words, her mind turning over various scenarios. It seems the one she decides on is: keep her talking, keep her engaged. 'I shouldn't have spoken to you like that. You know how I hate it when people swear.' Her blue eyes drill into mine – no sign of tears now. 'I know you're right. About the suppliers. I agree with you. They should be compensated.' She takes another mouthful of whisky. 'I'm sure you and I, between us, could work something out. I do regret not telling you everything at the time, you know. Even if you don't believe me, I need to say it. And it's not just because we're here, now, in these circumstances. I really mean it. There were so many moments during the trial when I wished I'd been open with you. But it was too late by then. I felt trapped. It was a terrible time for all of us, Christine.'

That's not how I remember it.

My feet have gone to sleep, and I uncurl my legs and stretch my toes, then put my shoes back on. She waits until I am still again before continuing.

'It might make sense if you and I were to fly to Geneva together. Why don't you think about it? I'm happy to explain to you how everything works. It's actually not that complicated.'

I notice her eyes flick over my shoulder. The curtains are open, and she can see out into the garden – all those pretty lights twinkling away. It's not those she's interested in though. She is wondering whether the gardener is still out there, and when the security man will turn up. She'll be hoping to see him, patrolling with his torch. I turn and draw the curtains.

'Let me get you another,' I say, jumping up and taking the glass from her, as if we are back in our old roles again. Perhaps she thinks that is what I want. For things to go back to the way they were. I pour her another generous measure.

'Thank you, Christine,' she says, as if we have slipped back in time and are having a drink at the end of a busy working day – she, mistress, me the servant. 'What about you? Won't you have one more?' One more. As if I'm about to leave.

'You know me – better pace myself.'

'So, what do you think? Does that idea appeal? You and I going to Geneva together?'

'Oh dear. It's started to rain again,' I say. I love the sound of the rain on the shingle drive outside. I put my feet back up, not bothering to remove my shoes, and stretch out my legs. I hear her bite into a cube of ice in frustration. I will not be hurried.

I think about what it would be like, to sit by her side again, in first class. I have never been to Geneva and I allow myself to imagine walking with her along the edge of the lake, the air bitterly cold, the sky blue, the sun shimmering on the water. We would stand together and look into the lake's depths. She would see her reflection, and I would be tempted to push her, to watch her drown in her own image. But that's not how I want it to be. So instead I picture us sitting in a café, sunglasses on, drinking strong coffee, squares of chocolate wrapped in gold sitting in our saucers, their edges softening from the heat of our cups.

I blink the image away, and am overwhelmed with the

feeling I need to get out. This house is closing in on me. It is eating me alive. I am too comfortable in this window seat.

I stand up and walk over to the desk, closing the laptop and stacking the papers in a neat pile, putting the pens back into their holder, doing the usual tidy at the end of a working day. She watches me as I switch on her phone. It springs to life, as do her eyes. Alert, looking for an opportunity. There are a few messages waiting, but her out-of-office announcement has kept most callers at bay. Nothing that can't wait. I switch it off again and pick up my bag, feeling her eyes on me as I walk to the door, take the key from my pocket and unlock it.

'Shall we?' I say. She is confused. 'Have a walk around the gardens. For old times' sake.'

'Yes, good idea.' She tries to sound normal, but her words are slurred, and she almost trips in her hurry to escape the room. I reach out to catch her, but she slips past me, into the hallway.

'You'll need a coat,' I call after her as she stumbles towards the front door. I watch her reach for the catch, turn it, pull at the door. It won't open. It was one of the first things on my to-do list this morning. The keys to all the outside doors are tucked safely in my handbag. The house is quite secure. 'Here,' I say, holding her coat open for her. 'Let me help you.' She slips her arms into the sleeves. 'Let's go out the back way,' I say, and follow her through the hallway, along the corridor, towards the kitchen. The bread knife is still on the table where I left it, and I pick it up, before she can, and return it to its holder. She makes a rush for the back door, pushing and pulling at the handle. She should have remembered how thorough I am.

'Here,' I say, holding out her boots. 'It's wet outside.' She leans down to put them on, and I notice she is trembling. I expect her head is swimming too. She will be regretting that third whisky. I added a little something to the bottle – she really shouldn't have been so greedy. I watch her, wondering when the full effects will take hold. *Sedation, muscle relaxation, a reduction in anxiety.* I can't say she seems particularly relaxed. *Be careful not to accept drinks from strangers* – I read that on the internet. Then again, I am not a stranger. But they're right to warn people: Rohypnol is surprisingly easy to get hold of.

Her lips are moving. She is trying to say something. I have to lean in close to hear her.

'Fresh air,' I think she says. There is life in her yet. That mind of hers, ticking away, albeit not at its usual whip-like pace.

I look around for my boots, but they're not there. Someone has thrown them out – or given them to the jumble. She leans against the door like a dog desperate for its walk. I shake my head. She pulls at the handle. But I don't want to muck up my new shoes and, besides, she's bound to try and make a run for it – not that she'd get far. Even so, I don't have the energy to play chase.

'Second thoughts – let's stay in the warm.' Her look of disappointment is a joy.

50

I steer her to a chair in the drawing room and she collapses into it.

'You're freezing,' I say, her little hand like ice in mine. There's a blanket, neatly folded, over the back of a chair and I bring it over to her. As I wrap it around her shoulders, I'm reminded of the shawl she wore in court. 'You've always felt the cold. You need more flesh on your bones.' I rub her hands between mine to warm them up, but her teeth still chatter. She needs brandy, and I open the cabinet and find a bottle. 'This should warm you up.' I press the glass against her lips, hard, until she opens her mouth and swallows it down. 'Another?' She shakes her head and says something I can't make out. Speech is one of the first things to go. It must surprise her – not being heard.

She watches me as I move around the room – switching on side lights, making the place cosy, myself comfortable, flopping down on the sofa and putting my feet up.

'It's been a long day,' I say. 'You must be hungry. Margaret didn't leave supper but I'm happy to make you something. You can have it on a tray in bed. You'd like that, wouldn't you?' She doesn't respond. 'Come on then, let's get you upstairs.' I leave the comfort of the sofa, and help her to her feet, rearranging the blanket around her. She seems determined to try to walk unaided, so I stand back, expecting her to fall. It turns out she is stronger than I thought. A small stagger, but she holds her head high and I admire her for that.

She makes it up the stairs, her hand using the banister for support, and I can see the effort it takes her to hide her weakness from me. As we walk along the corridor, I glance into the pink room. How inviting the bed looks. I am tired too, I would love to lie down and sleep but I need to get her to eat something, and then I still have some work to finish up.

When I turn back she has hurried ahead towards her room. I know she wants to close the door on me, lock it from the inside, but I am too quick for her. My foot is there first, jamming it before she can slam it on me. I lock the door and put the key in my pocket. When I turn around, she is lying on the bed, fully clothed.

'Don't you want to undress?'

She shakes her head and turns on her side, facing into the room, her eyes open. They follow me around as I pick up her clothes from this morning – a job Margaret would have done, had she been in. I bundle them up, ready to take downstairs. I draw the curtains, turn on lamps, shutting out the night. I know she has another mobile hidden away somewhere, and I find it in a drawer of the dressing table and switch it on. A message from Andy, letting her know that he's been approached to do a magazine interview. Naturally, he must ask her permission first. *Absolutely, go ahead*, I text back. I imagine he'll be much in demand over the next few weeks.

I look around, pick up the cushion from the chair by the window and turn it around so its paisley pattern is the right way – fat side up, in my view. The wind is gaining strength. It blows against the windows. I can hear the familiar sound of the magnolia branches scraping against the glass. A storm is building up out there – no chance of the security man making an appearance. How frustrated she must feel; all that money she has paid over the years for security, and now, when she needs it, no one comes.

'I'll just be downstairs. I won't be long,' I say, closing the door and locking her in.

It is a strange feeling, being on my own at Minerva. Not quite alone, I know, but it almost feels as if it is my house. That I do, at last, really belong here. No longer eaten alive, but instead cocooned and protected.

In the kitchen, I take a Tupperware container of Margaret's vegetable soup from the freezer and defrost it on the stove. I think about having a bowl myself, but can't face eating. I add another dose to the bowl. It's not poison, it won't kill her. Relax her, that's all. Help her sleep. Flunitrazepam. In the same family of drugs as the diazepam Stella Parker used to feed me. I take the fruit knife from my pocket and slice an apple, placing the pieces on a plate. It's still beautifully sharp. It's been well cared for over the years. I set out a tray and carry it upstairs, resting it on the floor outside her room while I unlock the door.

When I walk in, she is not in bed. I find her in the bathroom. She must have crawled there, dragged herself along the carpet, for it is hard to believe she would have found the strength to make the journey on foot. There is broken glass on the floor around her, and I see she has smashed the window with the pretty milking stool on which a pot plant stood. There is soil everywhere and the poor fern lies on its side, looking almost as bedraggled as Mina, who is hunched against the side of the bath, shivering. I crouch down on the floor beside her. Her eyes are open but she won't look at me. Still, I help her up and take her under the arms, get her on her feet, then drag her back into bed. I think about undressing her and putting on a nightgown, but there's no point. Instead I sit her up like a doll, propping her against the pillows.

'Here.' I set the tray across her lap. She is too weak to take the spoon, so I feed her like a child. One mouthful at a time. 'It's Margaret's homemade vegetable. She'll be here in the morning. It will be Margaret who will find you,' I say.

She turns her head away, refusing to eat more. She certainly can't manage the fruit, but I put the plate on the side, just in case. Her head droops, her neck barely able to hold it up, and I take the tray away and sit on the edge of the bed. I could do anything I want to her, but, for now, I just want to talk.

'Have you ever been to Swainston Forest, Mina?' It's a rhetorical question. 'I have. It's beautiful. At least, it was the day I went there. The sun was shining and I walked through to the centre – deep into its heart. It was the middle of the day, the sun at its strongest, but when I looked up it seemed to disappear, and I remember feeling so cold. I thought, this must be the place. This must be where he did it. I began to shiver, just like I had in court when I heard John Fraser had killed himself.

'It was the week after the trial and I was in a bad way. I couldn't see the point in anything any more. I stood looking up at the trees and I thought I heard the echo of a gun going off – like a whip being cracked. I closed my eyes, and was sure it was John Fraser's gun I'd heard. I was taken back in time and saw him, his chin resting on the barrel as he pulled the trigger. The memory of it, trapped in that forest, repeating itself over and over. I saw birds scatter, shrieking in alarm, then returning and hopping around his body, as birds do, with their bright-eyed curiosity.'

It had been so vivid to me at the time and I wanted to conjure it up for Mina. For her to feel the same shame that had rushed through me. By then, I'd read the piece in the local paper – a few cold sentences recording the death of an old man.

'Did you know John Fraser's father, Malcolm, came down

from Scotland during the war? He bought a piece of land in Kent and cultivated it, built it up into something to pass on to his son. Under John, Fraser's grew and then Clifford took over. Clifford was a good farmer, Mina. The business flourished under him. He really poured his heart into that farm.

'Clifford has three sons. The farm was their inheritance. It was their future, but then you came along and took it away. I wish you'd been with me that day, Mina. If you'd felt what I had, perhaps it would have shifted something in you – pricked your conscience. Then you might have put things right.' I look down at her. Her eyes are closed but I press on.

'I took a rope with me to Swainston Forest. I was going to hang myself. I wanted my body to be found in the same place as John Fraser's. For people to make the connection – between him, and me, and you. I was angry that you weren't there to see it. And that's what made me leave the forest and go home. My rage at your absence. It's what's kept me going ever since.'

I twist a piece of flesh on the inside of her arm, squeeze it between my fingers. She doesn't flinch. She doesn't feel a thing.

51

I wait outside her door and listen. Nothing. I take the tray downstairs and walk through to the study and gather up our dirty glasses, returning to the kitchen. I load the dishwasher with her bowl, spoon, and the glasses, and set it going. It seems a waste for so few things, but they need to be spotless. The pan and wooden spoon I wash by hand.

The rain has stopped and I watch droplets fall from the fleshy leaf of a plant into the light cast by one of the outdoor spots. It looks magical. I see the security man is on the move. The beam from his torch looks ethereal through the misty damp. He is making a perfunctory circuit, taking his time, working his way around the paths. He is coming towards the house. Soon he will see me at the window, and I will wave and he will, no doubt, give me a nod. He will assume I am her, or Margaret perhaps. Intruders tend not to do the washing-up. Domesticity is a wonderful disguise.

I dry my hands on a tea-towel, then make a tour of the downstairs, returning the keys to their rightful places. Everything must look right when Margaret arrives in the morning.

I finish up in the study. The lights are on, the curtains drawn and the sound of the water trickling from the gutters comforts me, as always. I take out Mina's phones and turn them on. They ring at once with messages, and I take a quick look but ignore them. A *thank you* from Andy, the others, all work – even the invitations to dinner are about business, not friendship, though it's a blurred line in her world. Like the houses I used to pass on the way to Appleton's – domestic, business – hard to tell them apart with their pretty window boxes and their shiny black front doors.

I sit down at the desk and open her laptop and read through the changes we made to her memoir this morning. I enjoyed watching her face as she typed it out, and try to picture the faces of those who will read it later. I restore her original password, then do the same with her phones. No reason to block her access any longer.

I take my own laptop from my bag, open it up and begin to type. '*My name is Christine Butcher and I worked for Mina Appleton for almost eighteen years . . .*'

I answer all the questions put to me in court, and this time I tell the truth. It is only the confession of a secretary, but I give as full an account as I am able. Everything I know, everything I heard, everything I saw, everything I was asked to do, and everything I did. It will be enough to, at least, expose Mina Appleton as a liar, and a person capable of manipulating others to lie for her. She is a woman of extraordinary persuasive powers. I am sure they will understand that. I take the empty memory stick from my pocket and load it with my confession, then print out the pages and sign each one. As I hold them in my hand, I feel my anger slip away, and when I take out my phone, my hand is steady. Ed Brooks picks up straight away. He has been waiting for my call.

'Mrs Butcher? Christine?'

'Yes.' He asks me to call him Ed. 'I've typed up everything –

printed out a hard copy and signed it. Five pages. I'll get it in the post to you tonight.' He wants me to email it too – just in case. I feel we are colleagues working late in the office.

'Did you manage to record your conversation with her?' he asks, and is ever so pleased when I tell him I have. 'Well done. I know it can't have been easy.'

I don't answer.

'Christine? Are you OK?'

'Not really.'

'You're doing the right thing,' he says.

'I hope so. But I can't help it. I still feel I owe her some loyalty. You see, I've lied *for* Mina many times. But never *to* her.' He tries to reassure me, but I interrupt him. 'It's no good. I've worked for her for too long. I should at least warn her about your article.' He becomes agitated. Worried she will take out an injunction. 'You don't understand,' I say. 'I'm not used to keeping secrets from her. I've decided to drive back to Minerva tonight. Maybe she'll listen this time. Agree to make things right.'

'Christine, please don't do that. She'll put pressure on you to retract. I'm sorry, but she'll run rings round you.'

'What if I send everything to you first? There's a postbox right around the corner from my house.' There is. 'I promise I won't talk to Mina until it's safely on the way to you. She should be prepared, that's all, Ed.'

'No. That would be a mistake. You don't owe her anything, Christine.'

'I'm sorry. But I've made up my mind.' He's not happy.

We say our goodbyes and he tells me he hopes that one day, we can meet.

'Yes, I'd like that,' I say, but I have no intention of ever meeting Mr Ed Brooks.

I end the call, then play the sound recording on my phone, and Mina's voice fills the room.

'Yes, I drove those farms out of business – and yes, I bought their land. It was a good deal. It produced a healthy profit. No tax either. That's not illegal – nothing about my business practice was illegal.'

'You lied in court. You perjured yourself. That newspaper wrote the truth.'

'Yes. But then you lied too, didn't you . . . I'm sure you and I, between us, could work something out. Christine, we have worked together for eighteen years. You wouldn't betray me now, would you?'

It unsettles me to hear her voice in the room, knowing it will be the last time.

I download the file and email it to Ed and he emails me straight back. It's enough to get her back into court, he says. In the bin I notice the script I'd written out for Mina to deliver to her financial director. Screwed up and tossed away. A small scrap for the police to find. They will unfurl it, read it, and note that I tried to persuade her to do the right thing.

I put my typed confession into a jiffy bag, along with the now full memory stick. I hold the package in my hands, calculate its weight, then stick on stamps. A short walk before bed will do me good.

The postbox is only a few hundred yards down the road, and I push the envelope into its mouth. It only just fits.

On the way back, I pass The Laurels, and go in to pick up my car, tucked away at the side. The owners will think their tenant was a model one, though they'll never know her real name. When I closed the door this morning, I left it as clean as a new pin. All my belongings have gone – my clothes, books, anything that might give me away. I threw it all into the ornamental lake on my way to Minerva this morning, and watched everything sink to the bottom. Perhaps I have forgotten something. I don't claim to be a criminal mastermind. Far from it. One day, someone might discover my things in the lake. But then, why would they bother looking? And if they do, well, it will be an intriguing puzzle for someone to solve. I like the idea of there being some mystery to all this. Like the old-fashioned drawing room whodunits I read at The Laurels. A body in the bedroom. Signs of a struggle in the bathroom. Loose ends for someone else to tie up.

I drive back to Minerva, tap in the code on the electric gates and go through, parking my car in the driveway. I sit for a moment and hear the clunk of metal as they close behind me.

52

I let myself in, leave the keys on the side and walk through to switch the lamps off in the study. I think of the nights I stood outside in the garden, watching lights come on and off in the various rooms, following the movements of the woman inside. Now that woman is me.

I take my time, going back upstairs, feeling every tread of the plush carpet, running my hand along the balustrade, appreciating the smoothness of the wood. It will be the last time I take this journey. At the top, I look down, but it is dark, and as I stare into it, it turns into a mist that seems to come up the stairs after me. I walk along the landing, looking again into the pink room, but the idea now of getting into that bed does not appeal, and so I move on to Mina's room, unlock the door and go in.

She is still breathing, her pulse surprisingly lively. How restless she is. Her head moving back and forth on her silk pillow, trying, I imagine, to find a cooler spot to rest on. I turn away and walk into her dressing room. So many clothes, so many shoes, but I know exactly what she will want to wear. Something simple. A navy dress with a white collar. I hang it on the back of the door, choose underwear, shoes, and set them aside.

I sit at her dressing table and take a long, hard look at myself in the mirror. I try to stay objective, to see whether there is any trace of the old Christine Butcher, and I think I feel her somewhere inside, shivering. A little frightened, perhaps. I hold her gaze and tell her, there's no need to be. I am shivering too, and I swallow some pills and decide a bath will help me relax. Hot and deep.

I undress – careful not to tread on the shards of glass still strewn over the floor – and fold my clothes, setting them down on the closed toilet seat, then step into the bath, sliding my body into the water. I lie there, helping myself to a bottle of Mina's luxurious bath oil, and the smell of it fills the bathroom. I close my eyes. The hardest part is still to come, but I refuse to think about it, and allow myself a few moments more, holding my arm up under my nose and sniffing the delicious scent. My skin feels smooth, and when I get out of the water and towel myself down, I am as sleek as a racehorse. I go back into the bedroom to dress. The pale pink blouse, the grey suit.

The sun will be up soon. I pull back the curtain and see the sky is a deep mauve. I wonder whether the house will look different in the morning. Whether, overnight, it will have turned ugly. I hope not. I want it to be seen at its best – I would like the photographs to show a beautiful house, the sun stroking its bricks, the curtains drawn, Mina tucked up inside.

I can hear her behind me, mumbling in her sleep. Is it sleep? I'm not sure, and I move closer to watch her. Study her. When you look at her, up close, you can see how synthetic she is. Her skin unnatural.

I take her face in my hands and move it one way, then the other and something moves beneath the surface. All that stuff injected into her over the years, slipping and sliding. It slithers around beneath the surface as if there are things living inside her, moving around, trying to settle but they cannot get comfortable. She murmurs something – what, I have no idea. Shh, I say, and pull back the bedclothes and undress her. I leave her clothes in a pile, as she would have done, waiting for someone else to pick them up, and dress her in the outfit I have chosen. Her limbs are limp, easy to manipulate. Still, I find myself sweating from the exertion of pulling her around, re-making the bed, lying her on top. I walk around to the other side and lie down, exhausted, my head next to hers on the pillow.

'Hush now, I'm here,' I say. 'I hate the idea of anyone dying alone.'

I take her hand and hold it.

It will be Margaret who arrives first on the scene. She will walk in, and see a still life that, at first, will make no sense to her. It will take a moment for her brain to translate the scene. When she does, she will drop the tray with Mina's breakfast – a clatter of broken crockery. Tea and orange juice, staining the carpet. And she will scream and scream.

Or perhaps it will be Mina who screams. Perhaps she will wake before Margaret arrives. She will be covered in blood – everything around her will be soaked in it. She will open her eyes, all her senses alerting her that something is wrong. Only scraps will come back to her, though. Not enough for her to piece it all together. It will be a kaleidoscope of colours and shapes that won't make sense. That's the trick with Rohypnol – *strong amnesia. Limited or no memory at all.* For Mina, the previous twelve hours will be a blank. She'll tell them, over and over again: *I can't remember, I can't remember.* They will struggle to believe her. She is a woman who, by then they will know, is not to be trusted. She'll say, *I was drugged, she drugged me.* They'll find no evidence of that. By the time they test her, there'll be no trace of it left in her system.

And I will be there. My eyes closed. Dressed for a day in the office. Smart suit, shoes on, the brooch Mina gave me pinned to my lapel. I hope I look peaceful, though I will be covered in my own blood. I will have been leaking for hours, lying in the bed next to Mina.

It will appear, at first, as if I have been murdered. There will be a moment when they will look at Mina and think her capable of that. Revenge? Uncontrollable rage? A moment of madness at her secretary's betrayal? Things will become less clear when they examine me. They will find a slash across each of my wrists. Discover, too, that I have swallowed a cocktail of benzodiazepines. She did it to herself then? Perhaps. It will be untidy – drag on – as they piece the puzzle together. A mess. I like the idea of that. And, for once, it won't be me who has to clear it up.

Outside, the press will begin to gather, and they will not leave until Mina Appleton is led from the house. She will be a shocking sight, stained with my blood. Perhaps she will be handcuffed too. I hope so. Certainly, she will be escorted by the police.

Later, my body will be carried out, zipped up, perhaps, in a black bag. Minerva will become a crime scene – Mina's home once again crawling with police.

She may not go on trial for murder, but Mr Ed Brooks will make sure that justice is done. Her reputation will be destroyed. A stain on it forever.

I slip my hand from hers and wrap her fingers around the fruit knife, my hand over hers as the blade runs across my wrist. A muddle of fingerprints. An element of doubt makes a better story, to my mind.

And it is a story she will never be able to erase, or rewind – it will be out there in the public domain, strands of it peeling away and floating up. People will clutch at those strands, examine each one, hold them up to the light – this way and that.

They will try to put them all together, come up with a version of what happened that night. But in the end, it won't really matter what the truth is. However that story is told, Mina Appleton is always the woman with blood on her hands. An image that will stay for ever. A picture she can never erase.

Only one indisputable fact. Written over and over again: *The dead body of her secretary was found in her home.*

Acknowledgements

I was a secretary many years ago, but in writing this book I sought the help of two current professionals – Catherine Ahmad and Irene Haicalis. Both are highly skilled Personal Assistants and bear not the slightest resemblance to Christine Butcher, nor their employers to Mina Appleton. I am grateful for their patience and generosity in answering my sometimes bizarre, but more often banal, questions. Thank you both, for your time and good humour. The same goes for Patrick Rewcastle, who understood what I was after and showed me how to get there, as did Susannah Waters, whose skilful navigation helped me see the wood despite the trees. I am grateful, too, to Oliver Blunt, for giving me such an enjoyable tour of the Old Bailey and showing me things I would have missed without his expert eye. Thanks, too, to Rachel Farrer, who is not an archivist, but a real person who supported the work of children's cancer charity CLIC Sargent when she bid to have her name used for a character in this book. For their time, patience, kindness and sharp minds, I would like to thank my agents, Felicity Blunt and Lucy Morris at Curtis Brown. Also Melissa Pimentel, whose skill in selling this book, and the last one, overseas is mind-boggling. To my editor at Transworld, Sarah Adams: thank you for allowing me to believe I had all the time in the world and for shielding me from the horrors of deadlines. Your calm, steadying hand has helped steer me through the trickiness of this second book. Big thanks, too, to Kate Samano and Anne O'Brien for their painstaking copy-editing, and to Alison Barrow and Larry Finlay and all those at Transworld – it is a privilege to be published by you. In the US, I'd like to thank my agent, Jennifer Joel at ICM – lucky me to have you – and Mary Gaule and Jonathan Burnham at HarperCollins, whose critical eyes have made this a much better book. To Iris Tupholme at HarperCollins, Canada – thank you for giving me the benefit of your years of experience and gently encouraging this book out of me.

Lastly, I'd like to thank my friends and family, who've put up with the ups and downs of me having Christine Butcher in my head. Thanks to my sister Cathy Hughes for her invaluable help, and in particular for telling me the story of an old man and his fruit; to Beth Holgate for reading an early draft and giving me the confidence to keep going; and to Sara Olins for long walks, stimulating conversation and wise counsel. To dearest George and Betty – you make me very proud and are more than generous in your support of your mum. And to my darling Greg – it's safe to come out now, Christine Butcher has left the house.

About the Author

Renée Knight worked as a documentary-maker for the BBC before turning to writing. She is a graduate of the Faber Academy 'Writing a Novel' course, and lives in London with her husband and two children. Her widely acclaimed debut novel, *Disclaimer*, was a *Sunday Times* No.1 bestseller. *The Secretary* is her second novel.

ALSO BY RENÉE KNIGHT

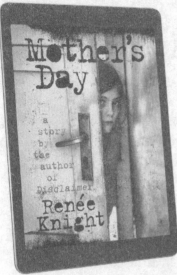

Mother's Day
A Short Story
Available in E-Book Format

Staying with her parents at Beauwater Manor, a luxury hotel in the English countryside, is the happiest memory of Laura's young life so far. She's excited at the prospect of returning to the hotel a few years later. But in this riveting short story, Laura will discover that even though some things about Beauwater Manor are familiar, others are very, very different from what she remembers....

Disclaimer
A Novel
Available in Hardcover, Paperback, E-Book & Audio Formats

Finding a mysterious novel at her bedside plunges documentary filmmaker Catherine Ravenscroft into a living nightmare. Though ostensibly fiction, *The Perfect Stranger* recreates in vivid, unmistakable detail the terrible day she became hostage to a dark secret, a secret that only one other person knew—and that person is dead. Now that the past is catching up with her, Catherine's world is falling apart. Her only hope is to confront what really happened on that awful day . . . even if the shocking truth might destroy her.

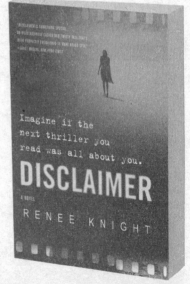